CRIME WITHOUT PASSION

CRIME WITHOUT PASSION

by

RICHARD GRAYSON

St. Martin's Press
New York

Library of Congress Cataloging in Publication Data

Grayson, Richard.
  Crime without passion.

  I. Title.
PR6057.R55C7   1983   823'.914   83-21103
ISBN 0-312-17205-2

First published in Great Britain in 1983 by Victor Gollancz Ltd.

First U.S. Edition

10 9 8 7 6 5 4 3 2 1

1

'IN OUR BELOVED France, gentlemen of the court, gentlemen of the jury, justice has never had her eyes blindfolded.'

Although Maître Bonnard had been speaking for not more than twenty minutes, an unbelievably short time for a defence counsel in a murder trial, one sensed that he was approaching the end of his closing speech. Expectantly the audience in the Great Assize court, the jury, the distinguished guests seated behind the three judges in their red robes and the public opposite them waited for his peroration.

'Justice sees all, justice understands all. Even now, gentlemen of the jury, she is looking through your eyes at the prisoner before you. What does she see? A young woman who has done wrong, who has killed, who has confessed. But she sees also a young woman who was shamefully wronged, who was exploited, who was betrayed. Mademoiselle Denise de Richemont was seduced, calculatingly and cynically, by a man for his ignoble ends. You have heard how, when he had won her innocent love and her confidence, he tricked her into trusting him with a secret. You have heard how immediately he published what she had told him in his newspaper, embellishing it with sordid details contrived by his own imagination, creating a sensation for the vulgar to enjoy. It did not matter to him that by so doing he destroyed the reputation and the career of the young woman's father, a man who had served France well. Indeed, you may think that this was his intention from the very outset, the object of his fiendish plan. You have heard how Mademoiselle de Richemont, distraught with anger and shame, went to see him. What could she do? Had she been a man she might have challenged him to a duel and so at least satisfied her honour. But, gentlemen of the jury, duelling is against the law; however, had she killed him at dawn in the Bois de Boulogne with a rapier or a pistol, would she now be on trial for her life? I think you may doubt

5

it, as I do. We have an unwritten law in France which allows a man to protect his honour. But women cannot fight duels. Even if they wished to, society would forbid it. So what did Mademoiselle de Richemont do? Bewildered, provoked past endurance, unable in her confusion to balance right against, wrong, she satisfied her honour and revenged her father in the only way a woman could. She shot the scoundrel dead.'

Maître Bonnard paused, took off his pince-nez and wiped them with a silk handkerchief in a way that suggested he needed time to master his own emotions. It was pure theatre, but he would never have become France's most successful and most highly-paid criminal lawyer without an understanding of the power of drama. He had only a few more words left to say and he wished them to have a profound and decisive effect on the jury.

'In the eyes of the law,' he continued slowly, 'Mademoiselle de Richemont has committed a crime. That cannot be denied. But it is not the law, gentlemen of the jury, that you have been brought here to administer today, but justice. And in our beloved France justice has always had a special compassion for Mademoiselle de Richemont's crime; the crime of a woman whose innocence, whose happiness, whose very life has been callously destroyed by a man; a crime of passion.'

Inspector Gautier, who had guessed what the advocate was about to say, watched the faces of the jury as Maître Bonnard spoke. They were twelve men, honest and well-intentioned no doubt, mostly artisans, shopkeepers and minor civil servants. Only three of them, who had given their occupations as 'proprietor' could possibly have claimed to be men of substance. Throughout the trial they had appeared ill-at-ease, as though uncertain of what was expected of them, their sense of duty in conflict with their sympathy for the prisoner in front of them. When Maître Bonnard spoke the words 'crime passionel' one could see the relief in their faces. Gautier sensed that the advocate had given them a way out of their dilemma.

When Bonnard had sat down, the Presiding Judge put to the jury the question they were required to answer. At one time judges used to give a 'résumé' or summing-up before the jury retired but the procedure had been changed and now the Presiding Judge simply told the jury that they must decide whether on the date in question the prisoner had murdered Jacques Le Tellier.

6

As soon as the judges had left the court, and the jury had been led away to start their deliberations, almost all of the many lawyers who had been watching the trial from a special enclosure left as well. They had come to see how the case was conducted and the arguments that were put forward and were not interested in the drama of hearing the verdict announced. Some of public spectators went out of the court to stroll and gossip outside the Palais de Justice in the pale autumn sunshine.

Gautier stayed seated. As the trial had been short, he felt certain that the jury's verdict would not be long in coming. He himself had played no part in the proceedings, given no evidence. His presence was a necessary formality because it had been he who had arrested Denise de Richemont and when, unexpectedly, the trial had been brought forward by several days he had been taken off another investigation so that he could attend.

He remembered the day, not so long ago it seemed, when he had been called from Sûreté headquarters to the editorial offices of the newspaper *La Parole* in Rue Réaumur. There he had found Mademoiselle de Richemont, silent and white-faced, sitting outside the office of the editor, Jacques Le Tellier. Members of the newspaper's staff had told him how, on arriving at the building a short time earlier, she had walked into Le Tellier's office, pulled a revolver from the muff she was wearing and shot him four times in the head and heart. She had not spoken then, nor given a word of explanation since, but had sat down calmly to wait for the police to arrive.

Gautier had not been aware then that she was the younger daughter of the Duc de Richemont, at that time French ambassador in Rome. Only when she had appeared before a juge d'instruction, later that day, had she explained her reasons for shooting Le Tellier.

She had met the newspaper editor, she had told the examining magistrate, a few weeks previously. Fascinated by his intellect and his charm, she had soon fallen in love with him and become his mistress, meeting him in his garçonnière in Rue Lamartine. While they had made love, he had questioned her, casually she had thought, about her home and her family. Trusting him and longing to unburden herself of a secret which had long distressed and shamed her, she had told him that her father was a pederast and, when he had expressed disbelief, she had shown him passionate

7

letters which the duc had exchanged with a young English boy while he was ambassador at the Court of St. James and which she had found hidden in their Paris home.

To her horror the story, along with the letters, had been published only two days later in *La Parole*. The scandal which had followed had forced the government to recall the duc from Rome, his career had been destroyed, his reputation ruined and he was no longer received in French society.

'So what could I do except shoot the villain?' Mademoiselle de Richemont had asked the juge d'instruction. 'You must agree he deserved to die.'

As he waited for the jury to return, Gautier looked around the court. Every seat in the public enclosure, and of those reserved for people of importance, had been occupied since the trial began, for it had caused an international sensation. Not only had the Duc de Richemont come of an old and illustrious aristocratic family, but as an ambassador he had been received in many of the most exclusive homes of London and Rome and St. Petersburg. Now his daughter was on trial for murder and titillating stories of his past had been published in the world's newspapers. The fact that the victim of the murder had himself been an editor of a well-known paper added piquancy to the affair and guaranteed that it would be voraciously reported in the world's press.

The ambassadors of several foreign powers were among the spectators but the British Ambassador was not one of them. Instead the First Secretary from his Britannic Majesty's embassy had been sent to the trial. He had been listening anxiously, one supposed, in case anything might be said that could damage the reputation of his country and endanger the fragile relationship between England and France. By no means everyone in France had welcomed the Entente Cordiale and there might well be those who would suggest that the Duc de Richemont had been tempted into pederasty by the corrupt atmosphere of English society. Memories of the scandal caused by the trial of Oscar Wilde still lingered and the position of the British Ambassador was not made any easier by the thinly disguised homosexual inclinations of one of his elderly attachés. Mockingly the French had christened the man 'La Tante Cordiale'.

Although there was a good sprinkling of women in the public

seats, Gautier could see only two in the reserved enclosure at the opposite end of the court. Both were heavily veiled and he wondered whether one of them might be the widow of the murdered man and the other the mother of the prisoner. Not surprisingly, in view of the scandal which the story in *La Parole* had provoked, the duc was not in court. One person whom Gautier recognized, and was surprised to see there, was Paul Valanis, a wealthy Greek businessman, who represented the British armaments firm of Lydon-Walters and Company Limited in France and lived in a vast house on Avenue du Bois. He had met and antagonized Valanis not long previously when investigating the murder of an art dealer. The Greek was a philanderer, a man of dubious background and even more dubious business interests, but Gautier had not supposed that watching the murder trial of a relatively unimportant and unattractive young woman would be one of them.

After about half an hour a bell was rung in the court to indicate that the jury would be returning. This could mean that they had already reached a verdict or that they only wished to seek the guidance of the judges on a point of law. Those spectators who had gone outside began scrambling back hastily as the three judges, led by the President, filed in and took their seats. Mademoiselle de Richemont was left waiting in the ante-chamber outside with her guards, for it was not the practice in French trials for a prisoner to be in court when the verdict was announced. Presently the jury was ushered in and when the Presiding Judge asked the foreman if they had reached a verdict, he replied that they had. Solemnly and rather self-consciously the man announced, using the formula which protocol demanded, that 'before God and before men' they found the prisoner not guilty of unlawful killing.

The verdict did not surprise Gautier nor did the scene that it provoked, for he could recall other trials when the defence of a 'crime passionel' divided the sympathies of the spectators. As soon as the foreman of the jury had made his announcement, many people in the public enclosure leapt to their feet and began to cheer. At once there was a reaction of disapproval and a counter-demonstration. Other spectators, women mostly, began to hiss and catcall and shout abuse at Mademoiselle de Richemont as she was brought by two municipal guards into court to have the verdict read out to her.

'It's a scandal! Why should she go free?'

'Disgusting! Is this justice?'

'To the guillotine with the whore!'

A crowd of more than a thousand had gathered outside the Palais de Justice and as soon as news of the verdict reached them, they began applauding or hissing as well. Gautier walked over to the dock where the prisoner was being congratulated by Maître Bonnard and his assistants.

'We must find a way of smuggling Mademoiselle de Richemont out by a back way to avoid the crowds,' he told the municipal guards.

'That won't be easy, Inspector,' one of the men replied. 'Some of those rascals outside know of all the exits at the back and the newspaper reporters of course will have men posted there already.'

'There is no need to try and hide me,' Mademoiselle de Richemont said. 'I am not afraid to face the crowd.'

'But Mademoiselle,' Maître Bonnard exclaimed, 'You will have to fight a way through. We cannot guarantee your safety.'

'I prefer to face the people. I have nothing of which to be ashamed.'

The young woman was completely composed. One might have expected that after the ordeal of a spectacular public trial and facing the possibility of imprisonment or even the guillotine, she would have shown some emotion, but she appeared to have accepted the acquittal almost as her right. Her face, in spite of its pallor and her long, thin nose might have been, if not attractive, then at least pleasant enough had she smiled more often and used her best feature, her dark deep-set eyes, to more effect. Instead her expression was cold and reserved with a hint of disdain.

Leaving the dock, the lawyers, the two guards and Gautier formed a ring around her as best they could and moved towards the doors of the court. Inside the building they were able without too much difficulty to force a way through the spectators who had left their seats and were standing about in the well of the court, but as soon as Mademoiselle de Richemont emerged outside, people surged forward towards them. There the crowd seemed more hostile than those who had been at the trial, perhaps because they had not heard the defence counsel's speech. Many shook their fists at the woman who was being freed and some who were close enough spat on her and would have struck her but for the protective cordon of policemen and lawyers.

The scene reminded Gautier of an occasion not many years previously when Emile Zola had been on trial for defamation after publishing a newspaper article with the headline 'J'accuse', in which he had accused government ministers and the army of conspiring to prevent the innocence of Captain Dreyfus being proved. When Zola had left the court each day, he had been surrounded by a hostile crowd whose hatred and anti-semitism had been stirred up by his words. As a young policeman, sent to help control the crowds, he had sensed that the mob's anger had been balanced on a fine edge of hysteria and violence. He had been frightened then and was far from comfortable now as he and his companions edged their way out of the court.

More police arrived, summoned hastily from Sûreté headquarters which were only a short distance away. With their help the lawyers and their client were taken slowly through the struggling mass of people and down the steps to where an automobile stood waiting. A chauffeur in leggings and a driving coat stood ready by the door of the automobile which, Gautier noticed, was a new Panhard et Levassor with gleaming headlamps of an unusual design.

As she was about to step into the automobile, Denise de Richemont turned towards Gautier and said calmly, 'I thank you for your courtesy, Monsieur, not only today but throughout my arrest and trial. When the time comes I will see that it gets proper recognition.'

2

CROSSING THE SEINE by Pont St. Michel, Gautier strolled through the Quartier Latin. That afternoon he would report back at Sûreté headquarters but for the time being he was in no hurry and in no mood to return to duty. Was this a sign, he wondered, that he was growing old, losing that sharp curiosity, that readiness to

11

meet a challenge which made him enjoy his work. He smiled at the thought. Still the youngest inspector in the Sûreté, he was in service at least ten years junior to most of his colleagues.

It may have been the end of the trial he had been watching that had provoked the slight sense of disillusionment which he felt. He was not a vengeful man and never expected nor wished that the law should impose its maximum penalty on all those who broke it, but he could not help believing that Denise de Richemont had not deserved to be acquitted. He recalled her icy calm as she had sat waiting for the police after shooting Le Tellier and her composure throughout the trial. In spite of what her defence counsel had said, there had been a curious lack of passion in her crime.

As he turned into Boulevard St. Germain, he heard music and singing. On the far side of the boulevard a group of street musicians was performing: a young woman singing to the accompaniment of a viola, a guitar and a trombone. A small crowd, mostly of students, had gathered to listen and applaud. Gautier recognised the singer as Emilie Pinot, a chanteuse who performed in café-concerts on the Left Bank as well as in the streets and was a great favourite of the students in the quartier, partly because of her cheerful, healthy appearance—more of a comrade than a 'petite amie' one critic had described her—and partly because of the political venom in her songs. La Pinot was an unbridled opponent of the government which she attacked wittily and often scabrously in her songs. For generations the Quartier Latin, with its population of intellectuals, poets and students, had been the focal point of unrest in Paris. In recent months dissatisfaction with what many saw as the mediocrity and cowardice of the President, Emile Loubet, and his ministers had found expression in demonstrations and occasional outbreaks of violence on the Left Bank. Now Loubet had gone, having finished his term of office, and his successor Fallières had inherited his unpopularity.

The many cafés in the quartier, where men gathered to talk and to argue, were the breeding grounds for discontent: the Café François Premier, where the poet Verlaine had found a brief refuge from his squalid, alcoholic existence; La Vachette, which had been favoured by another poet, Mallarmé, now also dead; Les Deux Magots, La Brasserie Lipp and the Café de l'Avenir. The café which Gautier frequented and for which he was heading that morning, had a much less radical clientèle. Lawyers, judges and deputies with an occasional journalist, made up the majority of the Café Corneille's regular patrons and Gautier was secretly proud of the fact that he was accepted by these professional men as a companion and by one or two of them as a friend.

When he arrived at the café that morning his oldest friend Duthrey, a journalist from *Figaro*, was already at their usual table with an elderly lawyer and the deputy for Val-de-Marne. The deputy had brought a friend with him, an Italian politician who was visiting Paris. As soon as Gautier joined them, knowing that he had come from the Palais de Justice, they began talking about the trial of Denise de Richemont. Rumour, which travelled faster in Paris than any man on foot, had already told them of the verdict.

'How was the verdict received?' Duthrey asked Gautier.

'By the prisoner? With astonishing equanimity. She showed no emotion whatsoever.'

'By the public, I meant.'

'They appeared divided. The majority of spectators in the court applauded, but outside Mademoiselle de Richemont had to face hostility and insults.'

'A verdict like that would not be possible in any other civilized country in the world,' the lawyer remarked.

'That is true,' the deputy agreed, 'and the reason is that we French have an innate sense of chivalry, a desire to protect defenceless women.'

'Chivalry? It has nothing to do with chivalry,' the lawyer replied. 'We have allowed ourselves to become obsessed with sex. Crime of passion, indeed! A young woman of good family gives herself wantonly to a married man, becomes his mistress and then when she shoots the poor devil we are asked to forgive her, as though the pursuit of sex is a vindication of any behaviour however criminal.'

'Aren't you being a little hard on the girl?' Duthrey asked.

'Certainly not! This deification of sex is destroying our country's morals. In your newspaper the other day, your editor boasted that Paris had become the artistic and cultural capital of the world. All I would say is this. For every visitor who comes here to enjoy art or music or poetry at least ten arrive to wallow in the lascivious pleasures which only Paris offers; to leer at the dancers at the Moulin Rouge as they lift their skirts, to listen to the bawdy songs of the caf' concs, to find illicit love in the luxurious houses of ill repute.

13

Why, even the King of England comes here incognito to exercise his lust on our courtesans.'

'And you, Signor?' Duthrey turned to the Italian, feeling perhaps that the lawyer's moralizing was becoming tedious. 'What is your opinion of our great courtesans, Liane de Pougy and Caroline Otéro?'

'Otéro!' The lawyer exclaimed scornfully. 'The illegitimate child of a Spanish gypsy!'

'And a Greek nobleman,' the deputy added.

'So she claims. And now she charges men 10,000 francs just to have supper with her.'

The Italian sighed and shook his head with an exaggerated show of mournfulness. 'Alas Messieurs! I have come to Paris to examine not your boudoirs but the corridors of power.'

'They can be equally dangerous,' Gautier said. 'One of our presidents died of over-exertion in his office.'

Everyone laughed, recognizing the allusion to a former President of France, Félix Faure, who had been found by a secretary in his private office dying in the embrace of his naked mistress. The presidents of the Third Republic since its creation in 1871 had failed dismally to inspire either public confidence or public respect. The first one, Marshall MacMahon, a bumbling, inarticulate soldier, had been renowned throughout Europe for his gaffes. Jules Grévy, a parsimonous lawyer, had allowed his son-in-law to set up a profitable little business selling France's most cherished decoration, the Légion d'Honneur. Faure, a megalomaniac, had insisted on sitting alone in the front row of the presidential box at public spectacles. Loubet, a timid little businessman, who looked as though he had just climbed down off a train from the provinces, had refused to wear the customary court dress on a state visit to England because his wife had laughed at him when he tried it on. And so over the years mocking the president had become a national pastime.

'What puzzles me about this affair,' Duthrey remarked when the conversation reverted to the trial of Denise de Richemont, 'is the behaviour of Jacques Le Tellier. I had always found him to be a man of high principles.'

'We know he was meeting his mistress secretly,' Gautier commented.

In the course of enquiries which he made after the shooting of Le

14

Tellier, he had been to the small apartment which the dead man had maintained. There the concierge had confirmed that Le Tellier had entertained a lady twice a week in the afternoons. According to the concierge the lady had always arrived veiled and on foot.

'How many men in his position do not have a mistress?' the deputy from Val-de-Marne asked. 'Precious few I would say.'

'That isn't what I meant,' Duthrey replied. 'I was talking of Le Tellier's professional principles.'

'Did he have any?' the lawyer asked sourly. 'He was a man who loved to tilt at windmills, a crusader. The government, the church, businessmen, bankers, he attacked them all. Remember how vituperative *La Parole* was over the Panama affair? And they crucified the wretched Grévy who was more of a fool than a knave. Le Tellier must have been delighted to print a story that attacked the morality of our diplomatic corps.'

'Doubtless he was. But I don't believe he would have stooped to such underhand methods to prise out the poor Duc de Richemont's secret perversion.'

'Nor do I,' the deputy agreed. 'He was a radical, I agree, but a man of integrity.'

'I am only surprised,' the Italian observed, 'that Mademoiselle de Richemont should have been willing to risk imprisonment, even the guillotine, on account of her father.'

'Do you know her then?'

'Oh yes. I met her and her family several times when the duc was your country's ambassador in Rome. She did not impress me as a girl who was devoted to her father.'

'Why do you say that?' Gautier asked. He had his own reservations about Denise de Richemont's character.

'More than once she quarrelled bitterly with him in public. In fact the scenes became so frequent and so embarrassing that she was sent back to Paris only a few months ago.'

'Yes. She's living with an aunt,' Gautier said.

'Children can quarrel with their parents,' the lawyer observed, 'yet still be devoted to them. My own never stop arguing with me but I believe that secretly they are quite fond of me.'

'But Mademoiselle de Richemont's attitude to her father was unnatural, even malicious. She once told me, calmly and without anger, that she hated him.'

*

'Now that the trial of that wretched girl has ended, let us hope, Gautier, that you will be available to do some work.'

'That is why I am reporting for duty, Monsieur.'

'I am pleased to hear it.'

Courtrand's tone was accusing, as though he believed Gautier had been on holiday, enjoying himself and leaving others to shoulder his duties. The director-general of the Sûreté was a self-important little man who nagged his subordinates with the same persistence as he ingratiated himself with his superiors. No pettiness was too mean for those who worked under him, no flattery too great for the Prefect of Police or anyone else who might further Courtrand's career.

'You can have no idea of the extra work which you caused me,' Courtrand continued.

'It was most inconsiderate of the authorities to bring the date of the trial forward without consulting you, Monsieur.'

'The gentle sarcasm was too subtle for Courtrand. 'Why did they do it?' he demanded. 'One knows of trials that are sometimes postponed to allow the defence more time to prepare its case, but never before have I heard of a trial being brought forward.'

'I understand it was at the request of Maître Bonnard, the defence counsel.'

'So I believe. And when I made enquiries I was informed that the request had been approved by a very important person indeed. That young woman must have friends in high places!'

'Do you wish me to resume the investigations I was engaged on before the trial started, Monsieur?'

When the trial of Denise de Richemont began, Gautier had been investigating a major robbery at the main branch of La Banque de l'Union Française. The affair had interested him for the robbery had clearly been the work of a highly skilled gang, using methods which he had not before encountered. He would have liked to be reassigned to the case, but was not hopeful that Courtrand would agree.

'No. Inspector Siméon has taken over the enquiries and is handling them most competently.'

'Then what are my instructions?'

'Do you recall that killing in Rue Fontaine? A woman named Callot was stabbed. Inspector Lemaire had been in charge but I now have a more important assignment for him.'

16

'So I'm to replace Lemaire?'

'Yes. Ask him to hand over the dossier of the case, copies of his reports and of the examinations carried out by the juge d'instruction.'

Courtrand would have had difficulty in finding a more unattractive case to give Gautier. Eva Callot, one of the many women who offered themselves to patrons of the Elysée Montmartre and other cabarets in that district had been found dead in a small street not far from Place Pigalle. A number of possible suspects had been brought in and questioned but there was no evidence worth anything. The woman might have been killed by an unsatisfied client, a jealous rival in whose territory she had trespassed, a passing drunk, almost anyone. After some weeks all the enquiries made by Inspector Lemaire had been fruitless and the Sûreté was almost ready to close the dossier for good. There were countless women like Eva Callot to be found in and around the cabarets, the café-concerts and guinguettes of Paris—too many some would say—and she would not be missed.

'One more thing, Gautier,' Courtrand added. 'Do try to use your own judgement in this assignment and please don't come running to me for help. I have been inconvenienced enough as it is and for the next few days I will be extremely busy.'

'I understand, Monsieur.'

'The Shah of Persia arrives here on his state visit in two days' time. I have been invited to the official reception in the Hôtel de Ville.'

'My felicitations, Monsieur.'

Courtrand looked at him sharply, as though this time he did suspect the sincerity of the remark. 'It was only to be expected. And naturally the Prefect of Police will wish to see me before then to discuss the arrangements that must be made to protect our royal visitor.'

The director-general paused to look at himself in the mirror which hung on one wall of his office, as though it were already time to start the painstaking preparations which would be needed to satisfy his vanity before he set off for the official reception. An injudicious friend had once told Courtrand that he resembled the then Prince of Wales and ever since that day he had gone to inordinate lengths to emphasize the resemblance, copying the style and the cut of the prince's suits, having his beard and his rapidly

17

diminishing hair trimmed to imitate those of the prince and even sending his dress shirts to be laundered by a firm in London who were reputed to be providing a similar service to Buckingham Palace.

Leaving him absorbed, like Narcissus, in his own reflection, Gautier went upstairs to his own office and found that Inspector Lemaire had already placed the complete dossier on the Callot affair ready for him on his desk. He began reading through the pile of documents, trying to suppress his apathy and a sense of impending boredom.

The first person to have been questioned over the murder of Eva Callot had been her 'protector', a man of mixed French and Algerian blood named Shaki, who had moved to Paris from Marseilles thinking that the pickings for his trade of pimp would be richer in the capital. Shaki had satisfied the police that he could have had no motive for killing one of the women on whom he relied for his livelihood and he had not been detained. Several other men and women had been brought in for questioning, and the most likely suspect was a refugee from Russia, now a naturalized French citizen, Igor Kratov.

When he had arrived in France several years previously, Kratov had joined an anarchist group, but then, tiring of politics, he had drifted into an existence on the fringes of the Paris underworld, picking up a living as best he could without taking to crime. The police had learnt that Kratov had been a regular client of Eva Callot, meeting her in a disreputable hotel near Pigalle, and that he had been seen with her in the evening before she was found stabbed. When first questioned by Inspector Lemaire, he had denied killing Callot but had been unable to give any coherent account of his movements on the night of the murder.

Later, however, when he had been brought before a juge d'instruction, he had recovered his memory. Not only had he been able to recall where he had spent the late evening and early morning, but he could also remember the name of his companion throughout that time. Gabriel Ibrahim was a young Persian of good family who had come to live in Paris not long previously and was employed by the Prince de Chaville as his secretary. Kratov's story was that on the night in question he had been showing the Persian round Paris, by which he meant the less respectable cabarets and brothels. Ibrahim was interviewed, discreetly, for one does not wish

18

to embarrass the protégés of princes, and had confirmed Kratov's story. He had explained, rather shamefacedly, that he was without friends in Paris and anxious to see something of the daring night life of the city, about which he had heard so much, had gone out on his own, met Kratov by chance in a café and accepted his offer of a guided tour of the seamier districts.

With no other suspects to interrogate, Lemaire and his assistants had made extensive enquiries in and around Boulevard de Clichy, hoping to find someone who might have seen Eva Callot that evening or at least have heard of what she had been doing. Gautier was not surprised to learn that the enquiries had been fruitless. The people most likely to have associated with Eva Callot were those who lived in the narrow streets of Pigalle, owners of shabby cafés, junk merchants, small-time thieves, pimps and street walkers. They had their own code of behaviour, a code which precluded giving the flics any voluntary help or information.

Lemaire had decided to have the woman's protector, Shaki, brought in for further questioning, hoping that by prolonged interrogation he might be able to wring something out of the man. But when the police had arrived at the Algerian's home he was no longer there and no one could say where he had gone. Shaki had disappeared, slipping into the Paris underworld where a wanted man could easily remain concealed for months or even years.

Faced with what looked like an impasse, Gautier read Lemaire's report of his interview with Gabriel Ibrahim again. Lemaire, whose reports were always lengthy and prolix, had noted that the Persian was an effeminate young man, fastidious in his dress, sensitive and shy. Gautier asked himself if this were true, how it was that he had become involved with Kratov, who by all accounts was coarse and violent and promiscuous in all his tastes.

Since he could think of no better starting point for what was likely to be a frustrating investigation he decided it would do no harm to have another word with Ibrahim. That at least would give him a pretext for getting out of the office. Sitting at a desk, writing reports or reading them, was for Gautier the least attractive part of his duties with the Sûreté and in his experience the least productive. He liked to be dealing with people, for it was from people, from what they said and what they did not say, from their admissions and evasions, from bluster, denials, bravado and cowardice, that one usually found the signs that pointed towards the solution of a crime.

The Prince de Chaville lived in Faubourg St. Germain, that district just south of the Seine and to the east of Esplanade des Invalides where 'Le Monde', the people who mattered in Paris society, lived. He had a large and rather ugly house in Rue de Varenne, which had belonged to his family for more than two hundred years and which had been fortunate enough to escape destruction when Haussmann, on the instructions of Napoleon III, had reconstructed the greater part of Paris—just as his family had been fortunate enough to escape the guillotine when the leaders of the French Revolution were reconstructing society. When Gautier knocked on the imposing doors of this hôtel particulier, they were opened by a footman in blue and gold livery.

'I wish to speak with Monsieur Gabriel Ibrahim,' he told the man after explaining who he was.

The footman clearly considered that police inspectors should be using the servants' entrance at the back of the house. He said stiffly, 'I regret that Monsieur Ibrahim is not available.'

'Are you saying he is not at home?'

'He is not in Paris.'

'Then where is he?'

'He has returned to his home in Persia for a vacation. We expect him to be away for at least two more weeks.'

3

EARLY THAT EVENING Gautier travelled on a horse-drawn omnibus towards Montmartre. His wife Suzanne and the former policeman from the fifteenth arrondissement with whom she was now living, owned a café not far from Place Pigalle. For some reason which Gautier did not understand, the promptings of conscience perhaps, Suzanne was anxious that he and her lover Gaston should be friends and she was constantly pressing him to drop in at the café for a meal or a drink. To please her he did go from time to time, not with any enthusiasm, for Gaston, although inoffensive enough, was a dull slow-witted fellow and they had long ago exhausted the only subject of conversation which interested them both—reminiscences of police work in the fifteenth where Gautier had also been stationed.

On this particular evening, however, his visit to the Café Soleil d'Or had an ulterior motive. Although a former policeman, Gaston had established a rapport with at least some of the customers who came to eat and drink and talk in his café and, merely by listening to them talk, he learned much about what was happening in the quartier. Many of the unsavoury characters to be found within a radius of one kilometre from Place Pigalle were known to him at least by reputation. Gautier hoped to tap this source of knowledge as the next step in his investigation into the murder of Eva Callot.

When he arrived at the Soleil d'Or, he found an atmosphere of gaiety which was unusual in a café of that type, where people gathered for the most part to talk seriously or to drink seriously. Gautier guessed that some kind of celebration was in progress.

Suzanne was delighted to see him. 'Jean-Paul, how wonderful that you should have come tonight!' She kissed him on the cheek and then, unaccountably, blushed.

Gaston shook Gautier by the hand with an enthusiasm that might have been mistaken for affection and thrust a glass of champagne into his hand. 'Delighted to see you, old friend!'

In a sudden flash of intuition Gautier guessed the reason for the celebration. Sensing from her blushes that Suzanne would be embarrassed to tell him, he said, 'You're pregnant, aren't you?'

'How did you know? Wasn't it clever of Jean-Paul to have guessed, Gaston chéri? Or did somebody tell you, Jean-Paul?'

She was prattling, a certain sign of embarrassment for in the normal way she was not a woman who spoke very much nor gave way to her emotions. Seeing the irony of the situation, Gautier wanted to laugh. They had been married for ten childless years and would certainly have still been together had they started a family, and now he was being asked to celebrate the fact that another man had succeeded where he had failed. But he had no wish to spoil Suzanne's pleasure so he kissed her on the cheek and pressed her hand without speaking.

She looked at him and he saw tears in her eyes. 'Jean-Paul you're a marvel, a saint!'

Gautier raised his glass first to her and then to Gaston. Several people in the café repeated his words noisily as he wished the couple good health. Champagne was not a drink which most of the habitués of the Café Soleil d'Or ever enjoyed, even when celebrating, and free champagne was not to be believed. Gautier supposed that Gaston must have had to send out for a supply from a wine merchant in a more prosperous part of Paris.

As long as the celebration continued, he was unable to speak to Gaston about the reason for his visit. After an hour or so, however, the champagne was finished and most of the customers drifted away, some to eat at home, some to one or other of the many unpretentious restaurants in the quartier. Finally, while Suzanne was busy serving the few remaining customers, he and Gaston were able to sit down at a table in a corner and open a bottle of armagnac.

'Jean-Paul, there's something I must discuss with you,' Gaston said, before Gautier was able to mention the Callot affair.

'What is that?'

'I'm worried about the child Suzanne is going to have. What name is it to have?'

'Are you saying you want Suzanne to divorce me?'

Gaston shook his head. 'Divorces are not for people like us. You know that.'

He was right. Although theoretically it was possible to have a marriage dissolved in France, the luxury of disposing of an unwanted marriage partner was only within the reach of the rich and the influential.

'Then what are you suggesting?'

'I was hoping you would agree to the child having my name. All that would involve is a simple legal formality and it costs very little.'

'Of course. If that's what you and Suzanne wish.'

'You're a good man, Jean-Paul.'

Seizing Gautier's hand, Gaston shook it with emotion. Then he refilled their glasses from the bottle of armagnac. Neither the compliment nor the armagnac gave Gautier any feeling of satisfaction, but he realized that now Gaston would be less likely to refuse the favour he was about to ask.

'There is something you can do for me, Gaston.'

'Of course, Jean-Paul.'

'Do you recall the Callot affair?'

'Eva Callot? The whore who was murdered just along the road?'

'Yes.'

'I thought that business was dead and forgotten.'

'The dossier is still open and I've been put in charge of the enquiries.'

'How can I help?'

'Callot's protector, a man named Shaki, has disappeared. I want to know where I can find him.'

'Shaki didn't kill the girl,' Gaston said.

'Then why has he gone into hiding?'

'Who knows?' Gaston shrugged his shoulders. 'He's from Algeria. One supposes that his papers are out of order. He may not even have any. On the other hand he might just be afraid that the police will pin the murder of Callot on him.'

'What makes you so certain that he didn't kill Callot?'

'He had no reason to. Shaki is not like some of the pimps in the neighbourhood; he's easy-going, lazy, not a violent man at all. And Eva was genuinely fond of him. She was happy earning enough money to keep him and have a bit put by. She wasn't interested in other men, except professionally of course. Anyway everyone knows it was that madman Kratov who killed Eva.'

'Do you know where I can find Shaki?'

'No.'

'But you could find out.'

Gaston was appalled. 'Do you know what you're asking, Jean-Paul? What would happen to this café if people believed I was an informer for the flics? No one would ever come here. Either that or one night some of Shaki's friends would come and wreck the place.'

What he was saying was right. Gautier knew it was unreasonable to expect the man to put his livelihood at risk, so he decided to change his approach. He said, 'Then just do this for me. Try and get a message to Shaki. Ask him if he will meet me. Anywhere. He can choose the place and the time and I'll go alone. I only wish to talk with him. Tell him that I believe he didn't kill Callot and I want his help to find out who did.'

'All right, Jean-Paul. I'll try. But I don't suppose for one moment that he'll agree.'

As he ate his evening meal, Gautier wondered what Suzanne would have thought had she known that he would be sleeping with

23

another woman that night. The café in Place Dauphine, less than five minutes' walk from Sûreté headquarters, was owned by a widow from Normandy and her unmarried daughter. He had been eating there for some time and had gradually become friendly with the two women. Not long previously the daughter, Janine, had let him know, shyly but unequivocally, that although she had no wish to marry, she would not be averse to having a lover. Now once or twice a week she would come and spend the night with him in his apartment.

Janine lived with her mother and she had made it clear from the outset that she felt it would be improper for Gautier to sleep with her at their home. Instead all three of them made a show of pretending that her mother did not know that he and Janine were lovers. Secretly Gautier could not help being amused at the way this pretence was observed. On the nights when they had decided that they wished to make love the old woman would find some excuse for leaving the café early: she would say she had to visit a sick friend or to do an errand for a neighbour or that she wished to attend evening mass at Notre Dame. Then before leaving she would kiss Janine, remind her to make sure that the café was properly locked and bolted and make her promise not to be home late. Sometimes Gautier wondered how the two women kept up the pretence when they met at the café the following morning.

That evening, when the old lady left, there were still half-a-dozen customers in the café. All of them had finished eating and were lingering over a glass of brandy or over what was left of their wine and, as they did not require her attention, Janine came to sit at Gautier's table. She was in her early thirties, only a year or two younger than Suzanne, he supposed, but although she had worked hard all her life, her eyes and her skin had retained the freshness of youth.

'We've sold more wine today than I can ever remember before,' she told him, 'and absinthe too.'

'Because of the trial I suppose.'

'Yes. Mama decided to open at six this morning because she guessed we'd be busy.'

'You must be tired.'

'I am.'

'Would you prefer to go home?' Gautier hoped she would reject the suggestion. During the day he had more than once found himself thinking with a pleasant anticipation of the night they would spend together. Now, sitting close to her, aware of the naked, sensual body beneath her clothes, desire suddenly sharpened.

'I would never be too tired for that,' she said smiling and then blushed at her own boldness.

He smiled back, touched her hand lightly but made no comment. Instead he said, 'What sort of people come here when a woman is being tried for murder?'

'Anyone. Everyone. Lawyers watching the trial coming in for a cognac to sustain them, journalists waiting for the verdict, messengers, coachmen, chauffeurs, disappointed would-be spectators who couldn't get a seat in the court and a good sprinkling of foreigners. I served at least three Belgians, a German and two Englishmen.'

'And afterwards? What were people saying about the verdict?'

'Most of them were angry that the woman was acquitted.' Janine laughed. 'Do you know some of them were even blaming the government for the verdict.'

'People blame the government for everything. One should not take it too seriously.'

'I'm not so certain about that. There's a lot of discontent in Paris. Here in the café we hear what ordinary people have to say. Nobody has a good word for the present regime.'

What Janine had said was true. The government in France, not only the present one but also its predecessor, had been intermittently under attack from public opinion for years. One had to accept that there had been reason for the criticisms. A succession of scandals, some grave some minor, Dreyfus, Panama, had unsettled confidence in the integrity of public figures, but the press and its political opponents were assaulting the government with more venom that it deserved. It was as though Frenchmen, having chosen to create a republic after the disastrous defeat by Germany in 1871, could only satisfy themselves by testing that choice to destruction point.

But after a long day Gautier was in no mood to brood over the political situation. Moreover as a policeman he had grown accustomed to neutrality, to standing back from political arguments. Wishing to deflect their conversation into less serious channels, he asked Janine, 'And you? What does a woman think of de Richemont's acquittal?'

'In view of Le Tellier's behaviour perhaps one should not have too much sympathy for him.'

'Are you condemning him for having a mistress?' Gautier knew he could tease Janine for she was a good natured woman with the sharp, dry sense of humour one often found in country folk. 'I never imagined you would begrudge a man that simple pleasure.'

'A mistress one could forgive, even applaud, promiscuity never.'

'Promiscuity?'

'He was living with his wife and had at least two mistresses.'

'How do you know that?'

'I heard it from a coachman who was here this morning.'

The coachman, Janine explained, worked for a family who lived in Neuilly and that morning he had brought the lady of the house to the trial of Denise de Richemont. While he waited for her, he had come to the café in Place Dauphiné to while away the time. After two hours and several bocks he had grown talkative and Janine had heard him boasting that the lady for whom he worked had also been the mistress of Jacques Le Tellier.

'How would he know?' Gautier asked.

'It appears that he used to drive the woman into Paris in the afternoons quite regularly. She would always make him put her down outside the church of Notre-Dame de Lorette, telling him to return and wait for her at the same place in two hours' time. Knowing that she was not of a particularly religious disposition, he decided one day to find out where she went really went. He watched from a distance and then followed her until she went into a house in Rue Lamartine.'

'The house where Le Tellier had his garçonnière?'

'Yes. Of course he didn't know that until the trial started and everyone was talking about it.'

'She may not have been visiting Le Tellier. I know the house. Several people have apartments in it.'

'That's true,' Janine admitted, 'but after Tellier was shot the visits stopped. The coachman has never been asked to drive her to that quartier since.'

Janine lay asleep with her head resting on Gautier's shoulder. He had cramp in his arm and would have liked to move it but was afraid that he might wake her. Her shallow breathing told him that

26

her mind was balanced on the edge of consciousness in that dream-coloured world of half-sleep.

In spite of her obvious fatigue she had made love eagerly, prolonging their embraces till the anticipation of fulfilment became almost unbearable. In the few short weeks that they had been lovers her shyness had evaporated, her first timid responses been replaced by an expert skill in giving pleasure. Physically she had changed as well. Although still generously built, she had lost weight and her breasts were smaller and firmer, her thighs slimmer, her stomach flatter. Gautier had often heard men say, without believing them, that sex kept one slim and he was tempted now to accept that it might be true. At the same time he could not help wondering whether for an unmarried woman, who had never had any permanent liaison with a man, their relationship might be causing her worry and nervous tensions which were affecting her health.

Suddenly she did wake and he saw her eyelids flutter. She said, 'Of what are you thinking, chéri?'

Gautier had observed that this was a question which women often asked, some through curiosity, some to revive a flagging conversation, some because they could not bear to be excluded from any part of a man's life, however trivial. At one time the question would irritate him. Now he had developed a technique of side-stepping it.

'About tonight,' he replied untruthfully.

'It was wonderful wasn't it? Why is it so much better when one is tired?'

'Because the body is relaxed, I suppose.'

'You will remember tonight, won't you?'

'Of course.'

'No, I mean it,' she insisted, not accepting his casual response.

'To hear you speak,' Gautier said lightly, 'one would think this was to be our last night together.'

Janine did not reply immediately. He could not hear her breathe nor feel the rise and fall of her breasts against his body and guessed that she was holding her breath, unsure of how he would respond to what she was about to say. From the street outside the noise of a drunken man cursing came up to them, bouncing off the walls of the building opposite.

'Not the last,' she said simply, 'but there will not be many more.'

A nuance in her words alarmed him. He twisted his body to look

27

at her, pulling himself up on one elbow and letting her head slip on to the pillow. 'Why do you say that?' he asked her quickly.

'An affair like ours could not last for ever. We both knew that before it began.'

'Are you saying you want it to end?'

'No chéri.' She placed a hand on his cheek. 'You know I don't.'

'Nor do I.'

'Not now. Not tonight. But you will, and before too long.'

If any other woman has spoken like Janine had, Gautier would have suspected that it was just a clumsy device, a way of persuading him into making some more permanent commitment or at least a declaration of his devotion. But Janine, he felt sure, was incapable of such artifice.

'Why do you say that?'

'I can't give you a logical reason. It's just what I feel; a presentiment of parting.'

She looked up at him in the darkness and there was neither unhappiness nor reproach in her eyes. With the practical realism of a countrywoman she had accepted what instinct had told her was going to happen. Gautier wanted to protest, to argue, to tell her she was wrong but he was afraid both that his denials might seem insincere and that time might prove them to be so.

Instead he took her naked body in his arms and they began to make love again.

4

MADAME MICHELLE LE TELLIER lived in a second floor apartment in Rue Miromesnil. The maid who opened the door to Gautier when he arrived there next morning had clearly been well trained for she showed no sign of surprise or concern when he told her who he was. Instead she took his visiting card and kept him waiting while she went to enquire whether her mistress would agree to see him.

Gautier had not met the widow of the editor of *La Parole* during the investigations he had made into the latter's murder. She had been questioned by the juge d'instruction, but as a courtesy to a bereaved widow the interview had taken place at her home and by chance that day Gautier had been required to give evidence in court at the trial of a different case and the judge had gone to Rue Miromesnil accompanied by another inspector. For a reason which he would not have been able to explain, he was curious to see whether in life Madame Le Tellier matched the picture he had formed of her during the investigations and trial of the de Richemont affair.

In the event he was not able to satisfy his curiosity, for, when the maid returned to say that her mistress would see the inspector and he followed her into the drawing room of the apartment, he found Madame Le Tellier dressed in a black coat and hat and wearing a heavy veil.

'I was about to go out for my morning walk, Monsieur Gautier,' she explained.

'My apologies, Madame, for calling at an inconvenient hour. May I return later?'

'I have a better idea, if you are not averse to walking that is. Why not come with me and you can explain the purpose of your visit as we go along?'

'Enchanted, Madame.'

Leaving the apartment they turned right heading, Gautier assumed, for the Champs Elysées and possibly, if Madame Le Tellier were energetic enough, for the Tuileries gardens. About a hundred metres in front of them, on the corner of Rue du Faubourg St. Honoré and Rue Marigny, stood the Elysée Palace. Policemen were stationed at the main gates and the side entrance in Rue Marigny and several others were posted in inconspicuous positions in neighbouring streets. The newspapers that day had carried a story of anonymous letters threatening the President's life and the authorities were taking the threats seriously. No doubt they still remembered that not long previously another president, Sadi Carnot, had died by an assassin's dagger.

'You must excuse me for wearing this veil,' Madame Le Tellier told Gautier. 'It's a silly habit and most unbecoming, but a veil can be a useful disguise.'

'A disguise, Madame?'

'Although my husband has been dead for many weeks, convention insists that I should remain in mourning. I am not supposed to leave my home except in a carriage and then only to put flowers on his grave. But to stay shut up indoors would be intolerable for me. I love walking. I love life. And so I go out secretly wearing this veil. In all probability the inquisitive old ladies among my neighbours are not deceived and they know it's me. That doesn't matter. I go out disguised and convention is satisfied.'

'I understand.'

They passed the Elysée Palace and continued under the chestnut trees along Rue Marigny. Although the skies were clear the weather had turned colder overnight with a heavy frost. Madame Le Tellier's ankle length coat had a broad fur collar and she wore a muff of matching fur.

'Have you come to see me in connection with my husband's death?' she asked.

'Yes, Madame.'

'But surely now that the trial is over the matter is closed so far as the police are concerned. Justice has at least been seen to be done.'

'You say that as though you do not agree with the verdict.'

Madame Le Tellier turned her head to look at Gautier through her veil. 'What reason that woman may have had for shooting my husband I do not know. But the reason which was put forward in her defence was false.'

'What makes you think that?'

'Mademoiselle de Richemont was not Jacques's mistress.'

Her statement, forthright and unhesitating, did not surprise Gautier. In his experience women were loyal to their husbands and widows were the most loyal of all. It was as though death with a single stroke could discount all the failings and misdeeds of a man, no matter how outrageous.

'Do you know that for certain?' he asked.

'Don't misunderstand me, Monsieur Gautier. Of course my husband had a mistress. I know that. During the course of our marriage he had several, but Denise de Richemont was not one of them. Of that I am absolutely sure.'

Gautier made no comment for it did not seem that there was anything he could usefully say. Moreover he had the feeling that Madame Le Tellier had more that she wished to tell him, but that

30

she would tell him in her own way and in her own time. She had spoken of being shut up in her home since her husband's death and she may have felt socially isolated as well, with no one in whom she could confide. If instead of questioning her Gautier would listen sympathetically, he might find himself in the rôle of confidant.

Leaving Rue Marigny, they walked through the gardens which bordered each side of the Avenue des Champs Elysées. In spite of the cold, children were playing on the lawns and around the shrubberies, the boys wearing velvet jackets and breeches beneath their topcoats, the girls with toque hats, short coats and high-buttoned boots. A group of them were playing 'prisoner's base', with a great deal of shouting and scurrying to and fro, all beneath the watchful eyes of their governesses who sat and gossiped on a nearby bench.

Opposite the rows of little wooden booths selling gingerbread, barley-sugar and toys, a man had set up a brazier on which he was roasting potatoes. Unexpectedly Madame Le Tellier stopped to buy one.

'I wonder if you would be so kind as to pay the man,' she said to Gautier. 'I did not bring my reticule with me.'

'With pleasure.'

She took the potato and slipped it into her muff and they continued their walk. Gautier had heard that women often used potatoes in this way to keep their hands warm during performances at the Paris Opéra where the building was notoriously cold.

'I've two reasons for knowing that Denise de Richemont was not my husband's mistress,' Madame Le Tellier continued as though neither their conversation nor her train of thought had been interrupted. 'The first is that Jacques, although a radical in his opinions, was obsessively conservative in his tastes. Only one type of woman appealed to him. I know that only too well. If ever his glance was drawn to a pretty girl, any girl, the daughter of a friend, a midinette delivering a new dress to our home, a girl selling flowers in the street, in looks and appearance she always belonged to the same type.'

'What type was that?'

Madame Le Tellier laughed, a short bitter laugh. 'I was going to say the same type as I am, but of course you have not seen my face. A rather conventional prettiness was what Jacques liked; blue eyes, pink complexion, very fair hair; faintly Teutonic if you like, a

31

Wagner heroine. And she must have a full figure. He detested those slim, angular, flat-chested figures which are becoming all the rage today.'

'No one could say that Mademoiselle de Richemont fitted that description.'

'My second reason for believing that Mademoiselle de Richemont's story about my husband was untrue is that I know the name of his last mistress; her christian name that is.'

'How did you find that out?'

'Poor Jacques was very careless. Perhaps he realized that I knew about his infidelities and didn't mind very much. At all events only a few days before he died I found a note from the lady which he had left lying about. Her name was Gigi, not Denise.'

'How very indiscreet!' Gautier remarked, thinking that a man in Le Tellier's profession, skilful enough in uncovering the secrets of others, should have had the prudence to conceal his own.

They had reached the bottom of the Avenue des Champs Elysées and Gautier expected that they would cross the Place de la Concorde and continue through the Tuileries gardens, but Madame Le Tellier stopped there and turned to face him. 'This is as far as I am going today, Monsieur Gautier,' she said.

'May I escort you home, Madame?'

'Thank-you, no. I have a call to make.'

'Then thank-you for giving me your time.'

'I enjoyed your company, Monsieur. Please do not hesitate to call at my house again if there is any further help I can give you.'

'There is one more question I would like to ask you, Madame, before you leave.'

'What is that?'

'If you do not know the surname of this woman, Gigi, can you at least guess who she might be?'

'No. I regret not.'

Turning away from him, Madame Le Tellier walked back towards Rue Marigny. Gautier found himself wishing she had not been wearing a veil for he would have liked to see her expression when she answered his final question, so that he could have decided if, as he suspected, she had not been telling the truth.

The new editor of *La Parole* was seated at the desk in the room where, on his last visit to the newspaper's offices, Gautier had found the body of Jacques Le Tellier. Monsieur Massart was an older man than Le Tellier, with a reserved manner and watchful eyes. Gautier wondered whether his appointment as editor reflected a deliberate change in policy by the owners of the paper and whether in future *La Parole* would be replacing its aggressive, crusading editorials with a more restrained and conservative approach. But when he explained that he was making a few last enquiries to tidy up the dossier on Le Tellier's murder before it was filed in the archives, Massart's response was not what he had expected.

'The authorities may wish to tidy up this affair and lock away their dossier,' he said angrily. 'No doubt they would prefer it that way. But you will find the French press less willing to forget this scandal!'

A copy of that day's *La Parole* lay on the editor's desk and picking it up he thrust it towards Gautier. Under the bold heading 'IS THIS JUSTICE?' was a trenchant article written, one supposed, by the editor himself.

IS THIS JUSTICE?

Yesterday in the Palais de Justice Mademoiselle Denise de Richemont, who by her admission and in the presence of witnesses had shot the former editor of our newspaper in cold blood and without provocation, was found not guilty by a jury and left the assize court a free woman. We should be asking ourselves how this bizarre verdict could have been returned. That de Richemont shot Monsieur Jacques Le Tellier, a distinguished editor and well-respected citizen of Paris, a good husband and a good servant of the Republic, cannot be doubted. Why then did a jury of honest Frenchmen acquit her? The plea put forward by her defence counsel in mitigation of her crime—and let us not equivocate, it was a crime—was one of 'crime passionel'. Are we then saying that any woman who believes herself to be wronged by a man has the right to punish him with death? A strange philosophy indeed! Are we saying that an editor of any newspaper who dares to expose the murky secrets of men in positions of public trust can be assassinated with impunity by the relatives of these ignoble men?

This is an argument which no right-minded person would accept. So we should be wondering, then, how this monstrous verdict came to be reached. Did the public prosecutor present his

33

case against the accused with sufficient conviction and determination? Did the judge question the accused with enough vigour and perspicacity to reveal the truth? Or may we believe that the government, for reasons of its own, did not wish de Richemont to be convicted? How much influence did people of eminence exercise on the trial and on the verdict? It was widely believed that the date of the trial was brought forward by the Ministry of Justice at the special request of an important person. We can now confirm that this was the case and that the person who interceded on de Richemont's behalf was Monsieur B———, a minister in the government.

Our readers may well ask themselves what is Monsieur B———'s interest in the young woman who shot Jacques Le Tellier. Could it be that it is he and not Le Tellier who has been her lover all along? Or is his motive for helping to bring about this mockery of a trial, this scandalous acquittal, something much more sinister?

Gautier handed the copy of the newspaper back to Massart. He realized now that he had misjudged the new editor who, assuming he had written or at least sanctioned the publication of the editorial, was likely to be at least as combative as his predecessor.

'Have you seen the other newspapers today, Inspector?' Massart asked. '*Figaro*? *Le Monde*? *Le Temps*? *L'Aurore*?'

'As yet no.'

'What they have published echoes the views I have expressed in my editorial; some even more strongly.'

'The press is united in this matter then?'

'Absolutely. If every fanatic who believes himself to have been defamed or insulted in print can feel entitled to shoot the journalist responsible, that will be the end of the freedom of the press.'

'But why have you suggested that the government was involved in the acquittal of de Richemont?' Gautier asked.

'Jacques was a constant embarrassment to them. He had a flair for unearthing unsavoury secrets: corruption, nepotism, underhand manoeuvres. And whatever he discovered he printed. Jacques was afraid of no one.'

Gautier did not ask whether Massart had any evidence of government complicity in the killing of Le Tellier, for he was certain there was none. The shooting of one of their colleagues had provoked a nervousness bordering on hysteria among journalists, which had only strengthened their suspicions of the French government. The fact that Massart had practically named a minister as being responsible for frustrating justice meant very little. In France the law of libel was lax and vaguely defined, so there was no chance of Massart being taken to court and the worst he might expect would be a challenge to a duel at dawn behind the grandstand of the racecourse at Auteuil, and duels never ended in anything more serious than a flesh wound, reconciliation over a good breakfast and congratulations from friends for settling one's differences like gentlemen.

On his previous visit to the offices of *La Parole*, Gautier had been told by the staff of the newspaper that they knew nothing of Denise de Richemont. No one had ever met her until the day of the shooting, no one could recall Le Tellier ever mentioning her name, even when the story of her father's indiscretions was about to be published, there was no record of any conversation between her and Le Tellier. Rather than go over the same ground again, Gautier decided now to follow a new line of enquiry.

'You have had time, Monsieur Massart, I suppose, to go through the papers which your predecessor left in his office?'

'Yes. I've done that.'

'Did you find anything to suggest that Monsieur Le Tellier might have been killed not for the reasons which the woman de Richemont gave at her trial, but for another completely different motive?'

'What other motive, Inspector?' Massart asked, puzzled.

'I really don't know. Let me put my question another way. Was there anything in your predecessor's papers to show that he was in any way involved in political activities? Not merely writing about politics but involved in political action? Was he part of any radical society or group?'

'You're asking whether he was part of a conspiracy.'

'Something like that.'

Massart shook his head decisively. 'No, Monsieur. Jacques was never one to join groups or societies. He liked to work alone. He was secretive. If he had an idea for an article to print in the paper, especially if it was an exposé, he would work on it alone, never telling his colleagues until he was ready to publish. For example, none of us knew the story he was writing about the Duc de

Richemont until the evening before it appeared in our paper. Sometimes his secretiveness could be embarrassing.'

'One can imagine that.'

'He kept a diary in the office and, do you know, the entries he made in that were cryptic, as though he did not want anyone to know the purpose of his engagements.'

Gautier felt a quickening of interest: a sensation not strong enough to be called excitement, but one which he knew from past experience often marked the beginning of a discovery, a first step towards finding the answer to a teasing puzzle. He asked Massart quickly, 'Do you have the diary, Monsieur?'

'I regret not, Inspector. It appeared to be of no value so I gave instructions for it to be destroyed.'

'Can you at least recall any entries in the diary which seemed particularly cryptic?'

Massart thought about the question for a time before replying. 'There was one entry, or rather a whole series of entries which I thought strange. They began some weeks before Jacques was shot. The first of them, I remember, simply read, "Rue Miromesnil—an interesting address!"'

'But Monsieur Le Tellier lived in Rue Miromesnil!'

'He was not referring to his own home. That became clear from later entries.'

'What were they?'

'The second one, as far as I recall, said, "Rue Miromesnil—an elderly beauty and three ambitious beasts." In the weeks after the first reference to Rue Miromesnil Jacques had made a whole series of entries all of them commencing with the same name.'

'There was nothing else which might explain what he was writing about?'

'Not really. On more than one occasion he mentioned three men and one woman and I thought at first that he might have uncovered a scandal; four people meeting secretly for immoral purposes. You may remember the public uproar not long ago when it was learned that young girls were being procured in a hotel room for two men of great eminence.'

'But you decided your guess was wrong?'

'Yes. The only woman mentioned—and she was mentioned more than once—was an elderly widow. And some of the entries alluded to music. One read, "Rue Miromesnil—a male voice quartet serenades the siren, but which voice is the leader?" In fact musical allusions appeared quite often in the entries.'

'I thought you said there were three men.'

'The first entries mentioned three. Later he always talked of four. And there was another strange thing. The meetings always seemed to take place on a Thursday.'

Gautier smiled. It happened to be Thursday that day as well. He realized it was just chance, but chance frequently helped to speed the course of an investigation. Luck had often served him well. He said to Massart, 'I have one more favour to ask of you, Monsieur, and then I will leave you to get on with your work. You have a lady who writes in your paper on society and social events, have you not?'

'Yes. Madame de Trémoille.'

'Do you suppose she might know who this widow in Rue de Miromesnil might be?'

'We can only ask her.'

All the daily newspapers in Paris, even those with radical leanings like *La Parole*, devoted many columns to reporting on the life of the Monde. Not only balls and soirées and dinner parties, but even events as trivial as children's parties were described in detail and the guests named. Some papers even published regular lists showing on what days of the week and at what times leading hostesses were 'at home' and would receive callers. The woman who compiled these columns for *La Parole* wrote under the nom-de-plume of Madame de Trémoille, a name chosen, one suspected, as a satirical jibe at *Figaro*, whose gossip writer Madame Estradère had dignified herself with the name of Princesse de Mesagne.

'This gives me an opportunity to demonstrate our latest acquisition,' Massart said proudly. 'An electric bell system. I press here once for my stenographer, twice for the deputy editor and three times for Madame de Trémoille and so on.'

He pressed an electric bell-push fixed to his desk and fortune was with him that day, for it worked. In a few moments the gossip writer appeared; a gross woman dressed in colours far brighter than any lady of conventional upbringing would allow herself to wear in daytime. Gautier remembered having seen her at a gala performance of one of Paris's finest circuses, at a charity bazaar, at the vernissage or preview day of an exhibition of paintings and at other events where the leaders of Paris society might be found. Massart told her about the entries in Le Tellier's diary and immediately she smiled.

'From his description, Monsieur Le Tellier can only have been referring to Madame Simone Pasquier.'

'Madame Pasquier? I don't think I know the name,' Gautier remarked.

'She is a wealthy widow, once very beautiful, who has retained enough of her looks and her charm to have a string of admirers, clubmen mostly.'

'You could call her an eccentric,' Massart added. 'She was the first woman to have a licence to drive an automobile and at her age!'

'Yes and her salon is considered rather bohemian,' Madame de Trémoille said, 'although a number of people from the Monde may be seen there.'

'Do you know the names of any of her gentlemen admirers?' Gautier asked.

'The most distinguished and the most loyal over many years has been the Prince de Chaville.'

5

'I AM HAPPY to receive you, Monsieur Gautier, but I should warn you that I am expecting guests shortly.'

'You are very kind, Madame. The questions I wish to ask you will take only a few moments.'

'I cannot imagine what they could possibly be.'

Madame Pasquier was sitting erect and straight in a hard-backed chair in her drawing-room. Although she must have been approaching seventy, she was still a handsome woman and that day she had pinned her hair up in a mass of tight curls, showing off her fine neck and generous bosom, which the very low decolleté of her dress scarcely concealed at all. She stared at Gautier with a more than polite interest. It was, he realized, the appraising stare of a woman who had always hungered after men and whose instincts had not changed, even though age might have dampened the fires of desire.

'I came to ask you, Madame, whether you knew the late Monsieur Le Tellier.'

'The editor of *La Parole*? Of course! He and his wife were neighbours of mine.'

'Did he ever visit your home?'

'Yes. At one time he and his wife were regular guests at my Tuesday salon. But not for very long. Jacques Le Tellier did not approve of most of my other guests, for political reasons. Why do you ask?'

'He left a diary in which he had made several references to you and your home.'

'Strange! I had no idea he took any interest in me or my affairs.'

'Did he ever visit you on Thursdays?'

Madame Pasquier's smile suggested that she was flattered by Gautier's question. 'So you have heard of my Thursday coterie, Inspector?'

'Coterie?'

'One might even call it a club, for its membership is exclusive; more exclusive than the Jockey Club I can tell you. No, Jacques Le Tellier was not one of the gentlemen who visit me every Thursday afternoon. He could never have aspired to that.'

'It is a small group then?'

'There are only four of them at present. Of course there have been more over the years, but the present four are so jealous and possessive that they have driven all others away.'

Madame Pasquier had finished the cigarette she had been smoking and now immediately she lit another. For a woman to smoke was almost unheard of and Gautier wondered whether this was an eccentricity, like driving an automobile, which she had deliberately cultivated. However many admirers she might have, a woman growing old, widowed and alone, might feel the need to draw attention to herself.

'It's Madame Le Tellier for whom one should feel sympathy,' she remarked.

'Yes. To have one's husband murdered in those circumstances must have been a most distressing experience.'

'That is not what I meant. At least she is now rid of a faithless husband. The mistake she made was ever to marry him.'

'Why do you say that?' Gautier asked.

'Jacques Le Tellier was nobody. A little bourgeois with ambitions and a malicious curiosity. His wife on the other hand comes of an excellent family. Before her marriage she was a Floquet, a lesser branch of one of the oldest families in France. She made the error of marrying for love, poor creature!'

'Love matches are not always disastrous.'

Madame Pasquier's sniff showed her contempt for love matches. 'A woman should marry for security and a proper place in society. I recall my father warning my sister and myself against marrying for love. "A few nights of passion in bed," he used to say, "and the rest of your life at the wrong end of the dinner table." And he was right. A woman can find passion enough and lovers enough after she is married, if that is what she wishes.'

Coming from another woman or a younger one the remark might have seemed a boast or an invitation. Gautier however, was beginning to suspect that everything Madame Pasquier was saying was no more than a distraction, a way of preventing him from pursuing the line of enquiry he had come there to make. 'Are you acquainted with the woman who shot Le Tellier?' he asked her almost brusquely.

'Of course. She has been to my salon. Denise is the daughter of the Duc de Richemont.'

'And the mistress of Le Tellier?'

'So they say.' Madame Pasquier appeared to phrase her reply carefully, as though she saw a trap in Gautier's question.

For his part Gautier began to feel that he was going to learn nothing from his visit to her house, which he had made on nothing more than a sudden impulse. Madame Pasquier, in spite of her willingness to see him, was a shrewd woman and she would not be tricked or surprised into any careless admissions, even supposing she had any secrets to admit.

'You have no idea, Madame, why Jacques Le Tellier should have written of your house in his diary?'

'How can I have, Inspector, when you have not told me what he wrote?'

Now she had forced Gautier into a position where he must decide whether or not to reveal his hand. It was a losing position, for even if

40

the entries in the diary, meaningless to him, meant anything to Madame Pasquier, she was not likely to tell him so.

In the event he was spared from having to make the decision, for at that moment the manservant, who had earlier let him into the house, admitted two more visitors into the drawing-room. One of them Gautier recognized. Pierre de Jarnac was a leading French politician and a well-known public figure in Paris. Not many months previously he had created a stir by resigning from his position as Minister for Foreign Affairs as a protest against the Government's shift in foreign policy. He was one of several politicians who could never forgive Britain for the insult of Fashoda and for what they saw as a condescending arrogance, and so they would not condone the Entente Cordiale. Handsome, persuasive and a brilliant orator, he now led a small but powerful band of supporters in the Chamber of Deputies and was popular with the people of Paris. The man who accompanied him into the room must have been approaching seventy but was slim and erect and appeared indestructible. He had white hair and a precisely clipped white beard and moustache and his eyes were small and dark and hard.

'My dear Jean!' Madame Pasquier exclaimed. 'Pierre! You're both early!'

'We met by chance on your doorstep,' the white-haired man explained. 'I strolled round here from the Cercle de la Rue Royale.' First he and then de Jarnac kissed Madame Pasquier's hand.

'I trust our early arrival is not inopportune,' de Jarnac said, glancing at Gautier.

'Not at all. This is Inspector Gautier of the Sûreté.' Madame de Pasquier's tone implied only too clearly that a visit by the police was of no consequence and would not be allowed to interfere with social distractions.

De Jarnac gave Gautier a practised, politician's smile. 'I know of your reputation, Inspector. The Prefect of Police thinks highly of your capabilities.'

'Monsieur Gautier is making enquiries about Jacques Le Tellier. I was not able to help him, but perhaps you gentlemen can.' Briefly Madame Pasquier explained about the entries in Le Tellier's diary. Then nodding in the direction of the white-haired man she added, 'Monsieur le Prince de Chaville knows something of Le Tellier and his newspaper.'

41

'I have no wish to speak ill of the dead,' the prince said disdainfully, 'but the man was a scoundrel, a sly opportunist and an unscrupulous peddler of scandal.'

'These references in his diary to Madame Pasquier's home,' de Jarnac said. 'One supposes that they were not complimentary.'

'Neither complimentary nor the opposite. Cryptic would be a better way of describing them.'

'You could not understand them, then?'

'Not fully.'

'But earlier you asked me if he had ever come to this house on Thursdays!' Madame Pasquier said, almost accusingly, as though she suspected Gautier of lying. 'You must have had a reason for that question.'

'Le Tellier mentioned in his diary that meetings were held here on Thursdays.'

'I knew it! He must have got to hear of our Thursday afternoon conversaziones.'

'He would imagine that they had some sinister significance,' de Jarnac remarked and laughed. 'Poor Le Tellier! Suspicion had become a mania with him. If he saw two women gossiping under a tree in the Parc Monceau, he would suspect a conspiracy.'

'What I do not understand, Inspector,' the Prince de Chaville said, 'is why you should be making these enquiries. You cannot still be investigating Le Tellier's death.'

'The dossier is not yet closed.'

'But we know how he was killed and who killed him!'

'It has been suggested that the motive which Mademoiselle professed for killing Le Tellier was not the true one.'

'What other motive could she have possibly had?' the prince demanded.

'That is what I am trying to discover.'

'Well, I regret that we cannot be of any help to you, Inspector,' de Jarnac said.

'As I told Monsieur Gautier, Jacques Le Tellier only visited my house once or twice,' Madame Pasquier said, 'and at that a very long time ago.'

Gautier realized that he had nothing to gain by prolonging his visit. As he had expected, he had learnt little at Madame Pasquier's house, but even so he did not regret calling on her. Sometimes a police investigation was not unlike a physician's examination, needing much patient probing in several places before the source of the infection was discovered.

As courteously as he could he took his leave and Madame Pasquier tugged on a velvet bell-pull by the fireplace to bring a manservant who would show him out of the house. Gautier followed the man down the main stairs and when the front door was opened he saw that two more visitors were just arriving. One of them was Paul Valanis and the other a tall man wearing the uniform of a colonel in the Hussars.

'We can expect news from Languedoc soon,' Gautier heard the colonel say.

'Inspector Gautier!' Valanis exclaimed, nodding at Gautier at the same time as he placed a hand quickly on the arm of the colonel.

In the normal way, Gautier was certain, Valanis would not even have acknowledged him if he met him by chance, much less have spoken to him. The Greek, wealthy as a result of his armament deals, had a vast house in the Avenue du Bois where he was amassing a fine art collection and he was aware that Gautier had once suspected him of conspiring to buy stolen paintings. Although no case had ever been proved or even brought against him, Valanis had not since that time been able to hide his hatred of Gautier. Was his greeting that afternoon then a signal, Gautier wondered; a warning to the colonel that they were in the presence of the police?

An automobile stood in the street with a chauffeur in attendance. After Valanis and the colonel had gone into the house. Gautier stopped to look at the machine. The chauffeur, who wore a peaked cap and a long driving-coat over his leggings, was polishing the paintwork with a chamois leather.

'That's a very handsome machine!' Gautier remarked to the man. 'A new model is it not?'

'Yes. The latest Panhard et Levassor,' the chauffeur replied. 'It was shown at the Salon de l'Automobile for the first time only last month.'

'Then there will not be many like it in Paris?'

'None,' the chauffeur said proudly. 'As you can see this model has a special type of headlamp; gold-plated instead of brass, which were made to the instructions of my employer, Colonel Charles Roussel.'

What the man had said confirmed what Gautier had suspected. The automobile and its chauffeur were those that had been waiting outside the Palais de Justice the previous day to drive Denise de Richemont away after her trial had ended.

Before leaving the Sûreté that morning, Gautier had given his assistant, Surat, two assignments. Surat was a loyal and fearless police officer who had been passed by for promotion, but had remained dedicated to his work. So when he arrived back at the Quai des Orfèvres, Gautier was not surprised to find that the first of the two tasks had already been completed and that Surat's report on it lay on his desk.

CONFIDENTIAL REPORT

for Inspector J-P. Gautier

With the assistance of the administration of the Palais de Justice, I established that there were two ladies among the spectators in the reserved seats on the last day of the de Richemont trial; the Duchesse de Richemont and Madame Geneviève Stahl. From enquiries subsequently made at a number of sources, I compiled the following information on these two persons:

The Duchesse de Richemont

Mother of the accused and wife of the former French ambassador in Rome, the duchesse was the only daughter of a wealthy bourgeois and brought a considerable dowry to her marriage with the duc, whose own family was generally believed to be impoverished at the time. The duchesse remained loyal to her husband in spite of the scandal which led to his resignation from the diplomatic service and they have been living quietly at their country château. She came alone to Paris for the trial and has been staying with a sister.

Madame Geneviève Stahl

Madame Stahl is the wife of André Stahl, head of the great banking family. Born Geneviève Grasset, she became an actress but was better known in the demi-monde for her great beauty than for any acting talent. In spite of her unconventional background, Madame Stahl was accepted by society after her marriage, no doubt because of the services rendered to France by her husband, his great wealth and his patronage of the arts, and for some years she had a fashionable salon in their home in St. Germain. Two years ago, however, Monsieur Stahl suffered a

44

severe heart attack from which he has still not fully recovered. The family moved to Neuilly for the sake of his health and are living there now.

As he put the report away in a drawer of his desk, Gautier smiled. He had asked Surat merely to find out who were the two women whom he had seen seated in the seats reserved for important spectators at the de Richemont trial. But Surat was never satisfied with simple, straightforward tasks and on his own initiative had assembled the facts set down in his report without asking himself where they were likely to be of any value to Gautier. It was this plodding conscientiousness, Gautier supposed, that had blinded his superiors to Surat's merits and prevented his being raised to a position of authority. No doubt he was now carrying out the second assignment Gautier had given him with the same time-consuming thoroughness.

The thought of Surat's conscientiousness reminded him that he had allowed himself to be diverted from the investigation which he was supposed to be making into the murder of Eva Callot. That at least was how Courtrand would see it. The director-general made his subordinates prepare regular reports for him on the cases for which they were responsible and he expected these reports to contain accounts of routine police activities which he understood: searches of premises, searches for people, interrogations, the apprehension of suspects. Gautier, on the other hand, preferred his own methods of solving a case, methods which were often oblique and even tortuous and which relied to a great extent on deduction and logic. Courtrand could not be expected to understand that in his own way he was investigating the death of Eva Callot.

Reluctantly he decided that simply to satisfy Courtrand and maintain some kind of peaceful relations with the man, he must put on a show of activity. Taking a sheet of paper, he began sketching out a plan for sending a dozen policemen to search in the Paris underworld for the man whom the police had first suspected of killing Callot, the anarchist Igor Kratov. Before he had set out the first stage of his plan, however, a messenger came from Courtrand.

'Inspector Gautier,' the man said, 'a force of fifty policemen is being assembled downstairs outside the building. The director-general wishes you to take command of them and proceed to the Esplanade des Invalides without delay.'

'Les Invalides? What is happening there?'

'A demonstration by unemployed workmen.'

'A demonstration against the government is a political matter. Why is the Sûreté being involved?'

'The Prefect of Police believes that the crowds may well start rioting. All available police officers are being mobilized to contain it.'

6

THE DEMONSTRATION WHICH was being staged on the Esplanade des Invalides that afternoon was meant to be a protest by unemployed workmen. Without doubt there were many people wanting work among the large crowd that had assembled on the open spaces in front of the Hôtel des Invalides, but those who led the protest were neither workmen nor unemployed. Among those who made inflammatory speeches attacking the government from a hastily erected platform, Gautier recognized left-wing intellectual writers, the editor of the socialist journal *Liberté* and a Pole, formerly a leader of the anarchist movement, who was now a professional agitator with an international reputation.

Gautier had left his detachment of uniformed officers in the horse-drawn police waggons which had brought them there from Sûreté headquarters, in a side street on the other side of the Chambre des Députés and gone on foot to Rue de Constantine, which bordered the east side of the Esplanade. There he found the commissaires of police from the seventh and fifteenth arrondissements, who had brought policemen to the scene and were discussing what they should do to ensure that the demonstration was kept under control.

'One of the speakers has just called on the crowd to march on the Elysée Palace and demand work,' Commissaire Druot said. Gautier had worked under Druot before he had been transferred from the fifteenth arondissement to the Sûréte.

'And they seemed to like the suggestion,' the other commissaire added.

'Professional agitators are circulating among the crowd, rousing their feelings.'

'How many people do you suppose there are here?' Gautier asked, nodding towards the crowd.

'At least twelve thousand, probably fifteen.'

'I'll divide my men into two groups and spread them across the bridges.' Gautier nodded in the direction of the Pont Alexandre III and the Pont de la Concorde. 'But if we are to prevent them crossing the Seine we will need reinforcements.'

'We could telephone from my commissariat and ask for the Brigades Centrales to be sent out.'

'That's a good plan. They could be brought up to the bridges on the other side.'

The three men also agreed that the police from the local arrondissements should be used to block off Quai d'Orsay to prevent the demonstrators moving along the river to cross further down. Messengers were despatched to relay these instructions. Meanwhile the demonstrators were making preparations to start their march. An improvised flag had been made by nailing a piece of black cloth to the handle of a broomstick and this was handed to one of the men on the platform who had evidently been chosen to lead the marchers. Presently he came down from the platform accompanied by the people around him and they set off shouting to the crowd to follow them. The demonstrators fell in behind them in ranks of about ten or twelve and the untidy procession moved off, not towards the river but along Rue Constantine towards Rue de Grenelle.

'They are not heading for the Elysée Palace,' Druot said. 'Where do you suppose they intend to go? The Palais de Justice?'

'This could be just a feint,' Gautier replied. 'A trick to make us move our men from the bridges.'

'What shall we do?'

'Let them go.'

He was right. Less than half of the crowd gathered on the Esplanade des Invalides fell in behind the group heading for St. Germain. A few minutes later another procession was being formed at the end of the Esplanade nearest to the river. Leaving the two commissaires Gautier hurried away, cutting behind the Chamber of

Deputies to join his men on the Pont de la Concorde. They had spread out across the bridge, forming a cordon half-way along its length.

Presently the procession of demonstrators appeared, moving along Quai d'Orsay towards the bridge. They intended, Gautier supposed, to cross the Seine and then march through Place de la Concorde, up Rue Royale and along Rue du Faubourg St. Honoré to the president's palace. The procession, like the other one which had set off towards St. Germain, was led by half-a-dozen men, one of whom was carrying a black flag. Behind this symbol of defiance at least five hundred people marched in an untidy column which spread across the road. As they marched the demonstrators began to shout two simple slogans repeated alternately: 'Give us work!' and 'Give us bread!'

When it reached the Pont de la Concorde, the column began crossing it, moving towards the thin line of policemen. Gautier realized that with the token force at his disposal he could not prevent the marchers from getting across the river if they were determined enough to charge the police. Looking over his shoulder he saw no sign of any reinforcements arriving in Place de la Concorde.

When the column reached the line of police, its leaders stopped. The man carrying the black flag came up to Gautier.

'Instruct your men to move aside,' he said. 'We wish to cross the bridge.'

'I'm sorry, Monsieur. We have been sent here to prevent you crossing.'

'This is a peaceful demonstration. We have a right to go wherever we wish.'

'As you well know the Prefect of Police has the authority to control and restrain illegal assemblies like yours.'

The man pointed with his flag towards the line of uniformed policemen. 'A handful of flics cannot stop us. We intend to march to the Elysée Palace and see that the President understands our demands.'

'In that case your demonstration will no longer be peaceful. You know the penalties for that, Monsieur. Would you really enjoy a sojourn in New Caledonia?'

In recent years several agitators and revolutionaries had been sent to France's penal colonies in New Caledonia, including Louise

48

Michel, the former communard. Louise, a plain and belligerant schoolmistress popularly nicknamed 'The Red Virgin' had spent seven years there before being pardoned. Faced with this reminder of the possible penalties to which he was exposing himself, as a ringleader of the demonstration, the man with the flag hesitated.

'Look, my friend,' Gautier went on, in the tone of one offering good advice. 'The Brigades Centrales have already been called out and they will be waiting for you at the Elysée Palace if not at the other end of the Place de la Concorde.'

The mention of the Brigades Centrales dispelled any lingering inclinations which the man with the black flag might have had for marching on the president's palace. They were a special detachment of police, picked for their size and strength and not noted for gentleness, who were deployed to deal with rioting or civil unrest. The leader of the march turned and spoke to his fellow ringleaders in low tones and presently they began to usher the demonstrators on the bridge back to the Left Bank. There they reformed in a column and set out marching, past the Chamber of Deputies and into Boulevard St. Germain.

Gautier realized that they must intend to join up with the other column that had already marched in that direction. Waiting for a few minutes to make sure that it was not just a ruse to trick the police into leaving the bridge unguarded, he followed in the wake of the demonstrators, taking half-a-dozen officers with him and leaving the rest to wait on the bridge until the Brigades Centrales or other reinforcements arrived.

The marchers moved quickly, evidently anxious to regroup with the other column as soon as possible, and within a few minutes the tail of the procession that had set off down Boulevard St. Germain came into sight. Gautier could hear the chanting of slogans and presently the sound of breaking glass. He realized that whatever the intentions of the organizers, the demonstration was no longer inoffensive and peaceful. Half-way along the boulevard there was a baker's shop where sometimes on his way home from the Sûreté he would stop to buy bread. Now the shop was a shambles, the door half-torn off its hinges, the windows shattered, the shelves inside empty. He looked into the shop and found the baker and his assistant looking in shocked dismay at the mess.

'Those ruffians looted my shop!' the baker exclaimed, pointing at two or three score of demonstrators who were running down the boulevard to catch up with the tail of the procession.

'What happened?'

'The leaders of the procession stopped outside my shop and one of them called out to the people behind him that if they wanted bread they should help themselves.'

'Did you recognize the man who shouted that? Or any of the other ringleaders?'

'As a matter of fact I did. He's a good-for-nothing student from the quartier named Marcilly. And I know some of the others as well. It's a fine thing when an honest tradesman is the victim of this socialist agitation!'

Following the end of the procession along the boulevard once more, Gautier saw that two other shops had been looted, a butcher's shop and another selling religious pictures, holy candles and plaster statuettes of the saints. He knew what this would mean. For that afternoon the police would try only to contain the demonstration, rather than risking further violence by arresting the ringleaders, but over the next few days all those who had been recognized among the leaders of the procession would be arrested. Lengthy interrogations would follow and in due course trials, at which, under the 'Lois Scélérates', passed in 1898 to curb anarchist violence, harsh sentences of imprisonment or deportation could be meted out.

Meanwhile the demonstration was starting to peter out as small groups of men, frightened perhaps of becoming involved in the looting and violence, were breaking off from the column and slipping away down side streets. Now that the march on the Elysée Palace had been abandoned, the demonstration seemed in any case to have lost its purpose. Not even the leaders appeared to know where it was heading and what would happen when it reached that objective. Gautier began to believe that in a short time what was left of the crowd would be marshalled together in some suitable place, would listen to a few final speeches and then be told to go to their homes.

Deciding that there was nothing further he could usefully do there, he made up his mind to return to Sûreté headquarters. Then he remembered he was only a short walk away from the neighbourhood in which the Prince de Chaville lived. It was to that district that Surat had gone on the second of the two assignments he had been given and it was likely that he would still be there,

50

drinking and gossiping in one of the humbler bistros or workmen's cafés. Gautier had asked him to find out as much as he could about the household of the Prince de Chaville. The servants of the rich, especially the coachmen, often had time to waste between finishing their daytime work and starting the evening's duties and many of them would spend it in nearby bistros or cafés. Surat, as Gautier knew, had a flair for making friends with the kind of people to be found in those places: servants from prosperous homes, shop workers, mechanics, lamplighters. And when he had won their confidence, they would talk freely, grumbling about the strictness or meanness of their masters and at other times boasting about the wealth or influence of the families for which they worked. A policeman could often learn more from listening to this idle gossip than from hours of interrogation.

Leaving Boulevard St. Germain, he cut down Rue Bac towards Rue de Varenne in which the prince had his hôtel particulier, an insipid seventeenth-century mansion. Surat was not in either of the first two bistros into which he glanced, but in the third Gautier saw him seated at a table, talking with two men. The first was small, ferret-faced, and wore blue trousers and a blue and gold striped waistcoat, while the heavy blue topcoat of the second suggested that he might be a coachman. Ignoring Surat, Gautier went to the counter, ordered a glass of red wine, pulled out a newspaper which he was carrying in his pocket and pretended to read it while he sipped the wine. He was close enough to Surat and his new friends to hear what they were saying.

'He's a proud man the prince,' the ferret-faced man said, 'proud and hard. You wouldn't believe how strictly he treats us.'

'Strictly yes, but always fairly,' the coachman said.

'I agree. And he'll always help any of us that gets into trouble.'

'I suppose he keeps you up till all hours of the night,' Surat remarked.

'And longer. Often I've been up till the morning waiting for him to return home.'

'Out making love to some cocotte no doubt,' Surat suggested and then added, 'My patron is the same. Spends all his time womanizing and leaves me to do his work.'

'The prince is not as bad now as he used to be,' the coachman said. 'A few years ago when he was younger he was out every night. I

51

couldn't count the hours I spent waiting outside the apartment of that Grasset woman.'

'Geneviève Grasset the actress?'

'She calls herself an actress.' The coachman grinned lewdly. 'But she spent more time on her back than on the stage.'

'I never knew she was the prince's mistress.'

'That was before you came to work for the family.'

'I've been with them ten years.'

'It would be a full twelve years since the affair ended. The prince was crazy about Gigi, as they called her. Spent a fortune on the woman! They say he once bought her a necklace costing half-a-million francs. And he'd take her out every night. Maxim's one day, Weber's the next or the Ritz hotel. All the best restaurants in Paris.'

'But he grew tired of her?' Surat suggested.

'No. It was the other way round. After taking all his gifts and spending all his money, she gave him up for another man. The prince never forgave her for being unfaithful. They had a flaming row.'

'Unfaithful? That's a laugh!' the ferret-faced man remarked. 'Women like Gigi will sell their bodies to whoever pays the most.'

What the man said, Gautier knew, was untrue. Many of the lesser actresses in Paris did have liaisons with rich clubmen or bankers or politicians who could pay their bills or advance their careers, but they and the great courtesans were selective in the men to whom they gave themselves. Many would-be admirers had been turned away by Geneviève Grasset. One of them, a rich cattle-farmer from the Argentine, was supposed to have blown out his brains in the street outside her apartment when she had refused him. Stories like that were now part of the popular mythology of Paris.

Listening to the three men gossip, Gautier began to believe that he was not likely to learn much from their superficial chatter. Surat had his own way of extracting information from people and, like much of what he did, it was thorough but slow and tortuous. He decided to finish his wine and get back to the Sûreté and wait for his assistant's report which would doubtless be presented to him before the day was out.

As he was paying the owner of the bistro he heard the ferret-faced man say, 'A Persian? That's Ibrahim, the prince's secretary. He's in Persia now but he'll be back here next week.'

52

'What sort of man is he?' Surat asked.

'Pleasant enough, though a bit girlish for my taste. He's devoted to our master; would do anything for him.'

'And so he should be,' the coachman commented. 'Didn't the prince take him in when he was destitute?'

'Destitute?'

'The prince met Ibrahim's father, who was a steward in Persia, on one of his many trips to that country years ago. A few months back, when he heard that both of Ibrahim's parents had been killed in an earthquake, he found a place for him in our house. He's like that, our master.'

That evening Gautier was making his way painstakingly through copy after copy of *Figaro* in a back room of the newspaper's offices. His friend Duthrey had arranged for him to be given access to the paper's collection of back numbers stretching over the past five years and, with no one to help him, the task of reading through them was both tedious and time consuming.

He was looking for any references he could find in the papers to the politician Pierre de Jarnac and he had decided to broaden his search to cover not only reports of the man's political speeches and editorial comments on them, but also any news items or scraps of gossip about his private life and social activities. All Gautier knew about de Jarnac was that he had the reputation of being an ardent republican and a popular demagogue. His resignation from the government was thought by many to have been a calculated manoeuvre, intended to disassociate himself from an administration which was becoming unpopular and not, as he had claimed, a course of action forced on him by his political conscience. Most of his speeches seemed to be based on the kind of appeal that seldom failed to rouse a Frenchman: appeals to French pride, French glory and independence.

The reports in *Figaro* showed that since resigning from the government de Jarnac had become one of the leaders of the 'revanchists' who demanded a war of revenge on Germany, but one sensed that he was using this popular cause mainly to promote his own popularity and his own ambitions. Apart from his political activities, however, the press had little to say about him. His name seldom appeared in lists of those who had attended charity balls, the opening of the autumn Salon or even the dinner parties of hostesses of the haut monde. Nor was it linked by the gossip writers with those of ballet dancers, circus riders or ladies of doubtful virtue. De Jarnac, it would appear, was leading a blameless—an almost surprisingly blameless—life.

Deciding that in his quick reading of them he might have missed small reports which could still be of significance, Gautier began looking through the back numbers for a second time and presently Duthrey came into the room. He was surprised to find him still there at that late hour. Duthrey's work on the staff of *Figaro* did not include the routine gathering of news nor reporting on each day's events, and the articles which he contributed on moral and intellectual issues could be composed at his leisure during the day. He was also a man of obsessively regular habits who liked to return home at precisely the same time every day for his lunch and again in the evening for his dinner. His friends often teased him, pointing out that it would be only too easy for his wife to deceive him. All she need do was to give her lover his hat five minutes before the hour when she knew her husband would be letting himself through the front door of their apartment.

'I did not expect you to be here still at this time of night,' Gautier said to him. 'What will your wife say?'

'Half of our staff are out covering the visit of the Shah of Persia,' Duthrey replied, ignoring the quip, 'and many of the others are covering the automobile race. So I was pulled in to lend a hand with tomorrow's edition. Thanks to that riot on the Left Bank I shall be late for my dinner.'

'But the riot must be over by now.'

'Yes, the rabble has dispersed. Now all that remains is to find the ringleaders.'

'Then at least you will be able to sleep safely in your bed tonight.' Gautier was teasing, for Duthrey was a nervous fellow, well known for his horror of physical violence.

Duthrey looked at him disapprovingly. His enforced presence in the office at that late hour was not a subject for frivolous remarks. 'I came to see if you have everything you require,' he said.

'Thank you, yes.'

'Have you found what you were looking for?'

Gautier knew that the question was prompted merely by a desire to be helpful and not by curiosity. Duthrey never attempted to take advantage of their friendship by prying into police matters. He

54

replied, 'I am not really sure what I am looking for. But you may be able to help.'

'In what way?'

'What do you know of Pierre de Jarnac?'

'No more than you, I am sure.'

'And the Prince de Chaville?'

'I once interviewed him some time ago for an article I was writing on the great French noble families.'

'What would you say are his political leanings?'

'He has none. I recall him telling me that politics were not a milieu for gentlemen.'

'But he must have some political sympathies at least.'

'If he had to make a choice I suppose he would be a monarchist.' Duthrey laughed. 'One might be excused for thinking he was of royal blood himself! He shoots with the Emperor of Germany, has shared the delights of the Shah of Persia's harem and at one time the Prince of Wales used to invite him to those ridiculous sailing races which the English love so at Cowes. He also used to be on christian name terms with the Tsar until he took offence at some supposed insult.'

'He seems to have a quarrelsome nature.'

'He has. It's his insane pride. He has quarrelled with all his friends at one time or another: the Tsar, the Prince of Wales, the last President, everyone. Once he disgraced himself by attacking another aristocrat, the Prince de Sagan, in a cemetery, after the funeral of a woman who had been his mistress. He is a man who has learnt little but forgets nothing, especially a grudge.'

As he finished speaking, Duthrey pulled out his watch and looked at it anxiously. Gautier would have liked to ask him more questions about the Prince de Chaville, but he knew that Duthrey was already late for the excellent dinner which was prepared for him at his home each night and the carefully chosen bottle of wine which would accompany it. So he decided it would be unkind to detain his friend any longer.

Once he was alone again, he resumed his search through the back numbers of the newspaper. He found nothing more about Pierre de Jarnac nor anything of interest about the Prince de Chaville, but a short news item which he had missed before caught his attention. It reported the appointment of Colonel Charles Roussel to serve as military attaché at the French embassy in London. Looking at the date on the paper, Gautier realized from the investigations he had carried out into the shooting of Le Tellier that the Duc de Richemont must have been the French ambassador in London at the time.

7

MORE THAN SIXTY automobiles had assembled to take part in the rally at the Bois de Boulogne the following day to coincide with the end of a race from Orléans to Paris. After a timid and protracted flirtation Parisians had finally accepted the automobile and constructors were vying with each other to create new models and to embellish them with novel accessories and increasingly luxurious fittings. Now, more recently it had been the invention of the windscreen, allowing drivers and their passengers to travel in complete cover, protected from the smell and noise of horses as well as from their hooves, which had convinced the rich and the conservative that the automobile was as practical and as stylish as the carriage.

The rally was no more than an excuse for proud owners to exhibit their vehicles. Speed was no longer the main attraction of the automobile since the Belgian, Camille Jenatzy, had broken the barrier of 100 k.p.h. without, as most people expected, his lungs exploding. Speed could now be left to special racing cars and to professional drivers, leaving members of the Automobile Club the pleasure of the rally, in which after a leisurely drive through the Bois they could station their vehicles on a stretch of grass not far from the Parc Bagatelle to be admired and inspected by envious spectators. A jury would also be examining them, for a Concours d'Elégance was being held in conjunction with the rally, and the day would end with a presentation of prizes to the winners in the afternoon.

Models from the factories of all the principal constructors were on view that day; Renault, Decauville, de Dion-Boutin, Peugeot,

Panhard et Levassor. They ranged in size from elegant little two-seater voiturettes of no more than three horse-power to heavy, cumbersome machines large enough to seat four passengers, built around the twenty-one horse-power engines of racing automobiles. Some were driven by steam, some by electricity and there was even one strange contraption, owned by a Russian grand duc, in which a converted landau carriage had been attached to a motorized base. The drivers and their passengers had emulated the variety of the vehicles they were displaying with the outfits they had chosen to wear for the rally: ankle-length driving coats, leather breeches, yachting jackets, top hats, flat peaked caps, dresses created for the ladies by the great courturiers of the day: Worth, Doucet, Paquin, Poiret, flower-decked toques, fur muffs, veils.

Gautier had come to the Bois de Boulogne after first calling at the home of Madame Stahl in Neuilly. There he had been told that the mistress of the house had taken her two small sons to the rally. They would be found, he had been assured, either in the marquee erected for members of the Automobile Club of France and their families or, later on, lunching at the Pavillon du Bois. He had made enquiries at the club marquee to learn that Madame Stahl was not there and, supposing that she might be out with her sons inspecting the automobiles on show, he began walking round the display of machines himself.

As a young man he had once seen Geneviève Grasset on the stage, but she had been playing the part of a man, Lorenzaccio, in a second-rate production of the historical drama by de Musset and he doubted whether he would recognize her now. In any case, although there were many society ladies among the crowds admiring the automobiles, he could not see one accompanied by two small boys. The only person he did see and recognize was Colonel Charles Roussel.

The colonel had clearly been taking part in the rally, for his Panhard was stationed among the automobiles with a large number affixed to its bonnet and he was standing beside it with his chauffeur, surrounded by a small group of spectators. Gautier realized that he might have expected to find the colonel at the rally. The owner of an expensive automobile, on which such care was obviously lavished, would take every opportunity of showing it off. If there was a coincidence it was not that Roussel was there but that Gautier had busied himself that morning before calling at the Stahl home, by making discreet enquiries about the colonel's army career and record.

The Ministry of War had given him, reluctantly, a list of the Colonel's recent postings. Before becoming military attaché at the embassy in London, Roussel had held similar appointments in Cairo and Washington. Gautier noted that he had been in London for only one year, a much shorter term of duty than was customary. Since being recalled he had served for a time as an instructor at St. Cyr, but was now on extended leave until a suitable appointment could be found for him. The last time he had actually served with his regiment had been several years ago in Languedoc. That was as much as the Ministry was prepared to reveal. Gautier would have liked to have seen the confidential reports on Roussel's conduct in his regiment had been several years ago in Languedoc. That was as been shifted from post to post with such frequency, but the army, a tight, closed élite, was jealous of its reputation and would resent any attempt by outsiders, especially by the police, to pry into its secrets.

That morning the colonel was in civilian dress, wearing a leather driving-coat with an astrakhan collar, which he had left un-buttoned, possibly by design, to show the tweed knickerbockers and belted Norfolk jacket which he had on underneath. A monocle hung from a black ribbon attached to the buttonhole of his jacket. The effect of the outfit struck Gautier as being strikingly English, although he had no real knowledge of what an Englishman would have worn on a similar occasion. Roussel was in his early forties and a bachelor, as Gautier had learnt from his enquiries, and handsome, in spite of an ugly scar across his left cheek.

As he stood receiving the compliments and answering the questions of visitors on his Panhard, Roussel noticed Gautier standing on the edge of the crowd. Presently he came over towards him.

'Inspector Gautier, is it not?'

'Yes, Monsieur.'

'If you are here on duty,' Roussel said insolently, 'Perhaps I could ask you to keep an eye on my machine while I go and have some lunch.'

'I would have thought you might have brought one of the men from your regiment to do that.'

The remark was made without any conscious malice and Gautier was surprised at the instant spurt of anger which it aroused in Roussel. The colonel's face hardened as he responded with a sneer, 'You're too busy watching out for pickpockets, I suppose. That would be a task more suited to your talents.'

He turned away angrily and returned to his automobile. Gautier guessed that it must be the resentment which Roussel felt at being placed on extended leave, with the humiliating implication that there was no post he could satisfactorily fill, that had made the man so bitter. He found himself wondering what had happened in London to cause Roussel's early recall from the French embassy.

After walking at a leisurely pace through the lines of parked automobiles, he returned to the club's marquee where one of the attendants at the entrance told him that Madame Stahl had returned there, and pointed her out. She was standing talking to an elderly man and holding a glass of the champagne which waiters were taking round to the members of the club and their guests. Like most of the women in the marquee she was dressed in black and grey, for bright colours were never worn during the day by ladies in society, whatever the occasion. Two boys, aged about eight and six, were chasing each other among the people standing nearby. Gautier waited until she had finished her conversation and the elderly man had moved away, before stepping forward to introduce himself.

'Inspector Gautier!' Madame Stahl exclaimed. 'Of course, I recognize you now.'

'Why Madame? Did you see me at the trial of Denise de Richemont?' Gautier asked. Sometimes it paid to be cruelly direct.

Learning that he knew she had attended the de Richemont trial disconcerted Madame Stahl, but she appeared injured rather than annoyed. 'I did see you there, yes, but I've also seen you on social occasions. You're something of a celebrity in Paris, you know.'

Gautier inclined his head and smiled to acknowledge the compliment. Geneviève Stahl was strikingly pretty, with long flaxen hair, which she wore pinned up under her hat, and a gaze that had none of the emptiness nor the hardness which were often to be found in pale blue eyes. Her complexion was clear, her figure rounded and she looked healthy, almost too healthy for an actress. One found it impossible to visualize her playing Marguerite in *La Dame aux Camélias* or other tragic roles. Gautier recalled Madame Le Tellier's description of the type of woman that had attracted her late husband. Geneviève Stahl matched it perfectly.

59

'I wonder if you would be kind enough to spare me a few moments of your time,' he said.

'Since you have gone to the trouble of establishing that I was at that woman's trial, I suppose that is what you wish to talk about.'

'Not the trial, Madame, no.'

She looked at him for a moment, irritably, and he guessed that she would have liked to refuse his request but something, it may have been curiosity, restrained her. 'We cannot talk here,' she said.

'It would be better somewhere else,' he agreed.

'My sons and I are going to lunch at the Pavillon du Bois. I will send the boys on ahead in my carriage and you and I can walk there. As you must know it is not very far.'

'A perfect arrangement.'

The Pavillon du Bois was an expensive restaurant, only a short walk away, which was much in favour with the gratin as a place to dine after the races at Longchamp or Auteuil. Madame Stahl called her two boys, led them out of the marquee and made them climb into a calèche which stood waiting outside the entrance. Gautier heard her tell the coachman to take them to the restaurant on a leisurely drive past the lake and by the paths where they would be able to see the cavaliers and lady riders of society out on their morning rides through the Bois. Then he and she set out on foot.

'I wished to ask you,' Gautier began, 'whether you believe that Denise de Richemont was in fact the mistress of Monsieur Le Tellier.'

'Why should I know?'

'You were on close terms with him, were you not?'

'What makes you think that?'

'We know about your visits to his apartment in Rue Lamartine.'

Madame Stahl glanced at him briefly and then looked away, without giving any sign of being angry or upset by what he had said. Actresses, Gautier had always believed, although well able to impersonate self-control on the stage, were volatile, excitable women and he had expected indignant denials, or demands by what right the police had been prying into her private life, or at the least bluster. As she made no comment, he continued, 'Monsieur Le Tellier left a note from you lying around in his home.'

'How do you know it was me?' she asked and he realized she was reluctant to admit the truth of what he had said.

60

'It was signed "Gigi". That is a familiar abbreviation of Geneviève Grasset, your maiden name, is it not?'

Madame Stahl sighed. 'Since you already know so much, there is no point in denying it. Yes, Jacques and I were lovers. I was always afraid that one day our secret would be discovered.'

Gautier wondered whether once Le Tellier was dead she had supposed their secret to be safe. He remarked, 'His widow refuses to accept that Denise de Richemont was her husband's lover as she claimed at her trial.'

'Of course she wasn't!' Madame Stahl's healthy pink cheeks grew even pinker with indignation. 'It was an outrageous lie!'

'How can you be so certain?'

'Jacques was dedicated to his work, obsessed with it. At any one time he would be working on half-a-dozen stories. He used to spend his days and much of his nights meeting people interviewing them, following up rumours and hints and suggestions. We had to snatch a few precious moments we could share together out of his frantic week. He could not possibly have found time for a second mistress.'

'I doubt whether you were the first woman he had entertained at Rue Lamartine.'

'I am sure I wasn't. Jacques liked women. He needed love just as he needed sex. But his women had to be fitted into his life in an orderly and methodical way. And I refuse to believe that he would ever have used any woman in the shameless way that Denise de Richemont suggested.'

Gautier made no comment. As yet he was not prepared to form any conclusions about Le Tellier's morals or personal integrity. From what he had so far heard, the dead man might have been a journalist of unshakable rectitude or equally an unprincipled opportunist. For his part, Gautier did not need to form a judgement. He had a growing conviction that Le Tellier's murder had not been a crime passionel at all, that it was not an isolated event but part of a much more complex pattern which as yet he did not comprehend. That was sufficient for the time being.

'You may be wondering,' Madame Stahl continued, 'why I did not denounce Denise de Richemont as a liar and a fraud. Had I done so, you might well have been able to prove that she had never been the mistress of Jacques. Evidence should not have been impossible to find. The concierge at his apartment in Rue

61

Lamartine would have been able to confirm what I have told you.'

They were passing close to one of the paths in the Bois along which riders exercised their horses. Several couples passed them, the men in tail coats, riding breeches and top hats, the women in black riding habits, mounted side-saddle. In spite of the growing popularity of the bicycle and the automobile, equestrianism remained the principal recreation of French society.

'Although he was handsome and rich,' Madame Stahl said, and Gautier guessed that what she was going to say would be a justification for keeping silent at Denise de Richemont's trial, 'I was not eager to marry my husband. I did not love him. But from the day we met he pestered me to do so. For almost a year he kept asking me and finally I agreed. We joke about it now. I tell him I married him just to get a little peace.'

'You exaggerate, Madame!'

'Of course. But after our marriage he fought no less than thirteen duels on my account. And when there was no one left willing to fight, society accepted me. André was so proud of me; not only for my looks and talent but because, as he still says, he stole me away from a prince!'

'And so you don't want him to know that you have been unfaithful?'

'He has probably guessed that. We have been married for nine years and for the last two he has been a husband only in name. André is not a fool. Oh, yes, he probably knows I have had a lover, but how could I admit publicly that it was Jacques? How could I humiliate my husband?' She glanced at Gautier and then added, 'And now the whole world will know.'

Gautier knew that the glance had been one of appraisal. Madame Stahl was trying to weigh him up, to calculate whether his silence could be bought and, if so, how: by persuasion or money or perhaps even by seduction.

'The world will not know from me, Madame,' he said to put her anxiety to rest. 'You can rely on my discretion.'

'But you are still making official enquiries into Jacques's death.'

'Denise de Richemont has been acquitted. To prove now that she was lying at her trial would serve no useful purpose. All I wish to know is the real reason why Monsieur Le Tellier was shot.'

They were approaching the Pavillon du Bois. Outside the restaurant stood a row of carriages, landaus, victorias and one or two smart little coupés. For some reason most of the wealthier spectators who had come to watch the automobile rally had preferred to drive to the event in a more leisurely style. Coachmen and footmen and grooms, several of them in livery, stood in groups around the carriages, gossiping as they waited.

'You will think me sentimental,' Madame Stahl said, 'but I chose this restaurant today because it was here that I met Jacques for the first time.'

'When was that?'

'Oh, months ago. He was lunching here with an old friend of my husband who brought him over to my table and introduced us.'

'Did he ever talk to you about his work?' Gautier asked. He had no wish to seem brutal in deflecting their conversation from her memories of Le Tellier but he was conscious that they did not have much time left to talk.

'Very seldom.'

'Did he ever mention Madame Simone Pasquier or any of her friends?'

'Not that I can recall.'

'Or the Prince de Chaville.'

'No, why should he?' Madame Stahl asked, rather more quickly than one would have expected, it seemed to Gautier.

'From some notes which he left it would seem that he was taking a special interest in Madame Pasquier.'

'Do not imagine that our relationship was purely physical and that we never conversed. On the contrary, when we were not making love we talked a great deal. Jacques was insatiably curious. He was always asking me questions; about people whom I know in society, my former lovers, royalty, everything and everybody.'

Madame Stahl must be a very trusting woman, Gautier decided, if not extremely naïve. It did not seem to have occurred to her that Le Tellier's inquisitiveness might have been purely professional, that all his questions might have been intended to extract information from her which he could later use in his newspaper.

They had almost reached the Pavillon du Bois and Madame Stahl stopped and turned to face him. She said, 'I suppose it was the de Richemont girl who told Jacques about the duc's secret?'

'Yes, it can only have been she who gave him the compromising letters.'

'But why? Through hatred of her father?'

'That may have been part of her motive. On the other hand she may have done it for the same reason as she invented the story of having been Le Tellier's mistress: to give herself an excuse for shooting him and a defence when she came to trial.'

'Why should anyone wish to murder Jacques?'

'That is what we have to find out.'

8

'IT WOULD APPEAR, Gautier, that I can no longer rely on you.' Courtrand's tone suggested that in truth he had never been able to rely on his subordinate.

'Monsieur?'

'Two days ago I assigned you to a simple investigation, a sordid crime of no account in the underworld of Paris, and I asked you particularly if you would handle it on your own, without involving me. That is so, is it not?'

'Agreed, Monsieur.'

'I asked you this so that I would be free to deal with important matters; matters of state one might say.'

To describe a visit to Paris by mere fringe royalty as a matter of state, it seemed to Gautier, was a flagrant exaggeration, but the director-general of the Sûreté liked to inflate the importance of his work. Gautier made no comment.

'And what happens?' Courtrand continued. 'Already I have received a complaint about your conduct. And it is the kind of complaint which has been made about you only too frequently, Gautier.'

'What complaint is that, Monsieur?' Gautier feigned innocence partly for his own diversion and partly because Courtrand would expect it. He was confident that he knew what the complaint must be.

'That you have been pestering people of impeccable respectability with questions. What else? People who cannot possibly have any knowledge or any connection with the crime which you are supposed to be investigating.'

'May I know who laid this complaint?'

'That is of no relevance.'

'Was it the deputy, Pierre de Jarnac?'

'It was not. If you must know it was Monsieur Marcel Bloquit, the Minister for the Interior.' Courtrand paused and looked at Gautier sharply. 'Does this mean that I may expect a complaint from Monsieur de Jarnac as well?'

'I hope not, Monsieur.'

'So do I! We all know that you have your own method of working, Gautier.' The sarcasm was by no means as subtle as Courtrand must have believed. 'But this time what you are doing is beyond comprehension! I understand the questions you have been asking relate to the death of the late Jacques Le Tellier.'

'That is correct, Monsieur.'

'Then how can they possibly have any bearing on the murder of the street walker, Eva Callot.'

'I believe that the shooting of Le Tellier may have been connected with the murder of Callot.'

Gautier made the remark on no more than an impulse, partly perhaps because he knew it was the kind of remark that usually infuriated Courtrand. To his surprise he said it with something like conviction and he wondered whether instinctively he was beginning to believe it. Until then he had not formed any views about the shooting of Jacques Le Tellier and the enquiries he had been making were motivated by inquisitiveness more than anything.

He was even more surprised to find that the remark did not provoke the indignation in Courtrand that one might have expected. 'Don't be absurd!' was the only comment that the director-general could find to make. Then he crossed the room from his desk to the window and stood looking out on the Seine without speaking. Gautier waited, expecting at least a further rebuke and even an order that he should desist from bothering important people with irrelevant questions, but nothing came. He realized then that some other more important matter must be troubling Courtrand and was the reason for his silent preoccupation.

Eventually Courtrand said, 'How much do you know of the Panama Canal affair, Gautier?'

'Only what I read at the time, Monsieur.'

'Do you believe there was a criminal conspiracy behind it?'

'Not a conspiracy, surely. Corruption, bribery of government officials and misuse of government funds, but the original intention to build the canal seems to have been honest enough.' Gautier was tempted to add that he had been too young when the project started, more than twenty-five years previously, to have formed a first-hand opinion, but he knew Courtrand was sensitive on the subject of his age and often hinted that Gautier was too young to have been promoted to his present rank.

'You may be right.'

The scandal resulting from the attempt to build a canal across the Isthmus of Panama had left an ugly scar on the reputation of many financiers and politicians in France. Hundreds of investors had lost their money when the company formed to build the canal had crashed and many were ruined. Revelations of blackmail and widespread bribery of officials had brought a serious loss of confidence in the government from which it had never fully recovered.

'If there were another financial collapse in similar circumstances,' Courtrand continued, 'people would demand a criminal investigation.'

'Do you think there is a danger of that?'

'I believe a scandal arising from remarkably similar circumstances is imminent.'

Turning away from the window, Courtrand began to pace the room, his hands clasped behind his frock coat. His face had the drawn, grey look of one who had been sleeping badly. Gautier could not remember ever seeing him look so dejected.

'Not long ago,' Courtrand said, 'a company was formed to mine diamonds in French North Africa. The project was supported by a major bank and by a consortium of financiers, and a limited number of prominent people were given an opportunity of subscribing to the new company. Later, when more capital was required, shares were sold to the public as well in small units.'

'And there are no diamonds?' Gautier guessed.

'Subscribers were shown the reports of geologists and mining engineers. They were even shown samples of diamonds extracted in a preliminary excavation. Then difficulties began to be experienced. The mine shafts had to be dug far deeper than had been anticipated and more funds were raised. The legality of the company's right to mine in the chosen area was challenged in a local court.'

'Was all this true or just the story that shareholders were told?'

'Probably the latter. We will know in due course no doubt. Now it appears that some weeks ago the bank supporting the project withdrew, selling its interest. Several of the larger private investors have also disposed of their holdings, some of them at a considerable profit. In the last few days there has been a strong rumour that the company is about to collapse and the value of the shares has plummetted. People have panicked and sold their shares for next to nothing to cut their losses.'

'Is there no chance of saving the company?'

'It seems not. An independent expert sent out to Africa by a group of shareholders has returned and reports that there are not and never were any diamonds and that no serious attempt was ever made to find any. The whole project, apparently, was a swindle.'

'In that case criminal charges must be possible.'

Courtrand made no reply but turned and looked out of the window once more. Now Gautier sensed the reason for his dejection. He asked, 'Do you personally have any interest in this speculation, Monsieur?'

'As it happens I do,' Courtrand answered reluctantly. 'I was rash enough to believe the advice of men whom I thought I could trust.'

'One hopes that your investment was not large.'

'Not more than I can afford to lose: 10,000 francs.'

Although as Courtrand said, the loss of 10,000 francs would not ruin him, for his wife came of a family of substantial merchants and had brought with her a handsome dowry, it was nevertheless a considerable sum. Few other men working in government service would have been able to invest on such a scale.

'Do you wish me to start investigating this business?' Gautier asked.

'Thank you for your offer, Gautier, but no. I would prefer that the Sûreté should not become involved, at any rate at this stage. A group of us who have lost money are having enquiries made privately.'

'I understand, Monsieur. Even so I shall keep my ears open. Sometimes one picks up rumours and—' Gautier left the sentence unfinished and spread his hands expressively.

'Quite. But you should not take that as giving you authority to pester bankers and other important people with impertinent questions,' Courtrand replied acidly.

After leaving the director-general's office. Gautier did not go directly to his own. He wanted to know why Marcel Bloquit, the Minister for the Interior, should have complained about him. As far as Gautier knew, Bloquit was the only member of the current French government whose name began with a B. He recalled that the newspaper *La Parole* had accused an anonymous Monsieur B, a member of the government, of using his influence to get the date of Denise de Richemont's trial brought forward.

Courtrand's secretary, a self-effacing civil servant named Corbin, worked in a room not much larger than a cupboard adjoining the director-general's office. Corbin was a patient, methodical man who collected any information that reached him which might be useful to his superior and kept it carefully filed. Not surprisingly, since Courtrand's main concern in life was that he and the Sûreté should be as helpful as possible to people who might in their turn be useful to him, most of the information locked in Corbin's files was about important people. He had a record of the names and addresses of leading politicians, senior members of the administration, field marshals, bankers, judges and advocates, together with notes on their past careers, family connections and pastimes. He also kept a special note of any of their eccentricities or predilections which might cause embarrassment. It was, for example prudent that the Sûreté should know if a foreign prince of royal blood had a penchant for visiting the male brothel in Rue Marigny or any similar establishments, so that he might not be arrested in one of them by mistake.

When Gautier entered Corbin's office, he found him writing out in his beautiful script a list of all the senior inspectors in the Sûreté with the cases which were currently investigating. Courtrand insisted that all records, even the most routine and trivial, should be kept rigorously up to date.

'What do you know of Marcel Bloquit?' Gautier asked Corbin.

Corbin looked up at him suspiciously. 'Are you asking that question because the Minister has laid a complaint against you?'

'No.'

'Then you have been reading the rumours published by that scurrilous rag *La Parole*.'

68

Corbin studied several of the leading newspapers every day and gleaned much of the information for his files from their gossip columns, especially little revealing details of the private lives of people in whom he was interested.

'Rumours? Are you saying that Bloquit did not use his influence to have the date of de Richemont's trial brought forward?'

'Perhaps he did, but that does not mean that he was Mademoiselle de Richemont's lover. What *La Parole* printed was a totally unjustified slander.'

'You may well be right but anyway what do you know of Bloquit?'

'Of what are you accusing him?'

The question, Gautier realized, meant that Corbin was not prepared to let him see his files. The director's secretary kept all the information that he amassed in a series of buff-coloured folders tied with red tape. He was usually prepared to open up the folders for most of the inspectors in the Sûreté, but he distrusted Gautier who had in the past embarrassed Courtrand by accusing important people of complicity in criminal offences and then having the impertinence to prove that the accusations were true.

'I only wondered whether Bloquit is a close friend of the Prince de Chaville.'

'If you are working on that hypothesis my friend, then you're following a false trail.' Corbin seemed pleased to be able to show that Gautier was fallible.

'What makes you certain?'

'The Minister is an ardent republican with strong anti-clerical views. The prince on the other hand is a monarchist and a devout Catholic, who makes no secret of the fact that he despises politicians. The two men are not on speaking terms.'

'Let me ask you another question then. Is Bloquit friendly with Pierre de Jarnac?'

Corbin stared at him again, unable to conceal his distrust. Then he answered reluctantly, 'As to whether they are friendly I cannot say; but de Jarnac is the Minister's brother-in-law.'

Later that afternoon the Shah of Persia arrived in Paris. He had travelled by sea to Marseilles and when his special boat train pulled in at the Gare de Lyon, the President and senior ministers of the French government were there to meet him. Royal visits to Paris provided the people with the innocent diversion of pomp and pageantry and the formula for them seldom varied. From the railway station the Shah and the President would ride in an open coach, escorted by a troop of cavalry, to the Elysée Palace. Next morning there would be another drive through crowded streets to the Hôtel de Ville for an official reception by the municipality of Paris. On the days that followed the visitor would be entertained to a banquet, a display of fireworks and a gala performance at the Opéra.

Gautier was at the Gare de Lyon with Surat when the royal party arrived. The Prefect of Police had given instructions that several inspectors from the Sûreté should be there, dispersed among the crowd. The Prefect had no special reason for expecting demonstrations against the royal visitor or the President, but he was a prudent man who believed in taking precautions. The mood of restless discontent which had been evident among the people of Paris for several months had been sharpened, first by the verdict at the trial of Denise de Richemont and then by the demonstration on the Esplanade des Invalides and the riot which had followed it.

In the event there was no trouble at the Gare de Lyon that day. When the President and the welcoming party arrived and walked along the red carpet towards where the train would stop, some of the crowd booed and others shouted abuse. Earlier in the forecourt of the station a handful of people were grouped around a banner proclaiming 'A Bas Fallières!', but they had been hustled away by the uniformed police before the President arrived.

When the train finally arrived and the Shah of Persia stepped out, he was greeted with applause and some cheering. The Shah was popular in France for he had been one of only two monarchs—the other being the King of Sweden—who had accepted an invitation to attend the Great Exposition of 1900. Royalty in other countries had been too suspicious of the Third Republic and of the French penchant for revolution, and their refusal to go to Paris for the exposition had been received as a deliberate snub.

After the President and the Shah had been driven away and the crowds were drifting out of the station, Gautier and Surat left, too, walking together towards the Place de la Bastille.

'Are you going back to headquarters, Patron?' Surat asked.

'No. As usual I'm off womanizing, leaving you to do the work,' Gautier replied, teasing him.

'Patron?'

70

'Isn't that what you told the Prince de Chaville's servants about me?'

Surat had evidently forgotten the remark he had made in the bistro and looked confused. 'I may have said that, but you were not supposed to overhear the remark.' Then recovering his composure, he added, 'What is it you wish me to do this evening?'

'Nothing this evening, but I have two tasks for you tomorrow. First try and discover the whereabouts of Denise de Richemont. It should not be too difficult. Send a couple of men out to make enquiries. Her mother has a sister living in Paris and the girl might be there. On the other hand she might well be a guest at the home of Colonel Charles Roussel.'

'Right, Patron. And the second assignment?'

'That's a different business altogether, a financial matter.'

Briefly Gautier told Surat the basic facts of the African diamond speculation and the circumstances under which the venture had apparently collapsed. He did not mention that the director-general of the Sûreté had allowed himself to become involved in the scheme, but simply said that a number of investors had lost money.

'This may be a case of fraud,' he continued. 'Find out as much as you can about the people behind the scheme. It may have been devised by crooked financiers, and a bank is supposed to have backed it but later pulled out. I want names if you can get them. Start by making enquiries in and around the Bourse. There will be a talkative clerk somewhere who will have heard about it.'

'Do I need to be discreet?'

'No. Try dropping hints that criminal proceedings will be started shortly. That may frighten people into talking, just to prove their own innocence.'

At the Place de la Bastille the two men parted, Surat heading west towards his home, while Gautier boarded a motor omnibus going up Boulevard Beaumarchais. He left the bus on the corner of Rue La Fayette and walked from there to Rue Lamartine. The concierge of the building in which Jacques Le Tellier had kept his garçonnière recognized him, for he had visited the apartment once before when making enquiries into Le Tellier's death.

'Who is occupying the apartment now?' he asked her.

'No one. The furniture is still there and the books and clothes Monsieur Le Tellier kept in the place, but no one is living in it.

Madame Le Tellier told me she has not yet decided whether she intends to dispose of the lease.'

'So Madame Le Tellier has been here?'

'Yes. On two occasions.'

'Did she come alone?'

The concierge hesitated. She was an honest, loyal woman who did not like to talk about her tenants, but the police, she knew, had a right to ask these questions.

'No. She met a man here.'

When Gautier told her he wished to look round the apartment, the woman made no objection. She took him up to the first floor, let him into the apartment and left him there.

Although small, the garçonnière was large enough to serve the purpose for which the dead man had acquired it, consisting of a living room, a large bedroom, a tiny kitchen and, surprisingly, a bathroom with running water. Such a luxury was rare in Paris and bathrooms were usually only to be found in the homes of the rich or in recently constructed buildings. In other households when a member of the family wished to take a bath a servant, usually a maid, would heat the water and carry it in jugs, often up three or four flights of stairs, and pour it into a metal bath.

The bedroom was suitably appointed, with a vast four-poster bed with a canopy, and its walls were hung with a series of erotic paintings. Naked ladies, plump, large-breasted sirens lay in suggestive poses; pretty serving wenches smiled naughtily at tipsy men whose hands were thrust, fumbling into their corsages. In a wardrobe Gautier found two suits and a selection of silk shirts, cravats, underwear and shoes.

By contrast the living room was austerely furnished, its only concession to dalliance being two armchairs and a Louis XV chaise-longue on which a mistress might at least recline to receive the advances of her host in some comfort. Otherwise it was a working room with a large oak desk on which stood a silver inkwell and a silver tray full of pens and pencils. The drawers of the desk were unlocked but contained nothing of any interest: a small supply of writing paper and headed notepaper bearing the address in Rue Miromesnil, envelopes, sealing-wax, a paper-knife with an inlaid handle and an empty snuffbox. Examining the locks of the drawers Gautier saw that they were rusty and the keyholes blocked with dust. It seemed safe to assume that Le Tellier had not used the desk to lock away any private or confidential papers, either because the keys had been lost or because he realized that the locks would be too simple to pick or to force.

And yet, he reasoned, his garçonnière would be the ideal place for a secretive man like Le Tellier to keep anything he did not wish others to see. In a man's home there might be a curious wife and at his office inquisitive colleagues. Returning to the bedroom, he searched the wardrobe and the drawers of the dressing-table and of the two bedside tables but still found nothing. Unwilling to give up hope, he asked himself what, if the apartment were his, he would choose as a hiding place and realised that the answer would depend on the nature of the article to be hidden. In the case of Le Tellier he supposed it would be papers of one sort or another, pages from a notebook, cuttings from newspapers, letters. He decided that there was nowhere in the apartment which would be proof against a thorough and diligent search, so the logical course would be to hide the papers where the longest and most time-consuming search would be needed to find them.

He had a sudden idea. Returning to the living-room he looked at the bookshelves which stretched along the full length of one wall. They must have held at least 500 books, probably more. His first thought was that he should take them from the shelves one at a time in turn, starting from the top left corner of the room and working his way along, opening each book and flicking through its pages. Then he looked at the titles on the spines. They had been methodically arranged; a section of reference books placed near at hand on the shelf nearest to the writing desk, historical works and the great classics of French literature—Voltaire, Rousseau, Châteaubriand, Taine—on the left, contemporary novels to the right. Gautier began looking for titles that were least likely to attract a visitor casually inspecting the books, the dullest, drabbest most unreadable books.

Ignoring the reference books which he could see from their condition had been frequently consulted, he searched the shelves and took out in turn a three volume history of the Punic Wars, a commentary on the lyrical dramas of Aeschylus and an eighteenth-century medical treatise on the therapeutical properties of blood-letting with leeches, but found nothing concealed among the pages. It was not until he held a book of poems by Omar Khayyam, in the original Persian, and shook it, that he made his first and only

73

discovery. A piece of paper slipped out of the pages and fluttered down on to the desk.

It was a single sheet of writing paper, badly creased, as though it had been crumpled up and thrown away only to be retrieved and smoothed out before being placed between the pages of the book for safe keeping. Written on the paper in a large, angular script, the handwriting, Gautier felt, of an aggressive extrovert, were the words CONCERT PROGRAMME, with underneath them a list of numbers.

CONCERT PROGRAMME
3971
3881
7581
9881
5681
7451

The numbers meant nothing to Gautier, but he folded the sheet of paper carefully and put it in his pocket. He flicked through a few more books from the shelves, but without any real expectation that he would find anything more. Then he let himself out of the apartment and went downstairs, stopping before he left the building to thank the concierge.

'It was a pleasure to be of service to you, Monsieur l'Inspecteur,' the woman said.

On an impulse Gautier asked her, 'Has anyone else been here to look around the apartment? Apart from Madame Le Tellier, I mean.'

'Only the lawyer and that was shortly after Monsieur was shot.'

'Madame Le Tellier's lawyer?'

'No, but he came with a letter of authority from her.'

'Did he tell you what he wanted?'

'No. But I thought perhaps he might be looking for a will.'

'Do you remember his name?'

'It so happens that I do. It was given in the letter of authority and it was an odd name. Not French I would think. Grout. Monsieur Emile Grout.'

After dining at the café in Place Dauphine Gautier returned home alone that night. He had arranged with Janine that he would go to the café again the following evening and that afterwards they would

74

spend the night together. Evidently she had put her gloomy presentiments of an imminent end to their affair out of her mind, for she accepted his suggestion with obvious pleasure, promising that the next night she would close the café as early as she possibly could.

As he climbed the four flights of stairs to his apartment, he did not feel that sense of depression which he had often experienced in the months after Suzanne had left him. Suzanne was settled and contented, so he need no longer be troubled by feelings of guilt for not having been able to give her what she had wanted from their marriage. And his own life had entered a settled phase. In place of the brief affairs and often unsatisfactory adventures with women which had been his only distraction after Suzanne's departure, he now had a mistress, one who was affectionate and dependable, free of ill-temper and caprice and who made no demands on him. He had often wondered whether he might not be temperamentally un-suited to marriage, too reserved or too self-sufficient and unable to give of himself freely enough and it now seemed to him that this new arrangement suited him much better.

When he reached the fourth floor and saw an edge of light under the door to his apartment, he thought at once that his satisfaction had been premature. Apart from the woman who cleaned for him, only Suzanne had a key to the apartment. So she must have come home. Had she quarrelled with Gaston or taken sudden, illogical fright at the prospect of childbirth and come to Gautier for comfort? Was there another explanation, even less pleasant?

But when he went into the living room he found not Suzanne, but a slim, coloured man who was standing by the fireplace. As Gautier went through the door, the man looked round, startled, his eyes wide with fear.

'You must be Shaki,' Gautier said.

'Yes, Monsieur.'

'You need not have come all this way. We could have arranged to meet wherever suited you.'

'No, Monsieur. I told Gaston I would not arrange a meeting, not even through him.'

'But why not?'

'I only came to see you because everyone says you are a good man, a fair man. But no one else must know that I have talked with you. So Gaston gave me the key to your apartment and I came without telling anybody.'

The irony of hearing himself described as a good man while knowing that Shaki had been given the key to his home by his wife's lover was not wasted on Gautier, but he made no comment. Instead he asked Shaki, 'Why have you been in hiding?'

'Do you need to ask, Monsieur? Because I have no wish to go to the guillotine.'

'But they say you did not kill Eva Callot.'

'I didn't. But will the flics believe me?'

'You were not arrested when we questioned you soon after she was murdered.'

'Things have changed since then. At that time you had a suspect: someone much more likely to have killed Eva than me.'

'Igor Kratov?'

'Yes, Kratov. He killed her and you would have forced a confession out of him eventually. But then he found a protector. Now no one can touch him and so the flics are hunting for me. Someone has to be put on trial and the flics will be happy to settle for me.'

Gautier wondered what kind of story he was going to be told. Shaki's choice of words were symptomatic of the way the mind of a petty criminal worked. Just as a girl must have a pimp to protect her from the exploitation of men and the jealousy of her rivals, so a criminal needed a protector, a person of influence who could protect him from the retribution of justice.

'Who is Kratov's protector?' he asked Shaki.

'A lawyer.'

'Tell me about it.'

According to Shaki, after Kratov had been questioned for the first time by Inspector Lemaire, he had been approached by a lawyer who had offered to advise him. Advising him in this instance had meant suggesting a story which Kratov could tell the police to account for his movements on the night Eva Callot had been killed and providing a witness who could corroborate it, the Persian Ibrahim.

'So you believe the story Kratov later told was a complete invention?'

'I know it was, Monsieur. Several friends of mine saw Kratov that night. He was in and out of the bistros around Pigalle, pestering the girls and getting drunk. There was no Persian with him.'

'Then why don't your friends come forward and tell the police?'

Gautier could not help thinking that Lemaire had not been very thorough in his investigation.

'In our quartier no one assists the flics, not even to help a friend. You know that.'

'Even if as you say Kratov has been cleared from suspicion by a fabricated story, that does not mean the police could make a case against you. After all, you are innocent.'

The Algerian shook his head. Although in the streets around Pigalle at night he could no doubt be brave enough and adept with a knife, he had an almost superstitious fear of the judicial system and of the guillotine. He said, 'If the lawyer has manufactured evidence to save that ruffian Kratov, he has probably invented some that will condemn me.'

'Then how do you imagine that I can help you?'

'You're a clever man, Monsieur. Go and see the lawyer. Make him tell you why he has done this thing. It cannot be for a fee since Kratov has no money.'

'Do you know his name?'

'Yes, Monsieur. I followed him once to his office in Rue Charlemagne. His name is Emile Grout.'

9

THE OFFICES OF Emile Grout were not at all what Gautier had expected. He had assumed that Grout must be one of those lawyers who operated on the dubious fringes of the law, handling cases which reputable advocates would prefer not to touch, picking up a fee wherever he could, and that he would be working from some garret or dingy back room. Instead, next morning, when he crossed the Seine to Rue Charlemagne, he found a suite of offices, conservatively but expensively furnished, with two clerks and a stenographer working diligently in the front room. Grout himself was a small, bald man, dressed in a frock coat which no one could have faulted, except for an ostentatiously large diamond pin in his cravat.

'Inspector Gautier!' the lawyer exclaimed smiling. 'To what do I owe the pleasure of this visit?'

'I am investigating the death of a woman named Eva Callot.'

'Really? I thought Inspector Lemaire was handling that case.'

'Not any longer. He has been moved to another investigation and I have taken over.'

'No doubt the director-general is dissatisfied with Lemaire's lack of progress. Weeks have passed but as yet he seems no nearer making an arrest. An affair like that, a crime of the gutter should not be difficult to solve.'

'Lemaire was not helped by your intervention, Monsieur Grout.'

The remark did not evoke the response that Gautier might have expected. Instead of protesting or even looking indignant, Grout smiled. 'Are you suggesting that the course of action I took on behalf of my client was in any way improper, Inspector?'

'As yet I have not made up my mind on that point.'

'Come, Inspector, what possible grounds can you have for doubting my integrity?'

'The sudden production of a witness who could exonerate Kratov was surprisingly convenient.'

'Are you suggesting that Monsieur Ibrahim committed perjury?'

'Several people appear to be convinced that he did.'

'Have you questioned him?'

'I have no doubt, Monsieur, that you are well aware that Ibrahim is no longer in this country. First he conveniently appears, then conveniently disappears.'

'I had no knowledge that he had left France, I assure you.'

Gautier knew that Grout was lying and he knew that Grout knew it. The lawyer was smiling complacently, as though challenging Gautier to prove that what he had said was a lie. He was not a man who could be bullied or frightened into giving away the advantage which he knew he held. It was possible, though, Gautier decided, that he might be vulnerable to a little bluffing.

'Accusing a lawyer of unprofessional conduct is not the behaviour one expects of a policeman.'

'You have left yourself open to such a charge.'

'In what way?'

'Possessing a forged letter of authority to enter the apartment of a dead man and search it is a clear violation of your profession's ethics.'

For an instant first surprise and then fear flared in Grout's face. Then, recovering his poise, he said coldly, 'I have no idea what you are talking about.'

'The concierge at Le Tellier's apartment could not possibly have invented the story.' Grout made no reply and, sensing his discomfiture, Gautier decided to capitalize on it. He said, 'What were you trying to find in the apartment? An article Le Tellier might have written and been intending to publish? Notes on enquiries he had been making which might have embarrassed your clients?'

'I have no idea what you are talking about,' Grout repeated mechanically in the same way as a witness bewildered by clever cross-examination takes refuge in meaningless denials.

'You did not search very thoroughly,' Gautier continued. 'Did it not occur to you that there might be papers or documents concealed between the pages of Le Tellier's books?'

'I thought you were supposed to be investigating the death of Eva Callot.'

'I am.'

Grout was silent. It was clear that more than anything he wanted to know what it was that Gautier had found in Le Tellier's garçonnière, but recognized that there was no way he was going to be told. Frustration drove him into making an injudicious and unprofessional remark.

'Your meddling may have dangerous consequences, Inspector. Do you know that?'

'Dangerous, Monsieur?'

'There are some who might decide to stop your interfering, by force if necessary.'

'Threatening a police officer,' Gautier replied, 'is not the behaviour one expects of a lawyer.'

'No one can doubt your own courage, I am sure.' Grout could not restrain a spurt of spiteful sarcasm. 'But you may also be putting those close to you in danger.'

When he arrived at the Café Corneille at mid-day Gautier found Duthrey sitting at their usual table with the elderly lawyer and a bookseller named Froissart. Froissart had been a regular patron of the Corneille for many years, longer than any of the other habitués. In addition to running his bookshop in the quartier latin, he was in a modest way a publisher, producing a literary journal and from time to time volumes of the verses of avant-garde poets. The conversation at their table that day, however, was not about poetry nor the law nor even justice, but the demonstration on the Esplanade des Invalides two evenings previously.

'The whole business was a disgrace!' the lawyer remarked indignantly. 'Rampaging through the streets! Looting shops! And we French pride ourselves on being a civilized nation, the most civilized nation in the world.'

'Surely we should be asking ourselves why it happened,' Froissart suggested. 'A demonstration like that is a symptom of discontent. Maybe the people who were there have a genuine grievance.'

'Violence is no solution to grievances.'

'How can you say that? It was only by revolution that we French won our freedom.'

'Perhaps the real question we should be asking,' Duthrey said, 'is why and how it started.'

'What do you mean?'

'Demonstrations like the one we are talking about do not happen spontaneously, they are organized. Someone printed the notice that a meeting was to take place that evening and passed copies of it around. Someone paid the travelling expenses of the speakers who were imported from Belgium and Russia.'

'We know who did that,' Froissart replied. 'It was the socialist newspaper *Liberté*. Its editor has already been arrested together with the other ringleaders.'

'Yes, I know. But where did *Liberté* gets its funds?' Duthrey persisted. 'The people who publish it have no money. It is run at a loss.'

'All kinds of people have helped that rag with money,' the lawyer said disparagingly. 'Writers, musicians, even society women with more money than sense. The Duchesse d'Uzés supported them at one time, and a rich widow, Madame Pasquier.'

'They are just harmless eccentrics,' Froissart commented. 'They give money to what they imagine are good causes, but usually only once before they are disillusioned.'

'I suspect an international revolutionary organization is funding *Liberté*,' the lawyer said, 'at least on this occasion.'

'Could it possibly be the Prefect of Police I wonder?' Duthrey asked Gautier, winking to show that the question was not made seriously.

'You'll have to ask him,' Gautier replied.

Duthrey was referring to a popular rumour circulating a few years previously concerning the secret activities of the then Prefect of Police, Louis Andrieux. With the complicity of a Belgian businessman, Andrieux had supplied financial backing for the radical newspaper *L'Intransigeant*. By making sure that the paper had enough money to survive and to pay contributors, the Prefect of Police provided a shop window in which subversive writers and anarchists could parade their views and themselves. It was a less costly and more effective way of keeping a check on potential troublemakers than maintaining an army of police spies.

'The police have no need to use such methods now,' Froissart remarked. 'The government has nothing to fear from radicals.'

'You don't believe that do you?' the lawyer demanded. 'If its power continues to grow, the C. G. T. could bring the country to its knees.'

'And it is being encouraged to do so by the socialists,' Duthrey added. 'Have you read George Sorel's new book?'

The Confédération Générale du Travail was a trade union founded some years previously and in his book *Reflections on Violence* Sorel had advocated the use of a general strike to win union demands. Sorel was no revolutionary, just a retired government engineer with time on his hands and Gautier did not believe that any of his friends at the Café Corneille took the book seriously. Their argument was tongue in cheek, no more than a light-hearted debating exercise.

'The government has the means to deal with the C. G. T. whenever it wishes to,' Froissart said. 'It has the legal power to impound its funds.'

'We are in greater danger from the small unions,' Gautier remarked. 'Only a recklessly brave man allows a barber to shave him these days.'

Everyone laughed. Some of the smaller trade unions had been urging what they called 'direct action' on their members as a means of getting their grievances redressed. Direct action meant deliberately shoddy or incompetent work and the barbers' union had even advised their members to sabotage their employers' businesses by inflicting 'non fatal' facial cuts on the clients whom they were shaving.

While they were still arguing flippantly about trade unions, the deputy for Val-de-Marne arrived to join them. He had been one of the guests at the reception which was being held that morning in the Hôtel de Ville for the Shah of Persia and to which Courtrand had been so proud to have been invited. The deputy listened to their conversation for a time without contributing to it. He appeared thoughtful and unusually serious.

Eventually he said quietly, 'I know you are only jesting, Messieurs, when you suggest that the government might be in danger, but I wonder whether perhaps you may be right.'

'Why do you say that?' Gautier asked quickly.

'Have you not sensed a change in the mood of the people these last few days? A growing hostility to those who are governing the country? Today when the President arrived at the Hôtel de Ville with the Shah of Persia, people standing by the entrance shouted abuse at him and as he descended from the carriage dung was thrown at him.'

'That's an affront to our royal guest!' the lawyer exclaimed. 'And an insult to France! One hopes the police took action.'

'One or two arrests were made.'

'Are you not taking the incident too seriously?' Duthrey asked the deputy.

'By itself it would not be significant. I concede that. But remember it comes immediately after Thursday's riot in St. Germain.'

'Even so, discontent among the masses will not by itself bring the government down.'

'Probably not, but for how long will it be restricted to the masses? I heard a disquieting rumour today: talk in financial circles of the imminent collapse of a business venture in which many small investors have speculated.'

'What kind of venture?'

'I have heard no details and no names have been mentioned.'

'Does anyone else know anything of this?'

Gautier said nothing. What Courtrand had told him was, he felt sure, intended to be in confidence. In any event the other habitués of the Corneille respected his position as a police officer and never asked him or expected him to talk about police matters.

'There is talk that members of the administration may be implicated,' the deputy for Val-de-Marne explained.

'In that case it could indeed be grave. Another financial scandal would embarrass Fallières. He was Minister of Justice, you may recall, at the time of Panama.'

When the Panama Canal venture had finally collapsed, with the loss of over 1,500 million francs, the government had been forced by the public outcry to hold an enquiry. Fallières, the Minister of Justice at the time, though promising speedy action, had procrastinated endlessly and there had been accusations that he was covering up to save his colleagues in the administration.

'A cabal of deputies and senators has been formed to attack the government, mainly on account of the riot in St. Germain. If a financial scandal breaks, it will give them another weapon.'

'Are they attacking Fallières himself.'

'No, he is safe for the time being. They will be demanding the resignation of the Prime Minister.'

'Who is leading the cabal?'

'Three or four people it seems.'

'Is Pierre de Jarnac one of them?' Gautier asked.

'Naturally. He likes nothing so much as intrigue.'

10

'FOR HOW MUCH longer must the people suffer? For how much longer must they endure poverty, hardship, neglect?'

The deputy, whom Gautier did not recognize, had worked his indignation up to a pitch of anger. He was a tiny, wizened man and had taken the monocle from his eye to gesticulate with it as he addressed the chamber.

'Can we be surprised when the out-of-work gather to protest? They have reason enough to complain. An empty stomach, a bare hearth, the despair of idleness will drive any man worthy of the name to anger. There are more than 12,000 people in Paris alone without work. Yes, 12,000. I challenge the government to deny that figure.' Without giving the government or anyone else time to argue, the speaker went on, 'And what is the government doing to correct this deplorable, this intolerable situation, to relieve the misery of the unemployed, to bring hope and dignity to the unfortunate? Nothing!'

Gautier heard the angry phrases of the man's speech but he was finding it difficult to give them his full attention, not because he had heard or read the same phrases before, nor because he was unsympathetic to the plight of the unemployed. He sensed that these early speeches by earnest but little known deputies were only a prelude to a much more penetrating and dramatic attack on the government which would follow as the debate developed.

In the meantime he had other thoughts to occupy him. Before leaving the Sûreté to come to the Chambre des Députés, he had received the report of the policeman whom Surat had sent to discover where Denise de Richemont was living. Since the trial, it appeared, she had been staying quietly at the home of Colonel Roussel except for a short visit which she had paid alone to Languedoc. Gautier recalled that when he had seen Roussel for the first time outside the home of Madame Pasquier, he had heard him remark to Valanis that they might expect to have news from Languedoc shortly. Although he had not the faintest idea to what the colonel might have been referring, he was curious enough to speculate why Denise de Richemont had gone there. Languedoc, he knew from his study of Roussel's army record, was one of the regions in which Roussel had served with his regiment.

'Four francs a day for a man,' the deputy was saying. In the course of his speech he had revealed that he was a socialist and the elected representative of Nimes. 'And less than half that sum for women and children. Can anyone here say, can the government say in all conscience that this is a living wage? And so we have decent working people struggling to live by doing what extra casual work they find in summer and pawning everything, their furniture, their clothes, even their blankets to stay alive in winter. And if by misfortune a family should fall behind in the payment of its rent, they are immediately turned out into the streets by rapacious landlords.'

When at last the deputy sat down another rose to continue the attack on the government. This time, however, it was not a radical but one of the still substantial number of monarchists in the Chamber. He began by saying, without much conviction, that he sympathized with the misfortunes of the workless.

84

'But that does not give them a right to anarchy and violence. Should we not also have sympathy for the honest, unoffending shopkeepers whose businesses were attacked and looted? What will the next outrage be? Are buildings to be burnt down, the lives of innocent people put in danger? Where were the police when this disgraceful demonstration took place? A handful of men, we are informed, were sent out to seal off the bridges and prevent the mob from attacking the President's palace. What about the ordinary people, women walking in the streets peacefully with their children? Who was protecting them? Evidently the authorities had no foreknowledge of what was to happen or—and this is more likely—were too lazy or too incompetent to take the necessary measures to prevent the demonstration getting out of control.'

More speeches followed, mostly in the same vein and all savagely critical of the government. Deputies who had attended the reception at the Hôtel de Ville that morning described the crowd's hostility towards the President and declared that if something were not done to counter the growing discontent of the people, such minor outbursts of public anger would erupt into much more dangerous violence. Even staunch republicans on whose votes the prime minister could almost always rely, rose to warn the government of the need for urgent action.

Eventually a spokesman for the government rose to reply. Since neither the prime minister nor the minister for the interior were in the chamber that afternoon—both were attending a banquet held in honour of the Shah of Persia—the defence of the administration's policies fell on a relatively junior and inexperienced minister.

'Messieurs,' he began, spreading his hands in a gesture that was meant to promise frankness, 'the government shares your concern over the looting of shops on the Left Bank the other evening. We share your concern for the workless and the poor. We deplore the ill-mannered display outside the Hôtel de Ville this morning. But are we not in danger of exaggerating the significance of these incidents?'

Several deputies shouted their disagreement. The spokesman for the Ministry for the Interior went on, 'Let us examine the facts. Admittedly there are people in our country who are without work. But this is not peculiar to France. Every country in Europe has its share of workless and most of them have a larger share than we do. It is a legacy of progress, of the new machinery and labour-saving

85

inventions which are being increasingly used in industry today. They bring benefits but also problems which require time for their solution. And we must remember that among those who are without work—this mythical number of 1,200 that has been conjured up—there are many who do not wish to work: vagrants, idlers, drunkards.'

Once again the speaker was interrupted by shouts and jeers and several deputies banged on their desks in protest. A republican administration was not supposed to condemn the frailties of the people. The government spokesman did not allow himself to be deflected from his task, but continued doggedly with his speech. He pointed out that the people of France might count themselves fortunate. They had enjoyed more than thirty years of peace and a growing prosperity. The wages of the lowest paid might not be high, but they were substantially higher than they had been only a few years before. And the economy of the country was stable, he declared. The purchasing power of the franc was the same as it had been thirty years previously. These were the fruits of peace and it was the government that had preserved that peace, winning allies for France to protect her against aggression.

The reference to the recent signing of the Entente Cordiale was ill-advised. Immediately, every deputy who resented the humiliation that France had suffered at the hands of the English at Fashoda, and there were many in the Chamber, began shouting derisively and banging on their desks. The junior minister began to lose his nerve and his temper. He had to wait for a full two minutes before the noise abated and he could continue speaking.

'You may criticize the government, Messieurs,' he said angrily, giving his opponents a cue to shout, 'We do! We do!', loudly and mockingly. 'Criticism is the prerogative of the irresponsible.'

'He's right,' a voice from one of the back benches called out. 'In eastern countries it is the eunuchs who criticize how men make love.'

'Every government has its problems,' the spokesman continued when the laughter had subsided. 'Unemployment, poverty, the threat of war are the scourges of our civilization. You may talk about them, you may attack the administration, but which of you can offer a solution to these problems? Which of you has ever offered the government constructive help and advice?'

The chamber fell silent. Gautier realized that this was not

because the deputies had no answers to the questions that had been posed. In his experience politicians were never short of a reply to a question, even when they did not know the answer. Most of the deputies present were looking expectantly towards one part of the chamber, as though they already knew from whom the reply would come. Once again Gautier had the feeling that the debate had been deliberately staged and that it was approaching its climax. He was in no way surprised when Pierre de Jarnac rose to speak.

'Messieurs,' he began quietly, almost diffidently, 'the government of France is asking for help and no one can say that this is not a reasonable request. Help is manifestly what the government needs, for it has shown only too clearly and painfully that it lacks the skill and the will to help itself. The gentleman who has just spoken tried to convince us that the root causes of the malaise which grips our country are not serious. Evidently the prime minister and the minister for the interior think so, for they have not honoured us with their presence this afternoon. We have seen rioting in the streets and an ugly demonstration of public anger outside the Hôtel de Ville. No doubt worse is to come and even now the banking fraternity is concerned over rumours of another financial crisis, one in which, as in the Panama Canal affair, thousands of small investors will be ruined.'

The mention of what Gautier assumed was the collapse of the African diamond mining company appeared to puzzle many deputies and startle others. Several of them began whispering, asking each other whether they had heard of this new disaster.

'Now you try to frighten us with rumours,' a supporter of the government shouted. 'We won't fall for that old trick.'

'You will learn soon enough whether it is a trick,' de Jarnac replied. He seemed composed, self-assured and in complete control of his audience. 'In the meantime let us return to the government's plea for help and advice. They are at a loss, it seems, to know what they should do to reduce unemployment and hardship among the people. Perhaps I can offer a piece of constructive advice, a plan. Let them bring in a law reducing the working day from twelve hours to ten.'

Immediately there were protests from the government supporters. The reduction of the working day was a measure that had been advocated before by radical thinkers, but no one in politics had ever taken it seriously.

'We know what that means,' a deputy called out. 'Prices of everything would go up. Food, clothes everything.'

'Perhaps,' de Jarnac conceded, 'but we have heard the government state that prices have remained at the same level for thirty years, but that wages have risen. Wage earners can therefore afford to pay higher prices and share some of their prosperity with the workless.'

A shorter working day was only one measure which he had to propose as a means of improving the conditions of the poor. The introduction of old age pensions was another. For too long the government had been content to rely on the rich and the prosperous bourgeoisie to look after the poor and the destitute. Every well-to-do family had its group of poor people, very often old people, who would come to the house regularly once a week or more to be given soup and bread and, when they were fortunate, discarded clothes. De Jarnac suggested that the relief of the poor should be a responsibility of local government and methodically organized. He outlined his social programme clearly and in detail, conscious perhaps that it would be reported in the newspapers the following day.

By no means all of the deputies in the chamber listened sympathetically to what he was saying. More than a few of them were men of well-entrenched conservative views, who believed that the unemployed and the poor were largely to blame for their own predicament and did not deserve help. Others were concerned at what any programme of social reform might cost and who would have to pay for it. De Jarnac must have anticipated their antipathy for he was ready to counter it.

'Of course the measures I am advocating will cost money,' he said smoothly, 'but the administration cannot be short of funds. Many of you will know that we in this chamber will shortly be asked to vote ourselves an increase in salary.'

The remark was intended to embarrass the government. For several weeks it had been rumoured that deputies were planning to vote themselves an increase of thirty per cent in their salaries, but the rumour had never been confirmed by either the government or the opposition in case it produced a hostile reaction from the public. The Prime Minister was probably hoping that the matter might have been arranged quietly and without publicity. De Jarnac's announcement must have seemed to many in the chamber that day a betrayal of confidence, but he gave no one time to protest.

'People may wonder where the money for the increase is going to come from,' he continued. 'We may allow ourselves to guess. The Minister for Finance has already instructed civil servants to draw up plans for his tax on incomes.'

The mere mention of an income tax was calculated to provoke an uproar in the chamber. The possibility of a tax on incomes, graduated so that those with lower incomes would pay least and the wealthy would pay the most, had been put before the Chamber of Deputies on more than one occasion by successive ministers of finance and had never failed to cause a storm of impassioned argument, which once had even resulted in lost tempers, shouted insults and blows. Landowners, the bourgeoisie and intellectuals, who made up the majority of deputies, all suspected that their section of society would be worst hit by an income tax and so they all attacked the idea. De Jarnac's announcement that the government was already working on the implementation of the proposal was greeted with surprise, consternation and anger.

The junior minister who had spoken earlier leapt to his feet and to Gautier's surprise de Jarnac sat down and allowed him to speak. 'That is a monstrous allegation!' he shouted. 'And completely unfounded. I can assure the chamber categorically that the government has given no such instruction.' De Jarnac made no comment so he went on, 'What we are witnessing today, gentlemen, is a shabby political manoeuvre intended to discredit the government. Monsieur de Jarnac has strung together an assortment of hints, innuendoes, rumours and deliberate falsehoods. None of the accusations he has made so freely can be substantiated. He knows that as well as I do. But then his speech was not made for the benefit of the chamber, but for the headlines it will provide in tomorrow's newspapers, for the popularity he hopes it will win him with the masses, the votes it might earn him in the future.'

When de Jarnac stood up to reply he was calm, relaxed and in no way upset at the attack which had been made on him. He said quietly and with dignity, 'You have the right, Monsieur, to disagree with what I am saying, but not to impugn my integrity. Like many others in this chamber I am gravely worried about the morass into which the country is slipping. Like a headless chicken, the government runs round in circles, flapping its wings and going nowhere. I have proposed measures which might be taken to deal with the problems facing us. They may or may not be the right solutions, but one thing is certain. We cannot, as the government appears to believe, sit back complacently and rely on others to solve our difficulties. A foreign alliance is no substitute for firm government at home. And what an ally they have chosen in England! Rightly has she been named 'Perfidious Albion'. No, Messieurs, the surest, indeed the only way to preserve our liberty and our prosperity is to make France strong once more. A strong, united France can stand alone, proudly, winning again the glory she has known in the past, dominating Europe as she has a right to do, fearing nothing and nobody. Only through strength and unity can we survive the crisis, a crisis of fear and cowardice, which faces our country today.'

He was ending his speech with the kind of rhetoric that Frenchmen loved to hear, ringing phrases, reminders of past glories, appeals to national pride and sheer bombast. The anglophobes in the chamber led the ovation when he sat down, standing up to clap and cheer, but deputies of other views joined in the applause: the revanchists who wanted a war of revenge against Germany, the monarchists who still hoped to see a king in France again, the socialists supporting the reforms he had suggested. Even his political opponents could be seen applauding. Gautier realized that what made the speech remarkable was not its content nor de Jarnac's delivery, but the skill with which he had won the sympathy and approval of men of widely different political opinions and ambitions, playing on the fears of some, the hopes of others, on discontent, on feelings of humanity, on chauvinism and on sentiment.

While de Jarnac had been speaking the Minister for the Interior had arrived belatedly in the chamber and now, after a hurried briefing by his junior colleague, he rose to exercise his right of reply. From his manner one could see that he was confident in his ability to expose de Jarnac's speech for what it was, a clever but shallow piece of political opportunism.

'As I listened to your words, Monsieur,' he began, 'I found myself listening also for other sounds; for noises in the streets, the baying of bloodthirsty mobs, the tramp of booted feet, the firing of muskets, all the harbingers of violent revolution. But what did I hear? Only the echo of your words falling on a derisive world. You have sought to frighten us with warnings and prophecies, drawing a picture of a nation seething with unrest, of a people labouring under oppression and ready to revolt. This is nothing more than fantasy. You have taken two unimportant and unrelated incidents, a meeting of unemployed workmen which got a little out of control and some minor damage was done; damage incidentally for which the owners of the shops will be fully compensated by the government. And a political protest outside the Hôtel de Ville which was no doubt staged by opponents of the government, perhaps even by you and your friends. From these two incidents you are creating a melodrama, one in which you see yourself playing a heroic part. The saviour of France perhaps? A twentieth century Jeanne d'Arc? A poor man's Bonaparte?'

The minister paused for the laughter which he felt his jibes deserved and he was not disappointed. De Jarnac took the opportunity to ask a question.

'And can you assure the chamber, can you assure us categorically that these little incidents as you have described them, are harmless, that there is no cause for alarm, that the republic is not in danger.'

'I can and I do. You have my assurance, Messieurs. And in truth what reason do our people have to be discontented?'

He continued his speech, defending the government's record and elaborating on the same theme as his junior colleague had used earlier. He spoke of the country's political stability, its recovery from the traumas and divisions of the Dreyfus affair and its growing prosperity. Gautier was surprised to observe that de Jarnac was listening to the speech with no more than polite boredom. He had expected that since the minister was now in the chamber, the confrontation would intensify, with angry interruptions and shouted insults which were all too commonly a feature of the French parliamentary scene. But de Jarnac seemed disinclined to fight. Presently however, Gautier noticed that a message had been brought into the chamber and was being passed along the rows of deputies towards de Jarnac. After reading it de Jarnac leapt suddenly to his feet, waving the note feverishly to catch the minister's attention. Finally he was given an opportunity to speak.

'Monsieur le Ministre,' he said evenly. 'Please forgive my discourtesy in interrupting you, but I have news which must not be withheld from our colleagues. This telegram comes from Languedoc. The army there has mutinied.'

11

BY LATE AFTERNOON Paris was in a fever. A statement from the Minister for War confirmed that there had been a mutiny in Languedoc, but no details and no explanations had been received. Some said that the telegraph wires from the region had been deliberately cut down. There were stories that two regiments were marching on Paris from different directions, that the staff in the Elysée palace were hurriedly packing the president's bags, that a curfew would shortly be imposed. The cafés were crammed, groups of excited men gathered at street corners and concierges locked and bolted front doors, only admitting people they recognized. The Prefect of Police was sufficiently concerned to put the Brigades Centrales on alert.

Early in the evening, as reliable news began to filter through, it appeared that the mutiny had been less serious than the first reports suggested, a purely local disturbance in which no other garrisons or regiments of the army had been involved. By then, however, it was too late to prevent the city living through a fearful night. Any official announcement would not reach the people until the following day and in the meantime more rumours would germinate and flourish in the foetid atmosphere of fear. There would be no shortage of people to exploit the situation: agents provocateurs employed by political groups, pickpockets preying on distracted crowds, café owners raising their prices or serving short measures and mischief-makers who merely enjoyed stirring up unrest.

As he rode back from Pigalle in a fiacre, Gautier reflected that he had never known Paris in such a mood before. Older colleagues had told him it was reminiscent of times when France had been on the verge of declaring war. But when it was all over, he supposed, people would remember it as nothing more than a fleeting bad dream.

He had been to Pigalle to have a brief word with Gaston at the Café Soleil d'Or. By good fortune when he had arrived there Suzanne had been busy in the kitchen and he had been able to speak with Gaston alone. All day thoughts of Grout's threat had troubled him. At first he had dismissed it as nothing more than spite, the snarl of a cowering dog. Then he had begun to reason that the lawyer could not be acting on his own account. If the clients for whom he was working were powerful enough and rich enough, Grout might go to almost any lengths to protect their interests. He had already shown his disregard for the ethics of his profession.

Gautier had told Gaston very briefly of the incident in the lawyer's office. Then he had added, 'When he spoke of people close to me, Grout can only have meant Suzanne. I have no other relations in Paris.'

'You think these people, whoever they are, mean to harm her.'

'Possibly. It would not be difficult to have such a thing arranged. It's unlikely, I agree, but they might.'

'But how?' Gaston demanded. He was not a man of much imagination.

'Someone could be paid to beat her up, injure her. They may know she's pregnant.'

'They wouldn't dare try! Not in our café. All our customers are friends and they are fond of Suzanne.'

'You're probably right, but don't let her go out alone, not even to slip across to the baker. Not for a few days at least.'

Gaston had agreed to be prudent and Gautier was easier in his mind as the fiacre took him away from Pigalle. He was heading not for the Sûreté but for Rue Miromesnil, for earlier in the afternoon when he had returned to headquarters from the Chamber of Deputies, he had found a 'petit bleu' waiting for him. The message sent only a short time previous on the 'pneumatique', or compressed air telegraph system, had asked Gautier to call at the home of Madame Le Tellier at 7.30 that evening as she had information for him.

When he reached the apartment and was shown into the drawing-room, he was surprised to find that she was not wearing mourning. The full skirt of her pale pink dress was decorated with crimson flowers and her corsage was of crimson roses. Her fair hair was tied up with a crimson ribbon, leaving her neck and shoulders bare and showing off a pair of pendant earrings. It was only in the

93

colour of her hair and eyes that she resembled the description she had given Gautier of the women who attracted her husband. She had none of the Teutonic robustness of Geneviève de Stahl and by comparison seemed pale and fragile. Gautier was reminded of the fairy stories he had read as a child, of the flaxen-haired princesses gazing out forlornly from castles in which they were imprisoned. He could not help wondering whether her pallor was a legacy of suffering, of grief at the death of her husband.

'It was good of you to come, Monsieur Gautier,' she said, after he had kissed the hand she held out to him and sat down. 'May I offer you a glass of port?'

The maid poured out two glasses of port from a decanter on a silver salver which stood ready on a table and handed one to Gautier and one to her mistress. Although port was a popular drink in society, Gautier did not much care for its sweetness. As an apéritif he preferred absinthe, the taste of a peasant he had sometimes been told mockingly by his friends.

'I hope I do not shock you,' Madame le Tellier said, 'by receiving you here alone and in this gaudy dress.' Her smile showed that she did not expect him to be shocked or to complain.

'In my profession we do not take much account of the conventions of society, Madame.'

'And are you good at keeping secrets?'

'I believe so.'

'This is my secret,' she said and laughed. 'My secret indulgence. Every evening when I am alone, and that is more often than not, I abandon the widow's weeds, dress up, have flowers brought into the rooms, drink a glass of port and dine in style.'

'That seems a modest enough indulgence.'

'I knew you would think so, but my friends would not agree. I am always afraid that one of them might call on me uninvited and be scandalized by what she found.'

'I suspect it may be just that danger that adds to your enjoyment.'

'Like a member of a royal family going in secret to watch the can-can at the Moulin Rouge? You may be right. But for me it's more than that. This is my rebellion, a rebellion against the loneliness and the boredom and the claustrophobic imprisonment which we women are forced to endure as a public manifestation of our grief, long after that grief has subsided.'

Gautier understood how she felt. The harsh, unbending conventions of society must seem monstrously unfair to any woman of spirit and intelligence. From the day of their marriage onwards a man could enjoy a freedom that his wife would never know. He could continue his liaisons with mistresses of bachelor days or start new ones or indulge in random sexual adventures whenever he chose. His wife, on the other hand, must stay at home and stay virtuous, tolerating his infidelities, looking after his home and his children, preserving a façade of conjugal happiness. If, as in the case of Michelle Le Tellier, her husband died while she was still a young woman, she must be prepared for months of a seclusion very little better than the cloisters.

There were signs of change, some of the conventions were being eroded. Divorces were becoming more common, women were occasionally to be seen in cafés and the other preserves of male privilege, the poetess Lucie Delarue Mardrus arrived at the church for her marriage wearing cycling bloomers and an Italian countess had even appeared in public dressed in leopard-skin trousers. But these were the defiant gestures of extrovert intellectuals or actresses or foreigners. In the closed world of the monde the precepts and taboos passed down from earlier generations still held unchallenged authority.

'I invited you here this evening,' Madame Le Tellier said, 'because I have some papers belonging to my husband which may interest you.' She pointed towards a number of sheets of paper which lay on the table beside her chair but did not hold them out to him.

'What are the papers, Madame?'

'Notes on stories he was planning to write for his newspaper, I should imagine, though they mean nothing to me.'

'And you believe I might be interested in them?'

'I look at it this way. If the de Richemont woman was not my husband's mistress, then her most likely motive for shooting him must have been to prevent him from printing a story, something so damaging or so dangerous to her that she would stop at nothing to suppress it.'

'That is certainly possible.' Gautier did not tell Madame Le Tellier that he had formed the same conclusion concerning the motive for her husband's murder. 'Where did you find these papers?'

'Looked in the safe in Jacques's study. I had noticed them in the safe before but had never really bothered to look at them.'

'Even though he had kept them in his safe?'

Madame Le Tellier smiled. 'That would not mean they were of special importance, except to Jacques of course. You see, Monsieur Gautier, my husband was quite paranoic about his work.'

Le Tellier, she explained, had an obsessive fear that other journalists might steal his ideas. Once, when he had been working in a junior position on another paper, a senior colleague had in fact taken the notes he had compiled on corruption in a government department, passed off the story Le Tellier had written as his own work and made a reputation for himself that had won him an editorial post.

'Jacques never forgot that,' she concluded. 'He claimed that it set his career back ten years at least. And so secrecy became a mania for him. He concealed every story he worked on, partly by writing his notes in a style that would be incomprehensible to other people and partly by keeping the notes locked up or hidden.'

She handed the sheaf of notes to Gautier. They consisted of perhaps twenty sheets of paper, of varying sizes and qualities; some evidently torn from a notebook, others embossed with the address of his apartment and others no more than scraps of whatever paper had come to hand. All of them were covered in a small, precise handwriting, the hand of a methodical, unemotional man. Gautier began flicking through the sheets rapidly.

One sheet near the top of the pile was headed: M.V.Q.—EXPENSES. Beneath the heading were listed sums of money, spent by Le Tellier one assumed, with a word or two of explanation against each. The accounting had been done meticulously, for many of the entries were for trifling amounts, the cost of a ride in a fiacre or two bocks in a café. There was a second sheet of figures, evidently a continuation of the same accounts. An entry half-way down the first sheet caught Gautier's eye. It read: To Mlle. N—for information, 5 francs.

Further down the sheet and on the second page more payments to Mlle. N. had been recorded, another of five francs, one of ten and two of twenty, all of them for information.

Studying the accounts more carefully, Gautier found one other person who had been paid for services rendered and his had been valued more highly. The item read: To Comte A—for introduction arranged in the Pavillon du Bois, 100 francs.

Madame Le Tellier had been watching Gautier as he studied the list of payments. Now she asked, 'Will the notes be of any value to you, Monsieur Gautier?'

'It is too early to say.'

'Of course they may not all refer to any story on which Jacques was working when he was murdered. My husband hoarded papers indiscriminately and some of the notes I gave you could be quite old.'

'To study them all thoroughly will take time. Have I your permission to keep them for the present?'

'I have a better idea. Why not stay and dine with me and we can go over the papers together afterwards?'

Gautier hesitated, remembering that Janine would be expecting him to eat at the café in Place Dauphine that evening. But Madame Le Tellier misread his hesitation for surprise at her boldness in inviting him to dinner. The idea appeared to amuse her.

'You must excuse my wanton behaviour,' she said, teasing him, 'but tonight I am burning my boats, tearing up all the conventions.'

'I will be delighted to dine with you, Madame,' he replied, feeling that if this were a challenge he must accept it.

'I can be of some help to you as you go through the notes. Any names that Jacques may have mentioned might well be known to me.'

'But what will you do,' Gautier asked flippantly, 'if any of your friends call here tonight?'

'We will hide in my boudoir,' Madame Le Tellier replied. 'and the maid will tell the caller that I have taken to my bed with a curious visitation.'

The dining room of the apartment was modest in size, with a table large enough to seat no more than a dozen people, but the furniture and the carpet and the curtains had been chosen with excellent taste. By contrast with those of most rooms in Paris homes, which were usually overcrowded with pictures, the walls seemed almost bare. The three paintings which hung on them, by Watteau, Corot and Veronese, would at that time only have been displayed by people of discernment. Even so they, like everything else in the room, would have commanded a substantial price in any art gallery or sale room. From what Gautier had heard, Le Tellier did not appear to have been a man of artistic sensitivity and he concluded that both the good taste of the apartment and the money needed to give that taste expression must have been brought there by Madame Le Tellier.

His hostess insisted that he should sit not at the far end of the table opposite her, but on her right hand so they could study her late husband's notes together. The dinner was excellent: quails' eggs, turtle soup, a gigot of lamb cooked in a subtle blend of spices and a soufflé with Grand Marnier. The wines were less good, a white wine from the Loire which was inclined to be sharp on the palate and a Volnay which Gautier thought was too fruity and not yet ready to be drunk. Only the champagne which they drank with the soufflé could not be faulted and Gautier had always believed that one did not need any special expertise to choose a champagne; one marque was much like another.

As they ate they talked. Madame Le Tellier was an accomplished conversationalist, skilful enough to arouse the interest of her listener and to draw the best out of him, impressing him with the breadth of her knowledge but at the same time flattering him in the most subtle way into believing that it was he who was inspiring her. They spoke of politics, of whether the Entente Cordiale was a diplomatic coup or cowardly expediency, of literature and Pierre Loti's latest book *Les Désenchantés* and of the symbolist poet Jean Lorrain who had died earlier that year; of the theatre and whether Sarah Bernhardt, now sixty-two, who had just made a farewell tour of the United States would really retire.

So absorbed was Gautier in their conversation, that it was only when dinner was over and they stood up to return to the drawing room did he realize that they had not even glanced at Le Tellier's notes. Madame Le Tellier must have noticed his expression when he gathered the papers up from the table, for she laughed.

'Are you thinking that I tricked you into staying on for dinner?' she asked. 'That the notes I produced for you were just an excuse?'

'If it was a trap then I walked into it willingly. And I would gladly take the bait again.'

'You shall take the bait away with you so that I won't be tempted to use it again. But of course, should there be anything in the notes with which I may be able to help you, you have an excuse for calling on me again.'

'Now it is I who am being tempted!'

In the drawing-room the maid brought him a glass of brandy and a cigar and Madame Le Tellier lit a cigarette. Gautier had seen a woman smoking no more than half-a-dozen times, since those few who did usually confined this eccentricity to their boudoirs and he wondered whether this was Madame Le Tellier's way of telling him yet again that she liked to disregard convention. He realized that it was almost ten o'clock and that he must soon be leaving for his rendez-vous with Janine in her café, but he had still questions to ask.

'Some journalists employ people to help them in their work,' he said as he lit his cigar. 'They pay people to bring them information, to attend social events, to frequent cafés where they may hear a rumour or a hint that might lead to a news story. Do you know, Madame, if your husband did so?'

'Heavens, yes! He had a whole regiment of informants drawn from all classes and all métiers, from comtes to chambermaids.'

'Comtes?'

'Yes. As I've already told you, though secretive, Jacques was not always very discreet. I found out that he had such an arrangement with Comte Robert de Argon poor man.'

Gautier knew that the Comte de Argon was an improverished aristocrat, whose rich American wife had turned him out of their home a year or two ago after he had wasted half her fortune. 'What kind of arrangement?' he asked.

'The comte would carry out small services in return for payment. He knows many important people and has the entrée to many salons. Jacques often used to say that a journalist's contacts were everything, much more important than a talent for writing. And the comte supplied contacts which Jacques could never have made for himself.'

'And the chambermaids?'

'That was alliteration.' Madame Le Tellier smiled. 'You were not supposed to take it seriously. Although no doubt Jacques had some on his payroll. Coachmen, valets, maids know so many of their employers' secrets and, as they are paid so badly, they are usually not too difficult to bribe.'

As soon as he decently could, after finishing his brandy, Gautier made his excuses and left. Janine was unlikely to be offended or even surprised that he he not eaten at the café, for she knew by then that a policeman's work did not allow him to lead the orderly, regulated life of other men and they would still have the night to spend together. Would she be so tolerant, he wondered, if she knew he had been dining alone with an attractive widow and one whose company he had found himself reluctant to leave. Although she had been living in seclusion since her husband's death, Madame Le Tellier had kept herself surprisingly well informed on the political and cultural life of Paris. Gautier, whose preoccupation with work had not allowed him to develop more than a sketchy knowledge of literature, music and art, had been fascinated by her breadth of interests and her wit. She had the capacity, he realized, to open a new window into his existence.

Thinking about the evening as he left the apartment, he could not help comparing it with evenings he had spent with Janine. Those too he had enjoyed but the enjoyment had been on a different plane. He put the thought out of his mind. Comparisons were unfair and he could not help feeling that by making them he was being disloyal.

There were no fiacres to be seen in Rue Miromesnil, so he set out walking. The absence of fiacres, he concluded, was explained by the excitement that the news of the mutiny in Languedoc had created. People, after leaving work had stayed on to talk excitedly and exchange views and rumours in cafés and restaurants and now they were hurrying home by fiacre to avoid being even later and having to face a scolding wife. As he passed the Elysée Palace, turning into Rue du Faubourg St. Honoré, Gautier noticed that extra police had been stationed outside on guard, but there were few people about and certainly no signs of any hostile demonstrations against the government. The President would be able to sleep easily in his bed that night.

When at last he reached Place Dauphine but was still some distance from the café, he was surprised to see that it was in darkness. As he drew nearer he understood why. The shutters had been closed over the windows and a policeman stood guard outside the bolted door. Gautier's first thought was that Janine and her mother had been obliged to close the café. Perhaps in the excitement that had gripped Paris that night there had been a disturbance and the police had been called to prevent the place being broken up and to take the troublemakers away.

'Why is the café closed?' he asked the policeman outside the door.

The man recognized him. 'Inspector Gautier! What brings you here?'

'Never mind that. Why is the café not open and why have you been sent here?'

'One of the women, the daughter of the owner was attacked.'

'Attacked? By whom?'

The man shrugged his shoulders. 'Nobody seems to know. Some voyou I suppose. He threw vitriol in the poor creature's face.'

12

JANINE HAD BEEN taken to the nearest hospital which was one run by the Little Sisters of Charity. When Gautier arrived there, he had to wait for twenty agonizing minutes before anyone could be found who could help him. Eventually an elderly nun appeared to answer his enquiries, even though she could not conceal her disapproval of a man who had the temerity to present himself at the door of a hospital so late at night and a hospital for women at that. He introduced himself.

'How could such a dreadful thing happen to a young woman?' the nun demanded. 'And she and her mother are respectable, law-abiding folk.'

'Is the demoiselle severely wounded?'

'Of course! And in great pain. She has had to be given morphia. Vitriol is a terrible thing!'

'Was she blinded?'

'Mercifully no.'

'How bad are the burns?' Gautier could not bring himself to ask whether Janine's face had been disfigured, whether her attractive, countrywoman's face would be scarred for life.

'I cannot understand, Inspector, how any of these questions can help your enquiries. All the police have to do is to catch the scoundrel who did this monstrous thing.'

'I am not here as a policeman, Sister, but as a friend of the family.'

The nun's attitude softened perceptibly. Life in the cloisters had not blunted her feminine sensibilities and she must have guessed that Gautier's relationship with Janine was more than that of a family friend. She said, 'Your friend was fortunate. She must have realized instinctively what the man intended to do as he approached her. As he threw the vitriol at her, she turned her face away. The acid splashed all over her shoulders and neck and apart from one burn on her left cheek, her face escaped injury.'

'Thank God!'

'Yes, Inspector. We should all thank him for protecting her.'

After scribbling a note to Janine on paper which the nun provided and giving it to her to pass on in the morning, Gautier left the hospital. As he walked away, the relief of knowing that Janine's injuries were not as devastating as he might have feared was replaced by a fury that he had difficulty in controlling. Most of his rage was directed at Emile Grout, for there could be no doubt that the lawyer must have arranged for the attack. Neither Janine nor her mother had enemies and, as the nun had remarked, they did not know anyone capable of such a despicable act. In Gautier's experience vitriol was the weapon of vicious, sub-human men, pimps for the most part, revenging themselves on girls who had left them for another protector. Only rarely was it thrown by a woman deranged by hatred or jealousy.

He was also angry at himself for not realizing that Janine had been in as much danger as Suzanne from Grout's threat, more in fact because many men would think that a man's mistress was closer to him than an estranged wife. The anger was reinforced by self-reproach. Had he eaten at the café in Place Dauphine as he had intended, instead of dining in style in a wealthy bourgeois home, he would have been able to protect Janine.

His first impulse was to go after Grout, to find out where he lived, drag him from his bed, take him to Sûreté headquarters and force a confession out of him. It was no more than a short walk from the hospital to Quai des Orfèvres and there he would be able to pick up two men from those on night duty to accompany him to Grout's home, not because he needed their assistance but for the impact which the arrival of uniformed policemen at their home late at night would have on the lawyer's family and servants. He wished to humiliate the man, have him brought away in handcuffs.

But in even the few minutes that it took to reach the Ile de la Cité, his fury subsided and reason returned. He had no evidence against Grout except for a threat and that had been made without witnesses and could be denied. To arrest the lawyer might give him the satisfaction of a quick retaliation but there could be a different strategy which would not only destroy Grout but unmask those for whom he was working.

Gautier was certain now that Jacques Le Tellier had been shot to prevent him publishing what he had discovered about a conspiracy which was being planned in the apartment of his neighbour, Madame Pasquier. He did not know what were the objectives of the conspiracy except that it was political and subversive and apparently intended to attack the government. He guessed but had no proof that it was linked in some way with the demonstration of unemployed workmen on the Esplanade des Invalides and the abortive army mutiny in Languedoc. Perhaps Le Tellier himself had not known much more than that but had been getting uncomfortably close to the whole truth. And now Gautier, following much the same line of enquiries had alarmed the conspirators to the point where he must be frightened off. If this were true then it was his duty to expose the plotters' intentions and by doing so he would amply revenge himself on Grout.

When he reached Quai des Orfèvres, he passed the entrance to the Sûreté and walked on, crossing the river to the Left Bank and making for his apartment. He had almost forgotten Le Tellier's notes which he had brought away with him from Rue Miromesnil and now he was eager to examine them, already certain that they would provide him, if not with firm evidence of a conspiracy then at least with sufficient clues to point him towards unravelling the truth. In his anticipation of what he would learn, he felt none of the depression which so often gripped him when he returned home at night to an empty apartment.

When he arrived upstairs he decided that before starting work on the notes he would pour himself a glass, not of wine, for he was not thirsty, but of home distilled calvados to sharpen his concentration. But the bottle of calvados, one of a consignment which had been sent to Janine's mother by her relatives in Normandy and which she had given Gautier, was empty. There was no absinthe in the cupboard either and all he could find was a bottle of whisky. He looked at it doubtfully. It had been a present given to him some months previously by Juliette Prévot, a young novelist whom he had met while investigating the murder of a priest and with whom he had shared a fleeting affair. All he knew about whisky was that it was a foreign eau-de-vie and Juliette had brought the bottle back with her from a visit to London. Whisky, people said, had become the after-dinner drink of English milords after the ravages of phylloxera on the grape had left the French with scarcely enough brandy for themselves and none for London. Now whisky was finding its way into France. Already it was to be found in the homes of those who thought it fashionable to imitate English customs and, Gautier had heard, it was even being served in the new American bar—a foreign imitation of a French café—near Weber's restaurant. There the barman had concocted a mixture of Scotch whisky and sweet cider which he had named a 'stone fence' and which he served to his clientele of jockeys, prize-fighters and circus performers.

Opening the bottle, he poured a little into a brandy glass and sipped it cautiously. Surprisingly the taste was not unpleasant, reminiscent of armagnac but more rounded in flavour and smoother. Taking a second, larger sip, he settled down to study Le Tellier's notes.

A glance through the various assorted sheets of paper showed him that most of the notes had no bearing on the meetings in Madame Pasquier's home, but referred to other stories on which the journalist had worked, some of which dated back several years. One which Gautier remembered had created a political scandal when *La Parole* had uncovered corruption among civil servants responsible for placing government building contracts. Another, the Gollan affair as it had been called, was provoked by the paper's allegations, never proved, that public money had been used to buy a château for a mistress of a former Minister for Foreign Affairs. The notes on these and other stories, although detailed and thorough, were lucid and easy to follow, giving facts and dates and the names of all the people involved.

In addition Gautier found six pages of notes, composed in a cryptic style using as few words as possible, initials where these would suffice instead of names and clearly intended to be incomprehensible to a casual reader into whose hands they might fall. The first page was headed CHAMBER MUSICIANS with underneath a list of names

104

BELLE AU BOIS DORMANT
HAUTS-DE-SEINE
PENSEE DU JARDIN
LEVANTIN
SOLDAT DE PLOMB

With the benefit of what he already knew, Gautier realized that the names were pseudonyms for the five people who made up Madame Pasquier's Thursday club and it was not difficult to identify them. The Belle au Bois Dormant, or sleeping beauty, was obviously Madame Pasquier herself, for Le Tellier had already referred to her in his diary as an ageing beauty. He may have thought her as an innocent who had fallen under the spell of the four men in her club.

The identity of the second name on the list was equally easy to guess for Hauts-de-Seine was a district to the south-west of Paris, in which Chaville was the principal town. Levantin, Gautier decided, must be the name Le Tellier had chosen for the Greek businessman, Paul Valanis. It was probably intended to be disparaging, although not so disparaging as Soldat de Plomb or toy soldier for Colonel Charles Roussel. That left only Pensée du Jardin and he puzzled over this for a few moments. A pansy was a gaudy flower of little consequence, which might make it a suitable epithet for an unimportant politician. Then suddenly he saw that the initials of the flower were also those of Pierre de Jarnac.

As he read the following five pages of notes, Gautier saw that they must have been compiled over an extended period, for changes, erasures and additions, using different inks, had been made to the original script at different times. The first page read:

BELLE AU BOIS DORMANT

Ran successful salon for several years and regulars included A. F. Foran, Clemenceau, Daudier. Salon broke up after the D.A. Lovers supposed to have numbered some of above and other men of importance. Radical leanings. Paid legal expenses of anarchist Vaillant and supported his family after he had been executed. Bitter because her husband was not given L.d'H. Too old at 69 to be courted, except for her money—inherited 39 million francs.

The abbreviations Le Tellier had used in his notes were not

difficult to interpret. A.F. must stand for the writer Anatole France, D.A for the Dreyfus affair which had split up many salons and antagonized many friends and L.d'H could only be the Légion d'Honneur.

By contrast with what Gautier found on the remaining sheets of paper, the notes on Madame Pasquier were easy to follow. She was the only person on Le Tellier's list who had been given a page to herself and the next four sheets were full of jottings, made apparently at random as the journalist's enquiries progressed, without any attempt to group them by subject. In order to marshal the information they contained in some sort of logical form, Gautier took a sheet of paper and began writing down all the facts he could extract from the jottings which seemed relevant to his enquiries. In this way he compiled a series of facts about each of the four other members of Madame Pasquier's Thursday club.

The Prince de Chaville
Former lover of Pasquier. Immensely wealthy. 1893 invested with Order of Golden Moon—Persia's highest decoration for promoting trade and cultural exchanges with France. Members of Shah's family often stay at his home on private visits to Paris. A late recruit to the organization, making the trio into a quartet.

Pierre de Jarnac
Junior Minister in Ministry for Foreign Affairs until Gollan affair brought downfall of Minister whom he replaced. At one time heavily in debt. Now apparently affluent. Substantial shareholder in Middle East and Ottoman bank.

Paul Valanis
Tried in both Turkey and Greece on charges ranging from living on immoral earnings to complicity in sale of stolen arms. Acquitted for lack of evidence. May have bought or blackmailed his way into present position as representative of armaments company. Appears to be supplying most of funds now being distributed by group. Source of these funds might be his firms if object is to secure government contracts or to provoke war. Funds could also be coming from Middle East and Ottoman Bank of which his uncle is a senior partner.

Charles Roussel
Dismissed by French ambassador from post of attaché in London for neglecting duties and 'inappropriate behaviour'. Appointment at St. Cyr terminated on complaints from commanding officer that he was a trouble-maker, stirring up discontent among students at academy. No prospects of further promotion in army.

As he looked through the material he had assembled, Gautier could not help but be disappointed. It was true that Le Tellier had unearthed facts about the members of Madame Pasquier's Thursday club which would not be known to anyone outside a very small circle of friends and relatives, and one had to admire both the diligence of the journalist and his wide range of sources, but there was nothing in the first five pages of notes to suggest that Le Tellier had any knowledge about the activities of the group so dangerous that he had been murdered to suppress it. Gautier began to wonder whether the motives for the journalist's murder might not be connected with something completely different, perhaps another story on which he had been working. And yet the fact remained that he had been shot by a woman who now appeared to be under the protection of Colonel Roussel. That might be just coincidence but Gautier had long ago learned to distrust coincidences.

When he came to the sixth and final page of notes, his interest quickened, for unlike the other pages it was dated and the date showed that it had been written only a few days before Le Tellier's murder.

The sheet of paper, like the other five, was covered in Le Tellier's small, precise writing but what he had written was not abbreviated jottings. Instead it seemed to be a brief résumé of the conclusions Le Tellier had formed as a result of his enquiries into the activities of Madame Pasquier's Thursday club and of the questions to which he had so far not found the answer. In the manner of a journalist he had given what he had written a headline.

STRANGE BEDFELLOWS

The secrecy of its meetings and the large sums of money which it seems to be dispensing (for what purpose?) prove surely that the group is planning something important and probably sinister. But what could bring such strange bedfellows together? What common theme could make such discordant voice sing in harmony—a disdainful aristocrat, a devious politician, a disreputable trafficker in death and a shallow, philandering soldier? (And incidentally why the recurring theme of music?)

Each member of the cabal has apparently been given a task. But what is to be the final culmination of these separate operations? If the objectives are political one can see how Pensée du Jardin, Levantin and Soldat de Plomb would benefit—political power for one, arms contracts for the second, promotion, perhaps supreme command for the last. Belle au Bois Dormant is a mischievous, silly woman who loves men and loves adventure and has enough money to indulge herself in both. But what about Hauts-de-Seine? What does he stand to gain? Why does his pride allow him to consort with shady adventurers? This is one question that must be answered.

The 'Concert Programme' is unintelligible, almost certainly a code. It may be vital to an understanding of this business. To learn more one must test the weak link in the chain but who is the weak link? Perhaps bluff is the solution. If the weak link believes I know more than I do he (or she) might take fright and run. I see no alternative.

As he finished reading the final page of the notes, Gautier had the macabre feeling that perhaps in those closing words Le Tellier had written his own death sentence. It seemed more than likely that he had tried his bluff and that the bluff had misfired. Believing that he had discovered too much about their plans, the conspirators—for that was how Gautier thought of them now—had swiftly devised a plan to eliminate him.

Le Tellier had concluded that the sheet of paper which Gautier had later found in his garçonnière held the secret to whatever Madame Pasquier's cabal were plotting. His bluff must have been to let them know that he had got hold of their 'concert programme' and to make them believe that he had deciphered it.

Gautier was still carrying the sheet of paper with him and now, taking it from his pocket, he studied it. The numbers meant nothing to him, but he noticed that there was only about half the space between the heading and the first number and the first and second numbers than there was between the subsequent numbers in the list. The obvious inference was that the first number had been inserted at a later date, perhaps as an afterthought, although one could see no reason why it had not simply been added at the bottom.

Each number was in effect a group of four digits which suggested some form of mathematical code, more complicated than any of the more commonly used ciphers in which numbers were merely substituted for letters. Taking a blank sheet of paper and a pencil he began playing around with the numbers to see whether he could find any mathematical relationship between them which might be significant. After an hour's concentrated thought he decided he was no mathematician. The code, if it was one, was still meaningless and the whisky had made him drowsy. Accepting that he had reached an impasse he locked Le Tellier's notes away and returned the whisky bottle to the cupboard.

It was only as he was climbing into bed that he recalled his conversation with Emile Grout. It would not be long before the conspirators guessed that he now had the list of numbers for which they had readily killed Le Tellier.

13

WHEN HE AWOKE Gautier lay in bed for a time thinking. After a few moments he realized that it must be Sunday. It was only on Sundays that his body, conditioned by years of habit in childhood and adolescence, expected the luxury of a few extra minutes in bed. He also knew by the silence that it was Sunday. On weekday mornings, long before seven o'clock, sounds would come up from the narrow street outside, bouncing, it always seemed to him, off the walls of the building facing the one in which he had his apartment, the creak of cart wheels, the hooves of horses on the cobbles, the cries of the vendors of meat and vegetables and milk.

In the days of their marriage, before Suzanne had left him to set up a ménage with Gaston, Sundays when Gautier was not on duty had been days of lazy, hedonistic pleasure. They would go to Mass first, not because either of them was deeply religious but because a small, symbolic act of self-discipline seemed proper on a day otherwise spent wholly in idle self-indulgence. Afterwards they would lunch with Suzanne's parents, her married sister and brother-in-law in any one of the many excellent bourgeois restaurants in Paris or, during the summer, outside the city in the country or by the river. Although as time passed Gautier had found himself missing Suzanne less and less, he still missed those long drawn-out, leisurely lunches which had become more jovial, more noisy and more relaxing as carafes of wine were emptied and followed by glasses of armagnac or calvados.

Today, he decided, he would work, not because he was obliged to but because he felt himself being drawn along by a sense of urgency which he could not explain. Intuition told him that whatever plot or conspiracy Madame Pasquier and the cabal were planning against the government—and he was certain after the events of the last few days that it was a political manoeuvre against the government— would reach its climax within days, if not hours. He would be powerless to prevent it until he could discover how and when the plot was to be brought into effect.

As it was Sunday he decided to allow himself one more luxury. He knew of an enterprising barber near the Gare St. Lazare who kept his business open on Sunday mornings and he went there to be shaved. The ritual of being shaved, of lying motionless to accept the soothing warmth of hot towels and the gentle rasp of a naked blade cutting through lather, always seemed to stimulate thought, honing his mind to the same sharpness as the razor.

Today however the stimulus was disappointingly slow to take effect. The numbers of the crumpled sheet of paper from Le Tellier's bookcase were by this time firmly planted on his visual memory and he could see each set of digits distinctly when he closed his eyes. He scrutinized them, troubled by an idea that would not take shape, a feeling that there was something about the sets of numbers, something startlingly simple that would at once explain their significance. He looked in vain for a common denominator, a hidden factor, a sequence or a progression.

Frustrated, he put the numbers out of his mind and tried instead to remember the salient points of Le Tellier's final page of notes. He had a feeling that it was the questions which the journalist kept posing and to which he did not appear to know the answer that should be occupying his attention. One of them was why the Prince de Chaville should have allowed himself to become involved in a plot from which he apparently stood to gain nothing which could matter to him. It was another question, however, that intrigued Gautier. Le Tellier had asked who might be the weak link in the chain, meaning, Gautier assumed, which of the conspirators was the most vulnerable and therefore the most likely to betray the plot.

As he was being shaved he thought about this, scrutinizing each of the five members of the cabal mentally. De Jarnac was an experienced politician, skilled in intrigue and clever enough, one supposed, to make sure that if the plot were sabotaged or betrayed, he would still be able to disentangle himself and not be dragged down with the others. The Prince de Chaville was an aristocrat, reserved and proud and safe in the knowledge that he was protected by powerful friends. Valanis, as Gautier knew from their last confrontation, was ruthless and single-minded. He was not a man to be taken in by either bluff or threats.

That left only Roussel and Madame Pasquier. Roussel might not be intelligent and he might be weak but he was a soldier, trained never to betray a comrade or a cause. Although one might be able to trick Roussel into an involuntary admission, it was Madame Pasquier, Gautier decided, who must be the weakest link in the chain. She was a widow, irresponsible by nature and with too much money and too much time on her hands, who had probably joined the conspiracy through love of adventure. He began planning how he could test her.

When the barber had finished his work, it was still too early to be calling on a widow on Sunday morning so he made for the Sûreté. On the way he saw a woman selling flowers by a street corner and stopped to buy some. They were autumn flowers, usually associated with funerals, but he was certain that Janine would not mind that. The horror he had felt the previous night when hearing that vitriol had been thrown at her still lingered. To have even a single scar on her face was bad enough, but women were clever at disguising these things, by changing their hair style for example, and Gautier would make up to her for what she had suffered when she came out of hospital. A group of urchins were playing in the street not far from the flower seller and he found one of them who was delighted to earn a couple of sous by taking the flowers and a note which he scribbled on a business card, to the hospital of the Little Sisters of Charity.

When Gautier arrived at the Sûreté, he was given a copy of a statement made by the Prefect of Police on the mutiny in

Languedoc. It had been the result of a minor riot by the farmers and wine producers of the region. An exceptionally poor vintage, resulting from the bad summer and partly from an undefined disease which had attacked the grapes, followed by the injudicious imposition of a local tax, had brought the owners of the vineyards out to make a protest. It had been nothing that the local police could not have contained but the mayor, taking fright, had unwisely called out troops from the 17th infantry regiment garrisoned there. This had inflamed the crowd into rioting and the officer in charge of the soldiers, losing his head, had ordered them to fire on the mob. The soldiers, all of whom came from the region, had refused to fire and instead had thrown down their rifles. One of the infantrymen had been shot and wounded by an over-zealous sergeant and forty others were under close arrest in the barracks, facing charges of mutiny. A telegraph message reported that all was now quiet and no further trouble was expected.

Upstairs in his office Gautier found lying on his desk Surat's report on the inquiries which he had been making the previous day into the collapse of the diamond mining venture. He was not surprised to find that the report was brief, for his intuition suggested that the business was a deliberately engineered swindle and, if this were true, it would have been skilfully contrived to conceal the identities of those responsible.

CONFIDENTIAL REPORT

For Inspector J-P. Gautier

There are many rumours about the impending collapse of the North African Diamond Mining Company but few ascertainable facts. The original survey was apparently carried out by a Dutch mining engineer who has now returned to South Africa. Sûreté records have no information on him and I have telegraphed both the Dutch and South African police to see what can be learnt. Replies may be expected after the week-end. It has proved impossible to establish who commissioned the survey and the three businessmen who originally formed the company are by a curious coincidence all either travelling abroad or at their country homes. It is generally believed that in any case they have all sold their shares in the company and that steps have already been taken to put it into liquidation. Estimates of the total sums lost by investors vary between 10 and 20 million francs. All I have been able to determine with certainty is that the company was substantially financed by the Middle East and Ottoman Bank. The Paris branch of the bank was shut down last week and the manager seems to have left France. The newspaper *Le Gaulois* is thought to possess enough information to prove that the whole mining venture was a deliberate swindle and it will be publishing this early next week.

As he read the report Gautier, although he could not help but sympathize with the many small investors who had been swindled, also felt a certain satisfaction. He recalled reading in Le Tellier's notes that one of the partners in the Middle East and Ottoman Bank was an uncle of Paul Valanis. Here was the first piece of hard evidence he had found that linked Valanis and the other men he had met at Madame Pasquier's house with the chain of events that were shaking public confidence in Paris. The evidence was too slight to have Valinis arrested or even to have him brought in for questioning, but it was enough to convince Gautier that the theory he had been forming was more than mere speculation. One piece of evidence always led to another and there would be time enough to assemble them, one by one until his case was complete.

When Gautier called at Madame Pasquier's house it was not a footman who opened the door to him but a maid. As it was a Sunday the footman may have been given leave from his duties to visit relatives in the country or he might be ill. Even servants were inconsiderate enough from time to time to develop a gripe or a crise de foie. The maid was fat and middle-aged, with the coarse, weatherbeaten skin of a countrywoman and the permanently frightened expression of a small, harmless animal that has inadvertently strayed into a noisy menagerie.

She kept Gautier waiting while she went to find out whether Madame Pasquier would see him and then returned to say that regretfully her mistress had guests for luncheon and would the inspector kindly return at a more convenient hour. Gautier, who knew from the number of carriages in the street outside, that Madame Pasquier must be entertaining guests and had deliberately chosen that time to call so that he could not be fobbed off with excuses that she was away from home or ill, had his answer ready.

'Tell your mistress,' he said to the maid, 'that it is imperative I should speak with her. She is in great danger of being compromised. I need only a few minutes of her time.'

The maid left and when she returned a short while later she led Gautier to a room leading off the entrance-hall of the house which must have been used as a study by the late Monsieur Pasquier. A portrait of a sombre man in a frock coat wearing a high collar, which made his neck seem even longer and stiffer than it was, hung over the fireplace. A photograph of a much younger and more seductive Madame Pasquier, by the society photographer Nadar, stood in a silver frame on the desk. Presently Madame Pasquier herself, her face pinched with anger, joined Gautier.

'You must understand, Inspector Gautier,' she said, 'that I am greatly displeased by the liberty you have taken in calling on me uninvited and on a Sunday.'

'Pray accept my sincere apologies, Madame. I would never have come had I not believed that what I have to tell you is extremely important.'

'What is it then?'

'We have established the reason why Jacques Le Tellier was murdered.' Madame Pasquier stared at Gautier without making any comment. Her face was still flushed with indignation but her eyes instead of being bright and hard, were watchful. Gautier continued, 'Le Tellier was shot to stop him revealing what he had discovered about a conspiracy.'

'A conspiracy?'

'Yes, a plot to throw France into confusion and anarchy and so to destroy the foundations of the Third Republic.'

'Even if what you say is true, and it sounds most improbable, what has this to do with me?'

'The conspiracy is the work of your friends, Madame; the little group of clubmen who come to visit you every Thursday.'

'But that's absurd! It cannot possibly be true!'

'I fear it is, Madame. Your friends the Prince de Chaville, Pierre de Jarnac and the others have been using their visits to your home as a device to conceal their seditious activities. It was they who engineered the riot on the Left Bank the other day and the mutiny of the army in Languedoc yesterday afternoon.'

As she listened to what he was saying, Madame Pasquier began to bite her lower lip. It was a nervous habit of which she was no doubt unaware and one which made her otherwise attractive mouth seem

114

grotesque and ugly. She had been totally unprepared for Gautier's visit and for the accusations he was making and now, feeling a trap closing about her, she began to look for a way of escape. Gautier had come prepared to give her one.

'I realize that you cannot possibly have known what these men were plotting,' he said. 'They have exploited your friendship for them, but unless you act at once you will be implicated, Madame; you too will be brought down when their conspiracy is denounced and they are arrested and brought to trial.'

'You are right, Monsieur. If what you are saying is true I am utterly confounded! I knew nothing of this!'

'I believe that.'

'What must I do?'

'You must disassociate yourself from them, refuse to see them, forbid them to come to your home.'

'Will that be enough?'

'Engage a lawyer to protect your interests. He will be able to advise you. And of course a willingness to assist the police will help to show that you were never a party to the conspiracy.'

'But how can I assist the police, Inspector. I know nothing of their plans.'

'You may think now that you know nothing, Madame, but give yourself time to reflect. Cast your mind back and try to recall your meetings with these men. They may have said something, a chance remark which would have meant nothing to you at the time but which, now that you know what they are plotting, might appear in an entirely new light. By doing so you may be able to provide us with important evidence.'

'I will do as you say, Monsieur Gautier. Of course I will!'

As Gautier was making to leave the room, Madame Pasquier asked a question. 'How soon do you expect their plot to come to fruition? When will these men make their move to bring the government down?'

Gautier saw the trap in the question just in time. If Madame Pasquier knew when the final and decisive move of the plot was to be made, and he had no doubt that she did, almost any answer he could make would show that what he had told her was little more than guesswork. So he took the only way out. 'There will be no finale for this affair, Madame. As soon as she returns from Languedoc Mademoiselle de Richemont will be arrested and taken

115

before a juge d'instruction. Once we have her confession the others will be brought in as well.'

After leaving the house, Gautier walked along Rue Miromesnil for a short distance, crossed the street and stopped on the opposite side. He knew that Madame Pasquier, although she was quick to flout convention and adopt modern attitudes in other ways, had not installed a telephone, and that left her only one way of communicating with the other members of the cabal. He had to wait for almost twenty minutes before his patience was rewarded and the maid who had opened the door to him on his arrival came out of the house, dressed in her outdoor clothes and carrying an envelope. She turned in his direction and walked to the bottom of the street where a line of fiacres were waiting. Gautier recrossed the street, timing his approach so that he came up to her just as she reached the first fiacre in the line.

'One supposes that your mistress has sent you on an errand, Mademoiselle,' he said. 'To deliver a letter?'

'Yes.' The woman stared at him, startled by his unexpected appearance by her side. 'How did you know?'

'And to whose house are you to deliver the letter? Monsieur de Jarnac or Monsieur Valanis?'

'Neither. To the hôtel particulier of the Prince de Chaville.'

Her reply surprised Gautier for he had formed the conclusion that either de Jarnac or Valanis must be the instigator of the plot. He told the maid, 'In that case I will ride with you, Mademoiselle.'

The maid looked as though she would have liked to protest, but she allowed Gautier to take her arm and help her into the fiacre. But when she heard him telling the coachman to take them to Quai des Orfèvres she grew alarmed.

'Where are we going?'

'First to Sûreté headquarters. Then you may continue to Rue de Varenne.'

'But why are you taking me to the Sûreté?'

'Because I wish to examine the letter you are taking to the prince.'

'You can't do that! When my mistress finds out she'll dismiss me.'

Gautier patted her hand reassuringly. 'Calm yourself, Mademoiselle. She need never know unless you tell her.'

'Me tell her? Do you think I'm mad?'

The fiacre drove past the entrance to the Elysée palace, turning into Rue du Faubourg St. Honoré. Small groups of people had

116

gathered in the street near the entrance to the palace as they always did in times of political tension or when bad news had arrived from the colonies or from a war, or when some prominent figure was known to be dying. It was a curious habit, and Gautier supposed people went to the palace for reassurance, not because they expected the president to come out and make a statement but because they found it comforting to be near the centre of power.

He said to the maid, 'It seems that you do not have a very high regard for your mistress.'

'She's a tyrant! A monster! Makes me work all hours of the day and night and is never satisfied, always finding fault with what I do. And, do you know, when my old mother was dying, Madame would not give me two days to go and see her.'

'She must be a hard woman.'

'Hard and selfish and so vain,' the maid replied; and then she added, with a little spurt of malice, 'a woman of her age doing herself up and fussing over men. It's disgusting!'

'So you repaid her by being disloyal?' Gautier suggested.

'What do you mean?

'Do you deny that you were paid by a journalist for information which you gave him about your mistress?'

The accusation was made on the spur of the moment, inspired by no more than a flash of intuition, but Gautier saw at once that his intuition had been right. The maid flushed with surprise as much as guilt and then said sulkily, 'All right, I did. And why not? Madame pays us servants next to nothing. And what I told Monsieur Le Tellier could have been of no value to him. The more fool he for paying me.'

'But you also gave him a paper that he wanted.'

She frowned for a moment, trying to think what Gautier might mean. 'Oh, yes, that's right. Once. A crumpled sheet of paper with numbers scribbled on it which I retrieved from the wastepaper basket. He had asked me to go through the wastepaper baskets whenever those men had been to the house. He seemed pleased with that. Gave me twenty francs and told me to keep a look out for anything more I could find.'

When they reached Sûreté headquarters Gautier told the driver of the fiacre to wait while they went inside. On Sundays not many men were on duty but he found one and gave him Madame Pasquier's letter, explaining that he wanted it opened carefully so

117

that it could later be resealed without leaving any traces that it had been tampered with. The operation would not be easy, for Madame Pasquier had sealed the envelope with a blob of blue sealing-wax into which she had pressed a signet stamped with the coat-of-arms of her husband's family, but there were men on the staff of the Sûreté who had been trained in that kind of work. Then he took the maid up to his office. While they waited for the letter to be opened, there were more questions he could ask her.

'Tell me Mademoiselle,' he said to her, 'what other information apart from the sheet of paper were you able to give Monsieur Le Tellier?'

'As I've already told you, nothing.'

'What did he ask you to do?'

'To search the wastepaper baskets and also to take the soiled sheets of blotting-paper from Madame's writing desk and give them to him.'

'Nothing more?'

'He suggested I might listen at the door when they were all in the drawing-room to see what I could overhear of their conversation but of course I refused. Whatever he might pay, it would have been far too dangerous.'

'But he paid you money more than once. That must have been for something.'

'It didn't amount to much. Once or twice I overheard remarks that the gentlemen made to each other on the stairs.'

'What remarks?'

'I don't remember.'

'Come, Mademoiselle. Try, please!'

The maid did as he asked, screwing up her face with the effort of concentration. Finally she shrugged her shoulders. 'One day I heard one of the gentlemen, the foreign gentleman it was, saying to the prince something about sharing out the work. Everyone should be made responsible, he said, for one operation. I remember he used the word operation.'

'And what did Monsieur Le Tellier say when you told him that?'

'He seemed very pleased. But not nearly so excited as when I told him about the money.'

'What money?'

The maid told the story in her own way. One Wednesday afternoon Valanis had arrived at the house carrying a small leather valise. As he was going into the drawing-room he had dropped the bag, which had sprung open, and money had fallen out on to the floor; bundles of notes and gold coins, according to the maid. Helped by the colonel he had quickly gathered the money up and put it back in the bag. About three or four weeks later she had seen him arrive again carrying the valise. This time he did not drop it but she could tell by the way he carried it that it was heavy, filled with money once more no doubt.

'After that I watched and he would bring the valise with him every three weeks or so, but by then Monsieur Le Tellier was dead, so it was no use to me.'

Gautier had a sudden thought. 'How long after you gave him that sheet of paper from the rubbish was he shot?'

'Only a few days later. I remember that.'

By the time the story had been told and she had answered his question, the policeman to whom Gautier had given Madame Pasquier's letter returned. The envelope was open and the sealing wax had been in some way lifted from its original position without being broken or even chipped.

'I will now read the letter,' Gautier told the maid, 'return it to its envelope and have it resealed. You will then take the letter to the home of the Prince de Chaville in the fiacre which is waiting outside. He will never know it has been opened.'

He did not feel it necessary to warn the woman not to tell either the prince or her mistress of how the letter had been intercepted and read by the police. Now that she had admitted spying on Madame Pasquier for Le Tellier, she was unlikely to do anything which put her position in the household any further at risk.

The letter read:

Cher ami,

Inspector Gautier has just paid me a visit. He knows why Le Tellier was murdered and has guessed a little more of our plans. He intends to arrest Denise tomorrow, so she must be made to leave Paris at once and stay away until our objective has been achieved. She will not wish to be parted from her lover but point out to her that it will only be a brief separation. I leave it to you to inform our other friends.

Yours in great haste,
Simone.

14

THAT NIGHT GAUTIER dined in a small café near Les Halles which was frequented by the porters who worked in the markets. The café in Place Dauphine would not in any case have been open on a Sunday but he had walked across there earlier in the evening, hoping that perhaps Janine's mother might have gone in to do her accounts or to finish tasks left undone after the unnerving experience of the previous night. But the doors of the café had been bolted, and pinned to one of them had been a handwritten notice which read:

INDEFINITE CLOSURE FOR REASONS OF ILL-HEALTH

From Place Dauphine he had walked to the hospital of the Little Sisters of Charity and asked for the nun to whom he had spoken the previous night. The news she had given him was reassuring. Janine's injuries were responding well to treatment and the doctors believed that the scars she would carry for the rest of her life, although unsightly would be less disfiguring than they had at first feared. With the help of morphine she had survived the first agonizing pain and had awoken from her drugged sleep only in the late afternoon. With proper attention and rest she might not need to be detained in hospital for more than a few days.

From the hospital Gautier had returned to the Sûreté. Feeling that there was nothing he could do either to help Janine or to lighten his persisting sense of guilt, he had tried to put the attack on her out of his mind by concentrating on the enquiries he was supposed to be making. Copies of the documents in the official dossier on the killing of Eva Callot were in the drawer of his desk and he took them out to study them. In his concern over the shooting of Le Tellier and the plot which he believed was being contrived in Madame Pasquier's salon, he had almost forgotten about Eva Callot. But common sense told him that there had to be a

120

connection between the two crimes—the shooting of Le Tellier and the stabbing of Callot—and the Russian emigré Kratov must be the link.

As Kratov had been cleared early on of suspicion in the Callot affair, Lemaire had not taken the trouble to investigate the Russian's background in any depth. Since it was likely that a foreigner who was also an anarchist would not have escaped the notice of the police, Gautier had gone downstairs to the records department. With the help of the duty clerk it did not take long to find a file on Kratov.

The Russian, he learned, had been an officer in the army of the Tsar, an engineer with an expert knowledge of ballistics and explosives. He had also been a philanderer, and an affair with a fellow officer's wife had been followed by a duel with pistols, during which Kratov had shot and killed the husband. Cashiered from the army, he had left Russia and come to France where he had tried to revenge himself on authority by joining an anarchist group. He had been imprisoned for being in possession of explosives stolen from an army arsenal, but the sentence had been light and although he had since often been under suspicion, the police had never been able to prove that he had been involved in any of the many bomb attacks which had been made on judges, lawyers and policemen during the closing years of the nineteenth century.

Over dinner in the café Gautier began to think once more of the list of numbers he had found in Le Tellier's garçonnière. He had left the original list safely locked away but had jotted the numbers down on a scrap of paper. Now after finishing a dish of cassoulet, bread and strong cheese from Provence, he pulled out the paper and, as he finished what was left of the rough red wine which they served in the café, he looked at them, still searching for the elusive idea that had nagged at him earlier, still convinced that there must be a simple key to the puzzle.

$$3971$$
$$3881$$
$$7581$$
$$9881$$
$$5681$$
$$7451$$

Suddenly he saw a common factor in each set of digits. All of them ended with a one. Almost immediately he realized that if the numbers were reversed, they might well be dates, all of them dates in the second millenium after the birth of Christ. He took a pencil and made the simple transposition.

1793
1883
1857
1889
1865
1547

The numbers must be dates. He was convinced of that, but any excitement he might have felt at the discovery was tempered by the knowledge that he had still to understand their significance. None of them, as far as he knew, were so well known as to be landmarks in history.

Two of them—1883 and 1889—were dates of years in his own lifetime and he concentrated on the two, trying to recall any events of special importance that had taken place during those years. 1889 had been a memorable year for him, as it had been in the summer of that year that he had joined the police force. But he could think of nothing which had happened either then or in 1883 that could possibly be related to the secret activities of Madame Pasquier's Thursday club.

Then he remembered that 1889 had been the year when the Panama Canal Company had collapsed, causing a scandal which had dragged on for four more years and ended in a trial for fraud of the company's founders and some members of the government. He recalled too his conversation with Courtrand and his discussion with his friends at the Café Corneille. On both occasions a comparison had been drawn between the Panama Canal affair and the impending bankruptcy of the North African Diamond Company.

He stared at the list of dates. Was it possible, he wondered, that the diamond mining swindle had been engineered by Madame Pasquier's friends and the date of a fraud on which it had been modelled used to identify it among themselves. If that were true then each date on the list must have been chosen for the same purpose and each must be a code name used for a sequence of events that were being carefully staged to create public unrest and destroy

122

confidence in the government. Following on this hypothesis, it would be logical to deduce that the events had been listed in the order in which they were planned to take place and the final stage would be the fall of the government, leaving the group to assume power.

Looking at the list again, he saw that 1889 was the fourth date of six. If Surat's report was correct, the scandal caused by the collapse of the African diamond venture would not break until the story was published by the press the following day. That meant it had been preceded by the abortive mutiny in Languedoc which, Gautier was certain, had also been contrived by members of Madame Pasquier's Thursday club. The mutiny in its turn had been preceded by the demonstration on the Left Bank and the riot it had provoked. But as far as he could recollect neither of the dates in the list immediately before the war of the Panama Canal scandal, 1857 and 1883, were in any way associated with a mutiny.

His glance travelled to the first number on the list, 1793 which, as he had already noticed, seemed to have been inserted after the original list had been compiled. As every Frenchman knew the 1790s were the aftermath of the French Revolution. He thought back to his schooldays, to the schoolmaster who had taught him history, to vivid descriptions of the dramatic events of those turbulent days, the story of the Bastille, the speeches of Danton and Robespierre, the tumbrils carrying aristocrats to the guillotine. Many of the historical episodes of the revolution had been depicted on canvas by artists. One picture by David came readily to his mind, for a reproduction of it had hung in his parents' home, and it gave him the answer for which he was looking: Marat dead in his bath, stabbed by Charlotte Corday. He remembered now that Marat had been murdered in 1793.

Whoever had compiled the coded programme of events planned by the cabal, had chosen the murder of Marat to represent the shooting of Jacques Le Tellier by Denise de Richemont. Gautier understood now why the date had been inserted at the top of the list. Killing Le Tellier had not been part of the original plan, but had been forced on the conspirators when they realized how much he had discovered about their plot.

Comparing the shooting of Le Tellier with the murder of Marat, one of the great figures of the Revolution, was fanciful to say the least, but it was a flattering comparison which Gautier was sure would have appealed to Denise de Richemont. She had impressed him as a proud, haughty young woman and to have her mean, cowardly act flattered by the comparison must have satisfied her delusions of grandeur.

He was convinced now that he had found the solution to the code which Madame Pasquier's friends had used to conceal the nature of their seditious activities. Each date must represent one stage in their plan and they had been listed in the order in which they would be executed. He was also satisfied that the riot on the Left Bank in Paris and the mutiny in Languedoc were both stages in the plan and since both had taken place they must be represented by the second and third dates on the list, 1883 and 1865. He was not worried by the knowledge that the two dates meant nothing to him. There would be time enough to work that out later. What mattered far more was that two stages in the master plan, the two final events or operations, remained to be carried out and they might be crucial to the success or failure of the conspiracy. He studied the two dates, 1865 and 1547. It was they he must decipher so that the police, forewarned, could prevent them being put into operation.

Half-an-hour's intense concentration brought him no nearer a solution. The early sixteenth century had not been a particularly glorious period in France's history and for that reason it had tended to be glossed over in the curriculum of schools. As a boy he had been made to learn the dates of France's kings by rote and he knew that 1547 had been the year that Francis II had died, but it had been an unspectacular death at the end of an unspectacular reign and he could not see how it could possibly be associated with any move that was being planned to bring down the government. The penultimate date on the list, 1865, seemed equally meaningless.

After paying for his meal, he left the café and set out on foot for his apartment. Neither Suzanne nor he had been particularly avid readers, but there were books on the shelves of their living-room that might help: an encyclopaedia given to him by an uncle who was a bookseller to mark his first communion, six volumes in a series of the lives of great Frenchmen which Suzanne had bought second-hand from a bouquiniste by the Seine because she liked the colour of the leather bindings, and an old copy of the Almanach de Gotha, which might be useful although it was mainly devoted to tracing the ancestry of Europe's aristocracy. It was not then eight o'clock and he had a long night which he could spend on research.

124

After crossing the river, he walked along beside it for a time. The night was cold, for the mild weather of the previous days had been driven away by a north-easterly wind and one could sense that sleet and snow were not far off. To his right he could see the twin towers of Notre Dame and further on the shadowy outline of the Palais de Justice. He asked himself whether it would be there that Madame Pasquier and her friends would finally pay the price for their ambitions. One could not be sure. The offences they were committing were difficult to prove. Organizing a peaceful demonstration was not against the law and it was the men who led the unruly march along Boulevard St. Germain, not those who had paid the agents provocateurs, who would face criminal charges, just as in Languedoc it would be the soldiers who had thrown down their rifles who would be punished and not the officer who had ordered them to fire on the mob. Many people would believe that what Madame Pasquier's cabal was doing was no more than a political manoeuvre, a legitimate weapon with which to attack an unpopular government. Even a coup d'état using force—if that was what they intended—would be condoned by the law provided that it succeeded.

When he reached the building not far from Avenue de Suffren in which he had his apartment, he began climbing the stairs. Until recently there had been a concierge to open and shut the main doors at night and to receive parcels and messages for the tenants, but the landlords, to make economies, had dispensed with the concierge. On the stairs between the second and third floors he met a neighbour, a good-natured woman who would sometimes shop for him and liked to help him in other small ways.

'I met a man on his way to your apartment not long ago, Monsieur Gautier,' she told him. 'He was returning the flowers which you sent to the hospital. I told him to leave them outside the door.'

Thanking her, Gautier continued up the stairs, surprised and hurt that Janine should have refused the flowers. Such a cruel gesture seemed totally out of character. He could not believe that she would blame him for the attack that had been made on her, even though he might blame himself.

The flowers were lying on the floor outside the door to his apartment. He was about to pick them up but then he checked, pulling his hand away. He was not by nature a cautious man but

125

reason as well as instinct told him that this was a time for discretion. The vitriol attack on Janine showed that he was dealing with dangerous and ruthless people. He saw that the flowers lying on the floor were of the same variety as those he had bought outside the Gare St. Lazare. The gas light on the landing was just bright enough for him to be able to count the blooms. There were fifteen of them and he had bought only twelve. He recalled wondering whether a dozen was enough or whether to take eighteen and then, surprised at the size of the bouquet as the woman bunched the flowers together and not wishing to seem ostentatious, he had settled for twelve.

Going downstairs to the second floor, he knocked on the door of his neighbour and when she answered asked her, 'Would you be so kind as to describe the man who brought the flowers back to me, Madame?'

'He was neatly dressed, with dark well-kept hair and a rather pale face.'

'Did he have a beard?'

'No, only a small moustache. And he was very courteous in an old-fashioned way. He spoke very carefully and very slowly. Why, is anything wrong?'

'I am not sure yet, but would you be kind enough to lend me a lamp and a broom, Madame?'

'Certainly, Monsieur.'

From the expression on her face it was clear that the woman thought Gautier was becoming an eccentric. That was only to be expected, poor man, after the shameful way in which his wife had treated him. A man who had been made a cocu and then lived on his own could not be expected to remain entirely normal.

On his way upstairs again, Gautier decided that if Madame Pasquier's cabal wished to have him killed, a bomb was the most likely weapon that would be used. Kratov now appeared to be under the protection of the Prince de Chaville and Kratov was recognized to be an expert on explosives.

When he reached his apartment, he placed the lamp on the floor of the landing beside the flowers and went down on his hands and knees. He peered into the leaves and under the stems of the blooms but could see no mechanical devices, no metal, no wires. It was unlikely in any case, he thought, that if anyone wished to place a bomb where it could kill or maim him, they would conceal it in a bouquet of flowers, to be left outside his door where it might be handled and exploded by a passer-by for whom it was not intended. More probably the bomb would be placed somewhere inside the apartment and the flowers would have been brought merely to give the man with the bomb an excuse for visiting the building.

Obeying his resolve to be prudent, he did not pick up the flowers but left them lying where they were and took the key to the apartment from his pocket. It would not be difficult, he supposed, for a trained engineer to fix up a device that would explode as soon as the door was opened. To give himself as much protection as he could, he did not stand in front of the door as he inserted the key into the lock, but flattened himself against the wall to its left at a point from which he could just reach the lock at full stretch.

Nothing happened when the key turned in the lock, so slowly and very gently he twisted the door handle. The click as the latch slipped out of its groove seemed much louder in the silence than he had expected and startled him. He stepped quickly away to his left, flinching, but there was no explosion.

Suddenly it struck him that there might not be a bomb. On the other side of the door Kratov could be waiting with a pistol. As Gautier stepped into the room he would be silhouetted in the doorway against the light from the landing and Kratov would only have to pull the trigger.

He had brought the broom upstairs thinking that if he held it by the bristles he might be able to turn the bouquet of flowers over gingerly. Now he could see another use for it.

He picked it up by the handle and standing well away and still to the left of the doorway, pushed the door wide open with it. It was only then that the bomb exploded with a force that hurled him into the wall on the other side of the landing.

15

STUNNED AND SHAKEN, Gautier lay for a time where he had been flung, staring towards where the bomb had exploded. The door to the apartment had been blown off its hinges and across the landing, where it stood, like an incapable drunk, leaning against the banisters of the staircase. Every pane of glass in the windows above the stairs had been shattered. The blast had deafened him, he had been winded when his body struck the wall and his right shoulder and arm throbbed with pain but after a time he managed to scramble slowly to his feet.

Walking across to the doorway, he looked into the apartment. The small hallway inside the door had been wrecked, most of the plaster of the ceiling had been brought down and the cupboard completely destroyed. As far as he could see, however, the main force of the explosion had been confined to the space inside the front door and there was no structural damage.

The oil lamp which he had borrowed from his neighbour still stood burning on the landing floor and he picked it up to go inside the apartment for a more thorough inspection. From the stairs below he could hear the sound of people running as the tenants from other apartments came hurrying to find out the cause of the explosion. The door from the hallway into the living-room of the apartment had been blown open, its lock shattered and it was only when he passed through the doorway that he smelt smoke.

By some freak effect of the explosion a fire had been started at a fractured gas pipe in the kitchen. By the time Gautier arrived, it had spread to the two bedrooms of the apartment and flames were leaping up the curtains in both rooms. Fighting the smoke, he turned off the gas at the main pipe and then began dragging down the curtains and stamping on them. Within a few seconds other neighbours arrived and with their help he fought the fire, throwing pails of water from the tap in the kitchen into the centre of the blaze and stamping out the smaller tongues of flame as best they could. Someone had called the fire brigade and half an hour later the horse-drawn engine came down the street at a gallop, the bells clanging loudly, bringing the people of the quartier out from their houses to watch the brave spectacle. When it finally drew to a halt outside the apartment building, the fire had already been extinguished.

When the firemen and neighbours had left and Gautier was alone, he looked around him. With the carpets saturated, the curtains no more than smouldering remnants, the bedclothes torn and stained, the apartment was no longer habitable. He had lost few possessions of any value in the explosion or the blaze, but that may have been because he had few to lose. He had never been acquisitive by nature and found no pleasure in possession for the sake of it. A painting which hung over the fireplace in the living-room had not been damaged and he was pleased at that. The artist from whom he had bought it for a few francs had been one of the struggling painters living in Montmartre. Her talent did not strike him as exceptional and he did not believe her work would ever become valuable, but she had been his mistress for a time and the painting was a poignant reminder of their affair. Juliette Prévot, the young author, donor of the bottle of whisky, had also been more than a close friend and he was glad when he found that the copies of her novels which she had given him were also undamaged. Ironically the only books too badly burnt to be readable were the biographies and the encyclopaedia which he had been hoping might help him to solve the code used in the plan of operations drawn up by Valanis, de Jarnac and their fellow conspirators.

The prospect of doing nothing, of leaving it until the next morning before continuing his enquiries, irritated him but he could see no alternative. No libraries were open on a Sunday evening. The jouralists of *La Parole* or *Figaro* who might have been able to help, for they would have access to reference books, would by that time have finished checking the proofs of the next day's edition and returned to their homes. For a moment he even entertained the idea of going to see Courtrand at his home. The director-general of the Sûreté might have the authority, even on a Sunday, to open sources of information that would be closed to lesser officials like inspectors. He thrust the possibility out of his mind immediately. Courtrand had an almost fanatical reverence for protocol and insisted that the rigid lines of demarcation in the hierarchy of the police should always be observed. A man who did not expect his subordinates ever to come to his office except when he sent for them, was not likely to welcome the intrusion of a mere inspector into the privacy of his home.

Aware that he must find somewhere to spend the night, Gautier locked up the apartment as well as he could, went downstairs and set out for Quai des Orfèvres. There was a camp bed which he could have put up in his office as he had done before when working late into the night on urgent investigations.

As he walked he thought again of the puzzle which the list of dates that he had found in Le Tellier's rooms presented. If his assumption was correct and the dates had been listed in the chronological sequence of the events which they were supposed to represent, then two more stages of the conspirators' plan remained to be executed after the collapse of the North African diamond venture. On that basis he might still have a little time before the final act was to be played out, bringing down the government. And yet he knew that the earlier stages in the plan, with the exception of the murder of Le Tellier which had been included only through force of circumstances, had all been arranged to take place within a period of a few days. It was as though the conspirators had deliberately contrived to concentrate the unrest and anxiety which these events would produce into as short a time as possible, so that the government would have no opportunity to take any counter action to restore public confidence and its own authority. If this were true then the final act in the plan might be imminent and Gautier might have no more than a day or two to discover what the last two operations were to be so that they might be forestalled.

He found himself wishing that Jacques Le Tellier were still alive. Although the journalist had left his notes, he must have known a great deal more about the people involved in the plot than he had committed to paper. And that knowledge surely must have allowed him at least to form a theory of how and when the plan would reach fulfilment.

Thinking of Le Tellier triggered off a sudden, impulsive idea. Hailing a fiacre which was passing, he climbed in and told the driver to take him to Madame Le Tellier's home. To call on a woman living alone, uninvited, at that time of night was a

130

monstrous breach of the conventions of society and one which would earn him a severe reprimand from Courtrand and even from the Prefect of Police if he should ever hear of it. Even so Gautier decided to obey his impulse, partly because Madame Le Tellier had given him the impression of being a woman who had no great respect for convention and partly because he sensed that she enjoyed and would welcome his company.

His instincts were proved right. When he arrived at her home not only did she agree to see him but received him in a style that flouted all convention. She was wearing a peignoir, had her hair down and was smoking a cigarette.

'I realize I should not be receiving you dressed like this,' she said as soon as he had entered the room. 'I would have changed my clothes but I was certain that you would not have called at this late hour unless your business was urgent.'

'Forgive me for disturbing you, Madame,' Gautier replied as he kissed her hand. 'I have two reasons for coming. First I can confirm that what you suggested when I dined with you yesterday evening was correct. Your husband was murdered for political reasons. He had discovered a conspiracy to bring down the government.'

'And the conspirators killed him so he would not be able to publish the truth in his paper?'

'Exactly.'

'They must be determined and desperate men.'

Gautier did not tell her that the conspirators had been desperate enough to try to have him killed as well. He had no wish to present himself in the role of either martyr or hero. He replied, 'They are ambitious and have a great deal to lose if their scheme should fail.'

Madame Le Tellier thought about what he had said. She showed no sign of anger or bitterness at knowing that her husband's life had been cheaply thrown aside to protect a shabby political intrigue. Instead her eyes held a distant expression which made her fair, fragile beauty seem remote and unattainable.

'If what you say is true,' she said, 'then Denise de Richemont invented the story that she and Jacques had been lovers, merely to justify shooting him.'

'I believe so, yes.'

'And as part of the plan she was ready to disgrace her own father. Would any daughter do that?'

'Very few, one supposes, but she did. She hated her father, no doubt because he had tried to put an end to her romance with Colonel Charles Roussel, his military attaché. He dismissed Roussel from his post with the French embassy in London. Denise de Richemont is arrogant and headstrong. By helping the conspirators she thought she could revenge herself on her father and at the same time further the ambitions of her lover.'

'But what if she had been found guilty at her trial? She would have been imprisoned or even sent to the guillotine!'

'That's one of the reasons why I believe they are planning a coup d'état. If they are confident they can overthrow the government and usurp power, it would not matter if Denise were found guilty. As soon as they formed the new government they could have the verdict reversed and give her a free pardon.'

'I can see that you've reasoned all this out,' Madame Le Tellier remarked. 'Were the notes that Jacques left of any help to you?'

'A great deal. But I need more assistance. And that is the second reason for my visit tonight.'

Gautier told her of the list of numbers he had found in her husband's garçonnière and how he had partly deciphered it. Now he needed reference books which would help him to decide the significance of the remaining dates in the list. Le Tellier had built up a sizeable library of reference books in Rue Lamartine and if Madame Le Tellier were agreeable he would go to the apartment now and get to work.

'I would be greatly obliged to you, Madame,' he concluded, 'if you could let me have the key to the apartment and a letter authorizing the concierge to let me in.'

'What makes you believe I have a key to the place,' Madame Le Tellier asked.

'I was told you visited the apartment not long ago.'

'And were you also told that I met a man there?'

'As it happens, yes.'

'So you have been making enquiries about me as well!' Madame Le Tellier laughed. 'You had no need to. The man who met me there was a decorator whom I have commissioned to redecorate the apartment.'

Gautier knew it was illogical to be pleased by what she had told him. When he had learned that Le Tellier had used the apartment for secret meetings with his mistresses he had been neither surprised nor shocked and there was no reason why he should feel differently if

132

Le Tellier's wife had assignments there with her lovers. He had always felt a sympathy for women who rebelled against the unjust rules that society imposed on them. And yet he was glad to know that the reason for her visit to Rue Lamartine had been an innocent one.

'I did not go to the apartment to make enquiries about you,' he told her, 'but to search it. That was how I found the list of numbers.'

'May I see it?'

He handed her the list of numbers which he had brought with him and on which he had written down the dates he had obtained by reversing the numbers. He also explained how he had deduced that the first and fourth dates on the list had been used as code names to identify two of the six stages in the plan which Madame Pasquier's Thursday club had devised.

'Your husband got hold of the document,' he said 'by bribing one of Madame Pasquier's maids, who retrieved it from a wastepaper basket. One can assume that it must have been made out at a time when the conspiracy was still being planned. It was also the maid who told him that each member of the group was to be given the responsibility for organizing one of the events in the plan and of how it was being financed.'

'How was it being financed?'

'Large sums were being divided between the members of the group, presumably to pay or bribe whatever people were required to carry out each operation. They would have had to finance the meeting on the Left Bank, for example and no doubt a number of vine cultivators in Languedoc were paid to assemble a crowd of protestors. The Mayor could have been bribed to call out the troops.'

Gautier's theory which he explained to her was that Madame Pasquier, who had previously supported radical causes, would have been given the task of organizing the meeting on the Left Bank. The mutiny at Languedoc must have been contrived by Colonel Roussel, who could have persuaded one of his former comrades to order his men to fire on the protestors, possibly with a promise of promotion once the new government came to power. Valanis, who had moved for many years in the world of swindlers and corrupt officials, would have had no difficulty in finding financiers to set up the diamond mining fiasco.

'I take it you have not been able to work out the significance of all the dates on this list,' Madame Le Tellier said, when Gautier had concluded his explanation.

'By no means. There are four which mean nothing to me.'

'Perhaps I may be able to help. We have reference books here too and that might save you a journey to Rue Lamartine.'

They looked at the list of dates together. Madame Le Tellier was sitting on a damask covered sofa and Gautier went to sit beside her. As he held the list out in front of them, she leant towards him and he felt her hair brushing his arm and then her shoulder pressing lightly against his. He realized that she was not deliberately trying to arouse the strong, sensual attraction he began to feel for her, but that did not make it any easier to suppress.

'If my theory is correct,' he said, 'the second date on the list, 1883, should stand for the riots which took place on the Left Bank last week. But I can see no obvious connection.'

'Wait a minute,' Madame Le Tellier said. 'Was it not in 1883 that Louise Michel addressed a similar meeting supposedly of unemployed workmen which ended in a riot and her arrest and imprisonment?'

'Was it in 1883?'

'I believe so. My husband wrote a long article after she had been sentenced, accusing the government of callous indifference to the plight of the poor. Of course he was not my husband then. I did not meet him until several years later but he was proud of the article and showed it to me.'

'I was too young at that time to remember it.'

'Implying that I was not!' Madame Le Tellier said with mock indignation. 'Not a very gallant remark!'

'You should know better,' Gautier replied smiling, 'than to expect gallantry from a policeman.'

'From you I do, for I know your reputation.'

Gautier sometimes wondered what his reputation in Paris society was supposed to be. Over the last few years he had been invited more than once to the salons of fashionable hostesses and his older colleagues at the Sûreté would tease him, remarking that it must be his good looks, youth and sexual appeal which had given him an entrée to society. He knew that this was untrue but had no means of knowing what Madame Le Tellier might have heard about him.

'Assuming you are right,' he said, changing the subject. 'And I

134

have no doubt that you are. We are left with only three dates to decipher. Logically the third one, 1857, should refer to the mutiny in Languedoc.'

'As far as I know there was no mutiny in that year. In fact I cannot recall any instance of a mutiny in the French army.'

'We need not concern outselves too much over 1857,' Gautier suggested. 'for it is that last two dates in the list that are important.'

'1865 and 1547?'

'Yes. They must signify operations in the plan that are still to come, the last two vital operations that are to bring down the government.'

'I can think of no event of any historical importance which took place in 1865.'

'Nor can I.'

'On the other hand, 1547, I wonder.'

'Do you have an idea?'

'Did you say that one of the men involved in this conspiracy was named de Jarnac?'

'Yes. Pierre de Jarnac.'

'Wait a moment.'

Springing up Madame Le Tellier lef the room and returned a few seconds later carrying a large volume bound in green leather. It was a dictionary of proverbs, metaphors and commonly used expressions in the French language. She sat down again, flicked through the pages until she found the place she was looking for and then handed the dictionary to Gautier. He read the entry which she was marking with her finger.

JARNAC, DE. Coup de Jarnac. An unforeseen and decisive blow. Derived from a duel fought in 1547 between two nobles, Jarnac and Chataigneraie in front of Henri II in which Jarnac confounded his opponent with an unexpected blow.

'That's brilliant!' Gautier exclaimed after he had read the entry. 'How did you think of it? I've never even heard the expression.'

'It must have been one of those inexplicable flashes of memory out of the distant past. I believe it was an expression my grandfather sometimes used, although as a child I did not know what it meant.'

'Well, it's an expression that fits the plan of these people perfectly. Coup de Jarnac. We may assume then that it is to end with a coup

135

d'état and that Pierre de Jarnac expects to be head of the new government.'

'But we still don't know how and when it is planned to happen.'

'No. I am sure it would help if we could work out what the last date but one is intended to signify. And we should be able to. It is not all that long ago.'

The two of them began thinking. No event which they could recall taking place in 1865 seemed to have any possible connection with a plot to overthrow the government. Madame Le Tellier fetched more books from her late husband's library: a history of France under the Second Empire, a collection of political essays written about that period and bound volumes of *La Revue des Deux Mondes* going back to the 1850s. They searched through them but could find no reference to any event which might cause enough public anger or discontent to bring down the government.

'It grows late, Madame,' Gautier said eventually. 'I do not think we are going to be successful tonight. Tomorrow I will look elsewhere, perhaps at the offices of one of the newspapers.'

'Now that I know what you are looking for,' Madame Le Tellier said. 'I will keep thinking. Who knows? Perhaps I will have a sudden inspiration.'

Gautier rose to leave, thanking her again for receiving him and for the help she had given him. As he leant over to kiss the hand she held out to him, she looked at him with curiosity.

'Forgive me for asking a personal question, Monsieur Gautier,' she said, 'But have you been near a fire today?'

'Why do you ask?'

'I thought I detected the smell of smoke about your clothes.'

'Holy mother! How could I have been so careless? I should have changed my clothes before coming to see you. Please forgive me, Madame.' Gautier could see no point in explaining that it was only after he left his apartment that he had decided to call on Madame Le Tellier.

'Then you have been near a fire. Was it a serious conflagration?'

'Not really.'

He explained the circumstances under which the fire in his apartment had started, saying simply that an explosive device had been left in the hallway. The word 'bomb' had sinister and emotive connotations and, not wishing to dramatize the incident, Gautier did not use it, nor did he say how narrowly he had escaped serious injury or even death. Even so Madame Le Tellier stared at him in horror.

'Do you think this was the work of the same people who are behind the plot to overthrow the government?'

'Not personally. They would have hired someone to do it.'

'It is past belief!'

'They had your husband murdered to protect themselves so why not me?' Gautier did not tell her about the vitriol which had been flung at Janine.

'Will they try again?'

'Very possibly.'

'Then your life is in danger?'

'I shall be on my guard.'

'Was your apartment completely destroyed?'

'No. Once the debris has been cleared away and the damage repaired it will be perfectly habitable.'

'Then where will you sleep tonight?'

'At Sûreté headquarters. It won't be the first time.'

'Why not stay here?'

Gautier was tempted to accept the invitation. Madame Le Tellier had given him no reason to believe she was in any way interested in him and he was sure that her offer of a bed was prompted by nothing more than kindness, but he was curious enough to want to find out whether he might be wrong.

Seeing his hesitation, she smiled. 'I do have two guest rooms.'

Gautier remembered that because of him Janine was lying in hospital in pain and partly disfigured. He replied, 'You are very kind, Madame, but I cannot allow myself to cause you such inconvenience. I will have to make a very early start tomorrow and it will be better if I stay at the Sûreté.'

'I understand perfectly.' He realized from her tone that she was mocking him gently. 'And no doubt you will feel safer there!'

FOR THE VAST majority of Parisians the day began early. Most of them would be at work by seven in the morning and many well before that hour. Only a handful of prosperous bankers, lawyers, politicians and journalists and those who did not need to work, the gentlemen of the Monde and their wives, rose at a more leisurely hour.

Another exception was Gustave Courtrand, who was seldom known to arrive at his office in Quai des Orfèvres before nine and was frequently even later than that. One of the reasons for this tardiness was the inordinate time which he spent on his toilet. In spite of an increasing embonpoint and a rapidly receding hairline, or perhaps because of them, Courtrand took enormous pains to pander to his vanity with regular visits to his home by a barber and manicurist, complementing the care lavished on his clothes by his tailor and valet.

Long before Courtrand had arrived at the Sûreté next morning, Gautier had completed a report and placed it on the director-general's desk. He had not intended to inform Courtrand of the results of the enquiries he had been making into the activities of Madame Pasquier's friends until he had deciphered all the numbers on Le Tellier's list and until he had found some stronger and more tangible evidence of their plot again the government of France. A night of reflection had caused him to change his mind. He asked himself why, obviously after the intervention of Pierre de Jarnac, the trial of Denise de Richemont had been brought forward to the date on which it had actually took place. The answer must surely be that the conspirators, having decided to make use of the trial as an event calculated to stir up public feelings, whichever way the verdict might go, wished to have it over and done with before the intended coup d'état. Since the trial had been brought forward by only two weeks or so, this must mean that both the coup d'état and the final operation in the plan which preceded it, were due to take place within the next three or four days.

Gautier had another reason for believing that the final act in the conspiracy was imminent and that was the attack on his life. If there had been more time at their disposal, the cabal could have used other means of silencing him. Renewed pressure on the Sûreté and the Prefect of Police might well have brought a direct order to Gautier from Courtrand to drop his enquiries. So, impelled by a sense of urgency, he had written a report setting out in detail his reasons for believing that the shooting of Le Tellier and the events that had followed, including the diamond mining swindle, were part of a criminal plot against the government.

Now, later the same morning, when a message reached him that the director-general wished to see him, Gautier went to Courtrand's office reasonably sure of what reception the report would be given and he was right. Courtrand's reaction was entirely predictable.

'This time you've gone too far!' he shouted angrily, shaking the report at Gautier.

'Monsieur?'

'Do you call this grotesque document a report? This farago of wild accusations, this ludicrous theory you have concocted? What is it based on? Answer me that if you please. A scrap of paper from a wastepaper basket; a list of numbers which you have chosen to imagine is a coded message and which by your own admission you cannot wholly explain. Do you call that evidence?'

'The evidence is largely circumstantial, I admit. But the theory is the only one which fits the facts, which will explain what would otherwise be an unbelievable series of coincidences.'

'Why can't you rid yourself of this obsession, Gautier?' Courtrand ignored what Gautier had said. 'This determination to prove that rich and powerful people are in some way involved in almost every crime you are asked to investigate?'

'In this case, Monsieur, they are.'

'What do you wish me to do with this report? Do you want me to have a prince, a leading politician and a colonel of a famous regiment dragged in like common criminals to be questioned?'

'Something must be done if the government is to be protected.'

'I won't do it, I tell you! I categorically refuse!'

'At the very least the President and the government should be warned. The guards at the Elysée Palace could be reinforced and precautions taken to protect the key ministries. It is those buildings which the plotters will try to take over at the outset when they make their coup.'

'I shall warn no one. Do you want me to be made the laughing stock of Paris?'

'What must I do to convince you, Monsieur?'

'Show me some real evidence to support your wild fancies.'

'It may not be evidence in the strict sense of the word, but the fact that these men should have tried to have me killed proves surely that they will stop at nothing to get their way.'

'Tried to have you killed?' Courtrand asked in astonishment.

Gautier had not mentioned the explosion at his apartment in his report mainly because it did not seem relevant to the theory which he had been advancing. Now in as few words as possible he told Courtrand about the bomb. As he listened, Courtrand's manner changed. The bombast and the shouting with which he had received Gautier had been an expression of extreme annoyance with an underlying fear in case what Gautier was saying might be true. Now he grew really angry. Although he was vain and petulant and lacked almost all of the qualities needed to direct an efficient police force, the director-general had an unshakeable belief and pride in the Sûreté as the upholder of law and justice. He thumped the desk in front of him.

'This is past belief! Intolerable! How could anyone dare to try murdering a police officer, a member of my department?'

'There can be no doubt that the bomb was intended to kill me.'

'Whoever did it will live to regret this cowardly attack.'

'One hopes so, Monsieur.'

Courtrand paused and looked at Gautier thoughtfully. 'I have another report here about a woman in Place Dauphine having vitriol thrown in her face two nights ago. Is there any connection between this incident and the bomb at your apartment, Gautier? I hear you often eat at a café in Place Dauphine.'

It was the first time that Courtrand had given any hint that he was interested in Gautier's private life. Gautier wondered how much more he knew about his affairs. He replied, 'Yes. I believe the attack was intended to warn me against pressing my enquiries into this plot.'

'Have you any idea of who might be responsible?'

'A lawyer named Grout suggested to me that if I persisted in my enquiries it might be dangerous for those close to me.'

'Do you know where he can be reached?'

'Yes, Monsieur. He has an office in Rue Charlemagne.'

Courtrand sprang to his feet. Gautier could not remember seeing him so enraged before. 'Have him arrested and brought in immediately,' he said. 'A lawyer indeed! I'll teach him respect for the law!'

'Certainly, Monsieur.'

'Wait! It might be more prudent if you did not arrest the man, since you are personally involved. Tell Beaudin to go with two men and to bring this man Grout back in a police waggon.'

'And what should I do about the Prince de Chaville and the rest of his group?'

'Nothing as yet.'

'But you will at least warn the government?'

'No, Gautier.' To Courtrand an attempt on the life of one of his men was obviously of much greater importance than any political intrigue. 'I must first be convinced that your theory is right. Doubtless there are plenty of people in Paris who have reasons for wishing you dead—criminals, not members of the aristocracy. We will see what this lawyer has to say first.'

'But Monsieur—'

'I have made up my mind.'

As Gautier moved towards the door, Courtrand reached out and laid a hand on his arm. He may have been regretting his sarcasm. 'I'm sorry about your little friend at the café, Gautier.' His use of the expression 'petite amie' showed that he knew or had guessed that Janine was Gautier's mistress. Then he added abruptly and unexpectedly, 'We have had our differences, Gautier, but I want you to know that I have the greatest confidence in your ability and your loyalty.'

When the police officers who had been sent to arrest Emile Grout had arrived at his offices, they had learned that he was not there. The lawyer had left for Brussels on a business trip, they had been told, catching the overnight train the previous evening, and he would not return to Paris until the end of the week. The more senior of his two clerks had been taken back to Quai des Orfèvres where Courtrand had questioned him sternly, but it had become obvious

141

that the man knew nothing about the attack on Janine nor about the bomb in Gautier's apartment and he had been released.

Gautier had then tried once again to persuade the director-general that he must take some action to counter the plot that was being engineered by Pierre de Jarnac and his supporters. But Courtrand had made up his mind and would not be swayed.

'I am by no means convinced that there is a plot,' he had said. 'Find me some real evidence, Gautier, if you can and then I'll act.'

Now, recognizing that he had reached an impasse and uncertain of what he should do next, Gautier decided to leave headquarters and make for the Café Corneille. Perhaps as he walked to Boulevard St. Germain, inspiration would come to him. He was still puzzled by the two unidentified dates on Le Tellier's list and thinking came more easily away from the distractions of the office.

As he was leaving the Sûreté he was given a letter which had been delivered there by hand a few minutes earlier. He decided that it must be from Janine, a note thanking him for the flowers he had sent her in all probability. The handwriting was neat and practical, developed by good instruction in one of the many excellent country schools. He found it strange that although he and Janine had spent several nights together and were on affectionate terms, he had never seen her handwriting before. The menus at the café were always written by her mother, even though the older woman had a less well-formed, a less literate hand.

He did not read the letter immediately, but waited until he was crossing the river by Pont St. Michel. Half-way across the bridge he stopped, leant against the parapet, slit the envelope and drew out the letter. As soon as he saw that Janine had started it with the words 'Cher Monsieur', he had a sense of foreboding. He read on:

I have to thank you for the flowers which you sent me. It was most thoughtful of you and they are very pretty. I have also to tell you that I shall be leaving hospital before the end of the week. There is nothing more that can be done for me here. Only time will heal my injuries. Also the bed should be used for a person more in need of it than I. When I leave here I shall travel with my mother to our village in Normandy for the doctor says I need rest and country air. We shall not be returning to Paris as my mother has decided to sell the café. She feels she can no longer live in a city of such violence and danger. We will get a good price for it.

Enough to live comfortably in Normandy. This means, Monsieur, that we shall not meet again. It is better that way. Please do not come to the hospital or try to see me when I leave. I know that you respect and have consideration for my feelings and will do as I ask.

Be so kind, Monsieur, as to accept the expression
of my most respectful sentiments.
Janine Croisère
P.S. You see, I was right about our parting!

Turning, Gautier rested his elbows on the parapet of the bridge and looked out over the water to the other bridges beyond. His first thought was that Janine had not meant what she said in a letter that she had written under the influence of strong emotion, of hysteria almost. She felt herself disfigured, scarred for life and could not endure the thought that he should see and eventually make love to her like that. But the mood would pass. He would wait for a few days, give time for the mental wounds to heal and then approach her gently, send her some more flowers, write to her.

Then he read the letter again. The language was temperate, the sentences well constructed. It was not the letter of a hysterical woman. The postscript was to remind him of how, when they had last made love, she had expressed her conviction that their affair would not last much longer. She had accepted the attack on her with stoical fatalism, believing that it was destiny, a preordained ending to their relationship. Her conviction would be difficult to shake. A little of her fatalism infected him and he let the letter slip from his fingers to flutter down on to the waters of the Seine.

When he reached the Café Corneille, he found it unusually crowded for that time of day. Every table was occupied by a group of men, many of whom he could not remember seeing there before and the air was thick with tobacco smoke. One could sense immediately that the mood was serious; faces were solemn and there was no laughter to be heard. The regular patrons of the café were for the most part tolerant, good-natured and witty, which was why the ambience there had always appealed to Gautier. He could recall no more than one or two occasions in the past when he had arrived at the café to find the same grave, tense atmosphere that he detected today and they had been at times of national crisis.

All his friends were at the café, the bookseller Froissart, the

143

elderly lawyer, the deputy from Val-de-Marne, a brilliant young judge, another journalist named Vence and, inevitably, Duthrey. Room was made for Gautier at their table and he found when he joined them that they were discussing the failure of the African diamond mining venture.

'Evidently,' the judge was saying, 'the fraud was devised by foreigners working in collusion with a foreign bank.'

'That makes it all the more reprehensible,' Duthrey remarked. 'There should be laws controlling the activities of foreigners in the French money market.'

'A very chauvinistic attitude if I may say so!'

'Not at all. As things are a foreigner can defraud investors here and then leave the country, having deposited the fruits of his swindle with a foreign bank. The investor had no means of redress.'

The deputy, a middle-of-the-road politician who liked to be fair, said, 'This debacle, coming so soon after the riot on the Left Bank and the mutiny at Languedoc is most unfortunate for the government. Its existence has been put in danger by a sequence of events for which it was not responsible.'

'On the other hand it is lucky for the government that they happened at this moment. The visit of the Shah will distract the people.'

'Yes,' Froissart agreed. 'The Shah is popular. The people will be lining the streets and cheering him as he passes on his way to the gala performance of the opera tonight. Some of his popularity will rub off on to Fallières.'

'I agree,' the lawyer said. 'But what will the Shah and his retinue be thinking. A riot, a mutiny, a financial scandal! France is being shamed in front of our guests.'

'One wonders what England will be thinking,' the deputy remarked. 'Will the king be regretting the alliance he has made with us?'

'Is it true that he is even now in Paris?' Froissart asked. 'Incognito, of course.'

'I understand so,' Vence replied.

'What a lucky fellow he is! When he comes to Paris his wife turns a blind eye on these little bachelor trips.'

'He's unfaithful to her but faithful to his former mistresses. What delicacy! What discernment!'

144

'He may see the fall of our government while he's here,' Vence said acidly.

'But that's not possible. It has a comfortable majority.' Gautier threw the remark in deliberately, wishing to know whether his friends really believed the government might be in danger.

'That may not be enough,' the deputy for Val-de-Marne said. 'Opponents of the Prime Minister are working up hostility against him. Several senators, deputies and businessmen are organizing a public meeting to be held this afternoon.'

'For what purpose?'

'There will be inflammatory speeches, demands for the government to resign and doubtless a petition will be signed.'

'Is Pierre de Jarnac to be one of the speakers?' Gautier asked.

'Surprisingly, no. He declined an invitation to attend, but his friends will be there in force.'

Gautier would have liked to know more about the meeting—where it was to be held, how many people were expected to be present, who would preside—but he did not press the matter with further questions. He suspected that it might well be planned as the penultimate operation devised by de Jarnac and his fellow conspirators before the final coup. Even so, if his friends at the Café Corneille, out of regard for his position, did not discuss matters involving the police in his presence, then it would be morally wrong for him to take advantage of friendship by questioning them on what might prove to be a criminal matter.

As it happened he was not even able to learn more about the meeting by listening to their conversation, for a waiter arrived at the table with a message for him. A lady was waiting in a carriage outside the café, he announced, and she wished to speak to Monsieur Gautier.

'Monsieur Gautier!' Duthrey exclaimed. 'Then it's not official business. See, his mistress cannot bear to be without him! She even comes to claim him from the café in the morning!'

'No doubt she wants him as her apéritif.'

'Really Gautier!' Froissart said with a show of mock severity. 'A man's café is sacrosanct, inviolable! You must discipline your mistresses. All this talk of women's rights is going to their heads.'

A closed Victoria drawn by two white horses stood in the boulevard outside the café. The woman inside it was wearing a veil, but from her figure and the way she was sitting with her head slightly inclined, Gautier knew she was Michelle Le Tellier. She beckoned him to join her, so he climbed into the carriage and shut the door behind him.

'Have you time to take a short drive?' she asked.

'Of course.'

'Then would you be so kind as to tell my coachman to proceed.'

He did as she had asked and the Victoria moved off at a gentle pace, heading down the boulevard towards Quai d'Orsay. As soon as they were alone Madame Le Tellier lifted her veil and smiled at him.

'What did your friends at the café say when a mysterious woman arrived to take you away?' she asked.

'They thought you were my mistress.'

'I shall take that as a compliment. But never fear, it shall not happen again.'

Gautier was about to reply that he would never object to leaving his friends for her company, but intuition told him that it was a meaningless piece of gallantry which he might one day regret. Now that Janine had rejected him, both Michelle Le Tellier and he were free and uncommitted.

'After you left me last night and again this morning I thought of what you told me. And I had an idea.'

'What was that?'

'The third date on the list, 1857. You thought that it might have been used to refer to the mutiny at Languedoc, did you not?'

'Yes, I did.'

'1857 was the year of the Indian mutiny. Indian soldiers mutinied against the British in India and many English were killed.'

'You must be right! I never thought of that.'

'Neither did I, and you know why? Because we both assumed that all the dates on the list must have been taken from French history.'

At once Gautier saw the implication of what she was saying. 'So the other date on the list, the only remaining one might also be drawn from the history of another nation?'

'Yes, I believe so,' Madame Le Tellier said quietly. 'From American history. 1865 was the year in which Abraham Lincoln was assassinated.'

Lincoln, Gautier knew, had been shot by a fanatic while in a box at the theatre. 'My God!' he exclaimed. 'They plan to assassinate the Shah of Persia at the opera tonight!'

17

'I AM MOST grateful to you, Monsieur le Préfet, for agreeing to see us and at short notice,' Courtrand said ingratiatingly. 'And I fear we may be wasting your time.'

'In that case,' the Prefect of Police replied with good humour, 'why did you come?'

'Gautier here is convinced that a serious crime is to be committed tonight; a political crime.'

'If Gautier has reasons for believing that, you were right to tell me.'

The prefect was a tall, lean man who gave the impression of being aloof and remote and not especially interested in his work, but the appearance was deceptive and his subordinates had learned that he had a surprising knowledge of how the various police departments were functioning even at junior levels and was merciless when faced with inefficiency. He had let it be known, unofficially, that he thought highly of Gautier and this must have been the reason why Courtrand, after Gautier had been to see him a second time, had grudgingly agreed that the prefect should be warned that there might be an attempted assassination at the gala opera performance that evening.

'When investigating the murder of a prostitute in Pigalle,' Courtrand replied, 'Gautier came across information which leads him to believe that a group of people intend to assassinate the Shah of Persia at the opera tonight.'

'One finds it difficult to see a connection between the two crimes.'

'I agree, Monsieur le Préfet. In my view Gautier has jumped to unwarranted conclusions. He has no evidence worth speaking about of a conspiracy and his interpretation of such facts as he has is imaginative, to say the least.'

'Perhaps it would be better if Gautier told me himself,' the prefect said drily.

As concisely as he could Gautier told the prefect what he knew of the group that had been meeting in Madame Pasquier's home and how he had come to believe that they were responsible not only for the murder of Jacques Le Tellier but also for the disturbing events of the past few days. He showed him the list of numbers which Le Tellier had retrieved from Madame Pasquier's maid and explained his interpretation of them, ending with his reason for concluding that the Shah of Persia was to be the victim of an assassination that evening.

'Why the Shah?' The prefect asked when he had finished. 'Why not the President.'

'I mean no disrespect, Monsieur, but the assassination of the President is not likely to inflame the feelings of the people against the government. The stabbing of Sadi Carnot did not generate much passion. The Shah on the other hand is well loved in France and, what is even more important, he is our country's guest. For him to be murdered while he was under our roof, so to speak, would be seen as a national disgrace, a stain on our honour, and the government would be held responsible.'

'I can see that, but where does this man Kratov fit into the plot?'

'He had been selected as the assassin. He has all the qualifications.'

Gautier's theory, which he now explained to the prefect, was that, having decided months ago on the assassination of the Shah on his visit to Paris as the final and key operation in their plan to bring down the government, the plotters began looking for a suitable assassin. There might have been any number of people who would have done the deed if the fee had been large enough, but the danger of hiring an assassin was that he might betray the plot. Then they learnt that Kratov was in trouble, likely to be charged with the murder of Eva Callot. It would not have been difficult for the Prince de Chaville to persuade his devoted protégé, Ibrahim, to give false evidence, and the price Kratov would have had to pay for being saved from the guillotine would be to assassinate the Shah. No doubt he would have been offered other inducements, money and the means to escape the police and France. If the government fell and de Jarnac and his friends took over, they would be able to arrange almost anything.

'And you believe that the assassination will be followed by an attempted coup d'état?'

'Yes, Monsieur, I do.'

'And how do you suppose that will be staged?'

'De Jarnac and his friends will be waiting somewhere this evening, probably at Madame Pasquier's home which is only a short walk from the Elysée Palace. When the news of the assassination reaches them they will march on the palace. More followers will join them. And they will be reinforced by people in the streets. The people of Paris will be shocked and angry, ready to defy authority with violence if necessary. Another group could be sent to take over the Ministry for the Interior.'

'This is just fantasy, Gautier,' Courtrand complained 'Coups d'état are a thing of the past. They can never succeed so long as we have a loyal police force.'

'The army matters more than the police. Would the army remain loyal if a popular officer was one of the leaders in an attack on the government? The army always believes it can run the country better than politicians. Remember Boulanger.'

Less than six years previously, at a time of political unrest, General Boulanger, a right-wing demagogue popular in the army and with the people, had won a parliamentary election with an astounding majority. Huge crowds had gathered on the night when the election result had been announced and had urged him to march at their head to the Elysée palace and take over the government. The army and all right-wing political groups would have supported him but, a coward at heart, he had flinched from making the decisive move and his chance had never come again. And so the third Republic had survived, but it had been the narrowest of escapes.

The prefect had been listening carefully to what Gautier was saying. Now, after a few moment of reflection he said slowly, 'I have to say, Gautier, that your theory is totally unbelievable.'

'That is what I have already told him, Monsieur le Préfet.'

'Nevertheless I find myself inclined to believe it. Incredible it may be but there seems to be no other satisfactory explanation of the events you have narrated. In any event it is sufficiently plausible for me to realize that we must take action. The question remains, however, what should we do.'

'Arrest all these people, including the women,' Courtrand suggested. 'That would put a stop to their plan.'

'Regretfully, Monsieur, it is too late for that.'

The conference with the prefect had been difficult to arrange, for, by the time Gautier had been able to convince Courtrand that higher authority must be warned, he had left his office to attend a banquet in honour of Sarah Bernhardt. When eventually they had assembled in the prefect's office, it had been almost three-thirty.

'These men are clever,' Gautier continued. 'They will not all be gathered together in a convenient place for us to bring them in, especially as they will know by now that the attempt to kill me failed. And even if we were to find and arrest them it would be too late. The plan to assassinate the Shah tonight will go ahead.'

'You are right,' the prefect agreed.

'Then we must have the Shah's visit to the opera cancelled,' Courtrand said.

'The Shah would never agree; nor would the President on such flimsy evidence as we have. No, we must protect the Shah and make certain that no one will have a chance to kill him. How do you suppose, Gautier, that they intend to assassinate him?'

'Either with a bomb or by shooting. Kratov is skilled enough to handle either method.'

The three men discussed the measures that should be taken to protect the Shah. They decided it was not likely that any attempt would be made to kill him while he was driving from the Elysée palace to the opera with the President, because to have the most dramatic impact the assassination should be witnessed by a large audience. Even so, as a precaution they agreed that police would be stationed along the route for the drive and that the whole area in front of the opera house, including the steps leading up to the entrance would be cleared and the crowds held well back. Spectators would also not be allowed in the foyer of the building or on the great staircase which led up to the floor on which the presidential box was situated and the president's party would enter the building and make its way to the box only after the rest of the audience were in their places.

'Have the whole building, including of course the presidential box searched for explosives,' the prefect told Courtrand. 'You can put men to work on that as soon as you leave here.'

'I will see to it myself, Monsieur.'

'That leaves only the most difficult task. We have to ensure that during the performance no one can get into a position from where he can fire a revolver or throw a bomb into the box.'

'We can find out who will be occupying the boxes adjoining the president's, including the box above it,' Gautier suggested, 'and if necessary they can be searched as they arrive.'

The prefect pulled out a gold pocket watch and checked the time. 'There is little time left, Messieurs, and there is much to be done. I am going to leave all the arrangements for security inside the Opéra to you, Gautier. You have my authority to call on as many policemen as you need from commissariats in the arrondissements and to give the staff of the opera house whatever instructions are needed. I shall be at the opera this evening should you need me, as I will be attending the performance.'

'So will I,' said Courtrand. 'My wife and I are guests of the banker Armand de Saules.'

As Gautier was moving towards the door the prefect added, 'If by any chance, Gautier, you come across any of the people whom you believe to be involved in this affair at the opera or elsewhere, treat them with discretion. They are men of influence.'

'I will of course. But does that mean, Monsieur, that you are still not convinced that there is a conspiracy?'

The prefect shook his head. 'I really don't know what to think. One can understand why an ambitious politician, a disgruntled army officer and a businessman with his eye on armament contracts might conspire against the state. But I find it impossible to believe that the Prince de Chaville would join in a plot to have the Shah of Persia assassinated. They have been friends for many years. I could imagine that he might conceivably be involved in a plan to kill the President, although even that seems most improbable, but not the Shah.'

'Then perhaps I am wrong,' Gautier replied. 'It may after all be the President who is the intended victim.'

18

AFTER AN INITIAL hostility and suspicion, Parisians had come to be proud of the imposing opera house which stood at the head of Place de l'Opéra, facing down the avenue of the same name towards the Louvre and the Seine beyond. The reason for the hostility was that the decision to build a new opera house had been taken by Napoleon III and work had been started on it in 1861. Before it would be completed there had come the disastrous war with Germany and the Emperor, blamed for the devastating humiliation to French pride, had been forced to abdicate. After the war and the rebellion of the Commune which followed, national confidence had been slow in returning but eventually work had been restarted on the building. It was finally completed in 1875 and inaugurated by MacMahon, the first president of the Third Republic.

Since then the opera had become an indispensable part of the social life of Paris. Monday was opera night and almost all the boxes around the auditorium were leased to members of the gratin, while gentlemen subscribers were allowed to visit the foyer de danse. There the ballet dancers who performed divertissements between the acts of operas would gather to receive admiration, gifts and discreet advances.

Gautier had been to the opera on only two occasions, both some years previously and when he arrived at the building that afternoon, he made a rapid tour of it so that he could decide what measures should be taken to protect the President and the Shah. Since it had been originally designed as a setting for the spectacular galas and social gatherings of the Emperor's court, the foyers, the vast staircases and balconies of the opera house had been given by the architect, Charles Garnier, an even greater importance and grandeur than the performance hall itself.

Their spaciousness, Gautier realized, would make the task of protecting the presidential party easier, for the audience would be in their places in the auditorium when the President arrived. A few policemen in plain clothes stationed at strategic points would be able to prevent any would-be assassin who might have concealed himself in the foyer or on the balconies from getting close enough to fire a shot or throw a bomb as the party made its way up the stairs towards the presidential box.

The twenty men whom Gautier had brought with him from the Sûreté were immediately put to work searching first the presidential box, then the adjoining boxes and seats and afterwards the foyers and balconies. They found no bombs, no concealed weapons, nothing.

Meanwhile Gautier went into the auditorium. If, as he assumed, the attack on the President or the Shah were not to be made on the journey from the Elysée Palace and since, after the precautions he would be taking, the entrance to the building, the staircases and the foyers would be reasonably secure, then any assassination attempt would have to be made when the presidential party was in its box. From the outset this was what he had expected would be the conspirators' plan; the assassin would throw his bomb or fire a shot at his intended victim, probably at a time when the opera was reaching its climax. In his own mind he had also decided that a pistol or revolver would be the weapon chosen, since a rifle would be difficult to smuggle into the building and bombs were not easy to handle and were unreliable at the best of times.

He looked around him at the horseshoe-shaped auditorium, sumptuously decorated in red and gold, with its splendid ceiling designed by Lenepveu to symbolize the hours of day and night and its immense gas chandelier. The rows of seats facing the stage could, with all the seats in the boxes, accommodate 2,000 spectators but no more than a handful of them would be close enough to the president's box to fire a pistol into it with any reasonable prospect of success. A pistol's effective range could be no more than 30 metres at the very most.

There were three tiers of boxes around the auditorium with a tier of baignoires below and a gallery above. If the assassin's attack was to be made from a box, it would have to be from one of those immediately adjoining the president's, and even from them the angle of fire would be difficult. From any other box in the house the range would be too great. Similarly, if the assassin were planning to fire from the rows of seats in the centre of the auditorium, it would have to be from one of the seats close at hand.

Leaving the auditorium, Gautier went into the front foyer which separated the head of the staircase from the main foyer and which opened on to two rotundas and on to the long buffet gallery. The main foyer, more than 50 metres long and with its high painted ceiling supported by gilded columns, was decorated with mosaics executed by Venetian craftsmen and tapestries hung in the spaces between its mirrors. Although it was lit by ten chandeliers, the light from which was reflected in the tall Saint-Gobain mirrors, the foyer and also the buffet gallery seemed sombre and shadowy. It was here and on the main staircase that the gentlemen and ladies of society would gather during the intervals of the performance to meet each other, and talk and be admired by the lesser mortals who could look down on them from the galleries above. Already the attendants who would usher the spectators to their seats or admit them to their boxes were arriving and moving about the foyers, while the waiters in the buffet gallery were laying out the refreshments and the champagne they would soon be serving.

The administrator of the Opéra was waiting for Gautier in his office. He was an effeminate, nervous man, appointed to his post, one supposed, more for his artistic flair and standing in the world of music than for executive ability. Having been alerted by the Prefect of Police, that precautions must be taken against a possible attack on the President, he had the manager of the building, a man named Lepelletier, with him.

'This is dreadful,' the administrator exclaimed. 'Unthinkable! An assassination in my opera house!'

'We must do all we can, Monsieur, to make sure that there is no assassination,' Gautier replied.

'How can people be so savage? An opera house is a place of culture and enlightenment.'

Gautier made no comment. He might have reminded the administrator that Napoleon III had only decided to build a new opera house after narrowly escaping being assassinated by Orsini while on his way to the old one in Rue Peletier.

'How can we help you, Monsieur l'Inspecteur?' Lepelletier asked. He was a practical man, not much affected by emotional outbursts.

'I noticed that the doors to all the boxes have locks. Does that mean that the person to whom the box is leased has a key?'

154

'No. The attendants have keys and open the door only to the person for whom the box is reserved.'

'Are all the attendants working here known to you personally?'

'Yes, I appointed them,' Lepelletier replied. 'And I am ready to vouch for them. We only appoint men who are thoroughly trustworthy and discreet.'

'Would it be possible for you to check, personally, that they are all here tonight?'

'Yes, it can be done.'

'But why are you asking this?' the administrator asked, petulantly, as though he felt that Gautier was in some way criticizing the way the Opéra was run.

'If a man were absent through illness, it might be possible for someone to take his place, might it not?' Gautier did not add that it was equally possible for one of the attendants to be bribed to give up his place for the night.

'I suppose so. A change would be noticed by the other attendants, but they might think that a newcomer had been engaged temporarily for the night. That does sometimes happen.'

'Then please be so good as to check, Monsieur. And should you find anyone among the attendants who is not known to you personally, see that he is held by my men for questioning.'

'These policemen are not going to be in the building during the performance, are they?' the administrator asked, and when Gautier nodded he complained, 'But what will our subscribers say? Many of them bring guests to the performance.'

'All my men will be wearing evening dress, as I will myself. We will not be noticed.'

Gautier explained very briefly the precautions he was proposing to take. The entrance to the opera building, the staircases and the foyers would all be cleared before the president's party arrived and men would be stationed at key points to see that they remained clear. The presidential box would be searched again before he arrived and two men would be placed on guard outside it. At the end of the performance no one would be permitted to leave the auditorium until the President and the Shah had left the building.

'You will spoil the evening,' the administrator complained. 'People come to these galas for the spectacle; to see the presidential party. And sometimes the President receives his principal ministers and their wives in his box.'

155

'That may be true, but the safety of our royal guest and the President must be our first consideration.'

'Is there anything else you require?' Lepelletier asked.

'Do you have a plan of the auditorium?'

'Certainly.'

From a cupboard in one corner of the room Lepelletier took out a rolled-up plan and spread it out on the administrator's desk. The plan was in two parts, one showing the layout of the seats in the well of the auditorium and the other the disposition of the boxes. Gautier pointed to the seats nearest to the presidential box and suggested to Lepelletier that those members of the audience who arrived with tickets for those seats should be directed to a separate entrance into the auditorium so that they could be searched before taking their places.

The administrator accepted the suggestion with ill humour. 'It will create a scandal.'

'I will need some of these seats for my men. Let us say ten in all, distributed equally in this area.' Gautier added.

'But all the seats are sold!'

'Then you will have to find the people who bought them places elsewhere in the house.'

'Anything else?'

'Yes. I will require an empty box to be placed at my disposal from where I can get a good view of the president's box.'

Lepelletier pointed at one of the boxes marked on the plan. 'Will this one do? It so happens that the gentleman who should be occupying it has sent a message saying he is indisposed.'

'Does that mean you know who will be occupying all the boxes?'

'Yes. Every box is leased to a subscriber. And we have a waiting list of people waiting to acquire boxes on Monday nights. That's the most popular night.'

'May I see the list of subscribers?'

Lepelletier produced a list of the box holders. In each of the tiers around the auditorium there were 39 boxes, all of them seating six people except the president's and the box above it which could take ten. Almost all of the people on the list of those holding boxes were well known figures in the Parisian scene: aristocrats, club men, society hostesses, ambassadors, bankers and government ministers. None of them, as far as Gautier could see, were people who might be associated with an attempted assassination and none of them, he felt

156

sure, would willingly admit Igor Kratov to their party of guests at the opera. He was about to return the list to Lepelletier, when he noticed a name that he had almost missed. The Prince de Chaville was down as having one of the less desirably placed boxes on the third tier. Did that mean, he thought immediately, that the box might be a recent acquisition, an arrangement made specially as part of the planned coup d'état.

But when he asked Lepelletier how long the prince had been a subscriber to the opera he was told, 'For many years. He has always been one of our regular patrons.'

'Yes,' the administrator agreed sourly, 'but it is not through love of opera, but for the love of the ladies whom he entertains in the privacy of his box.'

'Will he be here tonight, do you know?'

'As it happens, no,' Lepelletier replied. 'We have had a letter from him authorizing us to put the box at the disposal of one of his friends.'

'And may I know the name of the friend?'

'Madame Geneviève Stahl.'

Since Gautier knew he would not have time to go home and change, he had arranged for a man from the Sûreté to fetch his evening clothes from his apartment, and Surat brought them with him to the opera house. As he changed in a small office which the administrator had put at his disposal, he and Surat discussed what other measures were needed to be taken to forestall any assassination attempt.

'When the audience start to come in,' Gautier told Surat, 'I would like you to keep a surreptitious watch on box number eight on the third tier. It is rented by the Prince de Chaville but he has made it available this evening to a Madame Stahl. Make a note of how many guests she brings with her and their descriptions and tell me immediately.'

'Are you expecting that one of the guests may be the intended assassin?'

'No, I am merely curious. It would be impossible to fire a shot or throw a bomb into the president's box from where Madame Stahl will be. But in the meantime, did you get a description of Kratov?'

On Gautier's instructions, Surat had spoken that afternoon to

157

Inspector Lemaire and the other officers at the Sûreté who had questioned Kratov about the murder of Eva Callot, and asked them to describe the Russian emigré. He had written a description down and now he read it to Gautier. Kratov, everyone had agreed, was short and broad and inclining to grossness, had unkempt grey hair and a straggling grey beard and melancholy eyes.

Gautier sighed. 'I suppose it would have been too much to expect him to have a squint or a hairlip or to walk with a heavy limp.'

'I am afraid so, Patron. The man has no exceptional features.'

'I would like you to give every man from the Sûreté who is on duty here tonight a copy of that description.'

'I already have, Patron.'

'Then there is not much more we can do in that direction.'

'How do you suppose they intend to assassinate the Shah?'

Gautier explained why he believed that the most likely plan would involve the assassin being smuggled into the opera house, probably disguised as one of the attendants, so that he would be able to get near enough to the president's party to throw his bomb or fire his revolver. He added that the manager of the opera house had already checked to see whether all the attendants would be on duty that night.

'It seems that only one man did not report for work,' he said 'And he is known to have been ill for some weeks. No one has been engaged to stand in for him, so all the attendants here tonight can be accounted for.'

'The precautions you have taken are watertight. I cannot see how the Shah can possibly be in any danger.'

'One hopes not, but I don't underestimate the resourcefulness and determination of these people. We can only wait and see. Meanwhile were you able to put in hand the other measures we planned?'

Although at the meeting with the Prefect of Police it had been decided that there was insufficient evidence to justify arresting Pierre de Jarnac and his fellow conspirators, Gautier had thought it prudent at least to find out where the four men and two women involved in the plot would be while the Shah of Persia was at the opera. If the assassination attempt succeeded, the police would know from where the decisive move in the coup d'état would be launched.

'Yes, Patron,' Surat replied. 'I have sent men to watch Madame

Pasquier's home and also those of the Prince de Chaville, Roussel, de Jarnac and Valanis.'

'Excellent! and have any of the men reported back to you as yet?'

'Only two so far. The Prince de Chaville, it seems, is dining at home with guests this evening.'

'Are you certain of that?'

'Yes. Several well-known people are to be his guests. Meanwhile Valanis is at his home in Avenue du Bois, but he will not be there for long. His chauffeur is waiting even now to bring him here to attend the opera.'

'Then we will have to keep a watch out for him.'

Gautier had finished changing into his evening clothes so the two men left the office and made their way to the main entrance of the building. As the audience were beginning to arrive, they went up the grand staircase to a point from where they would be able to see not only the staircase itself, but the entrance to most of the boxes on the first tier. They watched those who had been fortunate enough to have seats or a box for the gala arrive: men in evening dress, carrying their top hats and ladies in the high-waisted dresses that were the fashion of the day, showing off their diamonds and rubies and emeralds for others to admire. They climbed the stairs at their leisure, stopping to exchange a word or a greeting or a rumour with friends. This evening they were shepherded, tactfully and unobtrusively up the staircase and to their places. They gave no signs of resenting or even noticing this unusual breach of tradition.

Presently Gautier saw Courtrand arriving. The director-general was with his wife in a small group of guests who were being entertained by the banker Armand de Saules and his wife, Renée, once considered to be one of France's greatest poetesses. Courtrand had done the banker small services on more than one occasion and Gautier supposed that an evening at the opera was to be his reward. Leaving Surat, he worked his way through the thickening crowds to the head of the staircase. The director-general, he noticed, was already looking round anxiously for him.

When they were face to face, Courtrand pulled him to one side impatiently. 'Is everything under control?'

'Yes, Monsieur. We have done all that is humanly possible to protect the Shah and the President, short of emptying the opera house or cancelling the performance.'

'It might have been wiser if we had done just that.'

'Well, it's too late to do so now. The President's party should be here in fifteen minutes.'

'You found no bombs?'

'None. And the presidential box is now well guarded. I am satisfied that no one will be able to make a successful attack on either the Shah or the President once they are safely in the box.'

'I wish I shared your confidence. If there is an assassination someone will have to take the blame. Heads will roll, Gautier, you can be sure of that.'

Courtrand hurried away to join his hosts. Gautier smiled as he recalled that not many hours previously the man had refused even to entertain the idea that an assassination or a coup d'état were being planned. Now he was obsessed with a fear that if any such disaster were to take place he would be held responsible.

As he was on his way to rejoin Surat, he noticed Paul Valanis approaching. The Greek was in a group among whom Gautier recognized the Minister for War. When he had arrived in Paris as the representative of an English armaments firm, Valanis had successfully ingratiated himself with the politicians and civil servants who controlled military expenditure and had the authority to place orders for rifles, canons and the deadly new machine guns for the French army. The commissions he had earned from their orders had already made him a wealthy man. Now, in spite of his dubious past, he was accepted in the highest strata of Paris society.

Gautier would have preferred Valanis not to have seen that he was at the opera, but pressed on both sides as he was by the throng of people arriving for the performance, he could not take evasive action. When they came face to face, Valanis stared at him coolly. He appeared neither alarmed nor even surprised, but Gautier knew from the past that he was a man who could keep his emotions under control.

'I did not know you were an opera lover, Gautier,' the Greek said. 'Or are you here on duty?'

Gautier deliberately ignored the question. 'It is not often that my duties give me the time to come here.'

The reply annoyed Valanis. As he walked past he turned to the Minister for War who was on his left and said loudly, 'How much further will society allow itself to be debased? Policemen at the opera! And they are even invited to fashionable salons!'

Similar remarks had been made in Gautier's hearing before and they never disturbed him. On this occasion he wondered whether Valanis's spurt of angry spite might be a sign that he was not as unconcerned as he appeared to be. Would he now take fright, having seen Gautier in the opera house and if so would he try to stop the planned assassination? To do so he would have to get a message to the assassin. Gautier decided to have the Minister for War's box watched in case the Greek should leave it during the performance, and to have him followed if he did.

When he rejoined Surat at their vantage point above the main entrance, he learned that another report had come in from the men who had been sent to keep a watch on the movements of de Jarnac and his cabal.

'De Jarnac left his home a short time ago,' Surat told him.

'Was he followed?'

'Yes, Patron.'

'You're going to tell me that he went to Madame Pasquier's home in Rue Miromesnil and is waiting there.'

'That's right. But how did you know?'

19

THE PERFORMANCE HAD reached a point half-way through the second act of the opera. On the stage, in front of Bellini's picturesque setting, Tristan and Isolde, in a frenzy of passion induced by the love potion that they had inadvertently drunk, were singing an ecstatic duet.

Gautier was not watching the performance and scarcely heard the music. From the box in the second tier which had been placed at his disposal, he had a good view of the presidential box. The arrival of the President and the Shah had passed off without incident and they had been received with warm applause as they entered the box. Now they sat watching the opera, unaware of the concern that Gautier had triggered off when he had told the Prefect of Police of

161

the assassination plot, and of the feverish precautions that had been put in train to protect them.

The Shah looked tired and unwell and Gautier recalled reading that he was facing difficulties in his kingdom. His attempts to raise money by selling trading monopolies to foreigners had led to unrest marked by riots, and recently he had been forced to grant his country a constitution which diminished his powers. In the circumstances it was understandable that his visit to Paris lacked the gaiety of a similar state visit made some years previously by his predecessor. Then the Shah of that time, captivated by the ladies performing in the ballet, had set all Paris laughing when he had sent his chamberlain backstage to negotiate the purchase of the whole corps de ballet, whom he wished to have transferred en bloc to his harem.

Now that the President and the Shah were safely in their places, it seemed to Gautier that the danger of an assassination attempt, although not entirely dispelled, had diminished. He could see officers from the Sûreté dispersed at strategic points throughout the auditorium. The occupants of the boxes adjoining the president's had been carefully scrutinized and were known to be people of good standing in Paris society and of unimpeachable reputation. No trace had been found of any person known to be connected with de Jarnac and his cabal except Paul Valanis and a watch was being kept on him.

Even so Gautier was uneasy. Although he still believed that the plot would soon be brought to a spectacular climax in a way which would destroy the last shred of public confidence in the government, he now began to question some of the deductions and assumptions he had made. The last but one number in Le Tellier's list, 1865, might well be the date of another event in history, as notable as the assassination of Lincoln but totally different in character. He felt he should also not ignore the possibility that Madame Le Tellier had deliberately misled him. In that case all the security precautions he had arranged would be concentrated at the opera and in the meantime the conspirators may have engineered some other attack on the government in another part of Paris.

He recalled Le Tellier's list of unanswered questions. The only one which still troubled him, intruding persistently on his awareness like an unwelcome memory, was why the Prince de Chaville should have allowed himself to become involved in an adventure from which he apparently stood to gain little and which would involve the killing of an old friend. The policeman who had been sent to keep a watch on the prince's movements that evening had reported that his guests at dinner were to include most of the leading figures in the old French aristocracy: the Prince and Princesse de Caraman-Chimay, Prince Edmond de Polignac and his wife the former Winaretta Singer, daughter of the American sewing-machine millionaire, and the Duc and Duchesse de Greffulhe. Gautier wondered whether this might be a deliberate device on the part of the prince to disassociate himself at the final critical moment from the assassination of an old friend.

Thoughts about the Prince de Chaville provoked another question, which intrigued Gautier rather than worried him. Why, he wondered, had the prince put his box at the opera at the disposal of Geneviève Stahl. Gautier remembered the prince's servant saying that he had been a passionate admirer of Geneviève Grasset in her courtesan days until they had quarrelled bitterly. He recalled too Duthrey's remark that the prince was a man who had learned little but forgot nothing, particularly a grudge.

Leaving the box, he went in search of Surat and found him standing with one of the men from the Sûreté in the front foyer. He asked him. 'Did you see Madame Stahl arrive and go into her box?'

'Yes, Patron. We both did.'

'How many guests did she have with her?'

'Only one. A plump, elderly man.'

'I thought at first it was the director-general,' the policeman said laughing.

'His wife would kill him if he dared to entertain a courtesan in a private box at the opera,' Surat commented. Like everyone else at the Sûreté he had little regard for the manliness of Courtrand.

Gautier hurried back to his box. An idea had exploded in his mind with all the startling brilliance of the fireworks that had been let off in the Shah of Persia's honour. Improbable though it seemed, if it were true most of the doubts that had been nagging at his mind all day would be resolved.

In his box he picked up the opera glasses he had borrowed from the administrator and focussed them on box number eight in the third tier. At first it seemed as though the box were empty. Then he made out the heads of a man and a woman who must have been

163

sitting well back to the rear of the enclosure. There was nothing unusual in his. A man who escorted another man's wife, who was also a former courtesan, to the opera would not care to sit right up by the front balcony in full view of everyone in the auditorium. Moreover, the shadowy recesses at the back of the boxes provided an opportunity for a little amorous dalliance. From what he could see through the opera glasses, he could not be sure who Geneviève Stahl's companion might be.

He had to know. Leaving the box again, he went downstairs, found an attendant and sent him into the box of Monsieur Armand de Saules with a message for the Director General of the Sûreté. Presently Courtrand appeared, sticking his head through the doorway of the box as though reluctant to leave even for a moment.

'What is it Gautier?'

'I wondered if by any chance, Monsieur, you knew who accompanied Madame Stahl here tonight.'

'Lower your voice, man, for heaven's sake! You are ruining the performance.'

'The duet of Tristan and Isolde was reaching a crescendo on the stage and Courtrand's suggestion that a whispered remark from where they were standing might be heard above Wagner's strident music was so ludicrous that Gautier wanted to laugh. The director-general had become so absorbed in and so entranced by the evening he was spending with the upper strata of Paris society, that he resented being distracted by prosaic police matters.

'But do you know, Monsieur?'

'Of course not! How should I?'

'I have reason to believe that Madame Stahl's companion tonight may be the King of England.'

Courtrand stared at him, astounded. 'And you have dragged me away from important friends just to tell me this? What business is it of yours, Gautier, whom Madame Stahl is entertaining?'

'If there is to be an assassination tonight, then perhaps the King of England is the intended victim.'

Speed of thought was not one of the director-general's most notable aptitudes. It took him a full minute to follow the line of reasoning that had led Gautier to this conclusion and even then his mind was reluctant to accept a possibility that would complicate still further a situation which he disliked and which was interfering with his social pleasure.

164

'Gautier this is preposterous! You are losing control of your imagination.'

'Can we at least find out whether it is the king with Madame Stahl? I might be mistaken.'

'And how do you propose we should do that?'

'The Prefect of Police may know.'

One could see that Courtrand's first impulse was to reject the suggestion scornfully. Then, remembering perhaps that in the past Gautier had been right more than once when he had been wrong, he had second thoughts. 'Oh, very well, I'll go and ask him.'

The Prefect of Police was also at the opera as a guest with friends. Courtrand and Gautier sent an attendant into the box from which he was watching, and when he emerged he seemed in no way upset at being disturbed. Rather he might have been quite glad of the interruption. Gautier decided that he must be one of the large number of men who had no love of opera but only went to the performances to please their wives or because it was expected of them by their friends.

When Courtrand had explained what they wished to know he said, 'It so happens that the King of England is here, although I do not know whom he is accompanying. Whenever he visits Paris incognito his private secretary, who travels with him, lets me know of his movements, merely as a matter of courtesy. But why do you ask?'

'Gautier here is now imagining that he may be the intended victim of the supposed assassination.'

'Good heavens! Of course! I should have thought of that possibility.'

'But why should these conspirators wish to assassinate King Edward?'

'I suppose because it would destroy the Entente Cordiale. Can you imagine what a hatred of France it would provoke in England if their much loved King were to be killed here? And the destruction of the entente would be a humiliating blow for the government.'

Gautier knew that what the prefect had said was true. The destruction of the fragile alliance between France and England would also disrupt the balance of power in Europe. As well as preparing the ground for a successful coup d'état, it would increase the possibility of war and a war would be welcomed not only by dealers in armaments, but by all those Frenchmen who still thirsted for a revenge against Germany.

165

'I may be wrong,' Gautier told the prefect. 'This is just speculation.'

'I realize that, but as a precaution we must protect the king.'

'We must place a guard on duty outside Madame Stahl's box,' Courtrand said.

'Forgive me, Messieurs, but would that be wise? A guard might prevent the assassin from striking here, tonight, but would we be able to protect him afterwards? He could easily be shot as he leaves the opera house or at whatever address he goes with his lady friend, anywhere.'

'That is true. He would never consent to being accompanied by armed guards, even if we were able to arrange it.'

'Then what do you suggest, Gautier?'

'That we should allow the assassin to make his attempt but make sure it does not succeed.'

'We could smuggle an armed policeman into the box, I suppose,' the prefect said.

'I do not believe that would work, Monsieur. The assassin or his confederate if he has one, is certain to be watching the door to the box.'

'You have another plan?'

'I have, but I hardly like to propose it. We could arrange for someone to take the king's place in the box. Someone who resembles the king and could be mistaken for him.'

'Gautier means me, Monsieur le Préfet,' Courtrand said quickly. 'That is so, Gautier, is it not?'

'Yes, Monsieur.'

Like many others who had worked under Courtrand for any length of time, Gautier believed he knew the man's character pretty well. Courtrand was pompous, self-important, ambitious to move in social circles above his own and for that reason obsequious to anyone who might help to achieve that ambition, while unable to resist bullying his subordinates in petty, spiteful ways. Now, Gautier realized, Courtrand possessed one quality which he and everyone else had overlooked, courage.

In spite of protests by the Prefect of Police that the director-general could not be allowed to risk his life in the way Gautier was suggesting, Courtrand insisted that he had a duty to do so. He had often declared that law and justice must be upheld and that every

166

man in the Sûreté must be prepared to defend them, whatever personal sacrifice might be involved, but no one had ever believed that he intended this admirable doctine to apply to himself.

Now, however, he joined the prefect and Gautier almost eagerly in planning how the affair was to be managed. Gautier's plan was uncomplicated. The Prefect of Police sent a message into Madame Stahl's box, asking her if her guest would be kind enough to go during the next interval to box number 23 on the first tier where the Prefect of Police wished to speak to him on a matter of great importance. The message added that the prefect apologized for not coming to Madame Stahl's guest, but because of circumstances which he would later explain this would be imprudent, even dangerous.

When the interval arrived, Gautier watched box number eight and presently Mr Windsor, as his highness had chosen to be known on this visit, emerged and went downstairs to the first floor. He looked displeased, as a man might well be who had his tête à tête with a beautiful woman interrupted. It was difficult to know whether he would have been more or less angry had he known that throughout his short journey downstairs he was under the protection of several policemen whom Gautier had stationed carefully and at a discreet distance, just in case the assassin might take this unexpected opportunity to make his attack.

Courtrand, armed with a concealed pistol, was waiting in the prefect's box and the exchange was effected, but only, as Gautier later learned, after a long argument, for the royal visitor had been disinclined to believe that his life could be in danger. From a distance, watching the director-general return to Madame Stahl's box, calm and composed and disguised by the anonymity of evening dress, Gautier felt reasonably satisfied that no one who did not know the King of England well would realize that a substitution had been made.

Once Courtrand was safely inside the box and the door had been locked, there was nothing to do but wait and watch. Gautier could not restrain a feeling of sardonic amusement as he pictured Geneviève Stahl's dismay when she found that her romantic prince—in his bachelor days Edward had mesmerized scores of women with his charm—had been suddenly transformed into a dumpy little frog.

On the stage in the opera house the performance of *Tristan and Isolde* continued, the singers and orchestra working their way relentlessly through the score, the audience silent and absorbed. Not many years before, the music of Wagner would have had a less tolerant reception. Some forty years previously attempts to stage his operas in France had been greeted with such a storm of protests from the chauvinistic Parisians, that they had to be abandoned. Even now, Gautier noticed, *Tristan and Isolde* was being received that night with far less enthusiasm than most performances at the Opéra. The choice of a German opera with which to entertain the Shah seemed maladroit to say the least at a time when France had just engineered an alliance with England which was ostentatiously aimed at Germany.

Presently Surat joined Gautier at the point where he had taken up his stance and from where he could watch the entrance to Madame Stahl's box without being seen to do so. He asked Gautier, 'If the target is the King of England, how do you suppose they will try to kill him?'

'He has been sitting well at the back of the box,' Gautier replied. 'So it would have been impossible to have shot him from anywhere in the auditorium.'

'Then it has to be with a bomb thrown into the box.'

'Not necessarily. They might intend to lure him out of the box by some trick and shoot or stab him as he emerged.'

'In that case we should have enough time to get there and restrain the man.' Surat was not aware that Courtrand had taken the place of Kind Edward in Madame Stahl's box.

'Let us hope so.'

Gautier did not tell Surat that his plan meant allowing the would-be assassin at least enough time to reveal his intention to kill the king by drawing out a pistol or raising a dagger. Only then would he have evidence that could be used to accuse de Jarnac and the other members of his cabal. It would require perfect timing and speed and more than anything luck. So much luck that he knew he was gambling with Courtrand's life.

After they had been watching and waiting for about fifteen minutes, they saw an attendant approaching the entrance to the box. As the man responsible for that particular section of boxes, his credentials had been thoroughly checked once Gautier had found out that King Edward was at the opera. He was a man who had been in the employ of the opera for fourteen years, and prior to that in government service. The manager of the Opéra had been prepared to swear that the man was not only loyal but incorruptible. What interested Gautier was that the man was carrying a package; a package that had been beautifully wrapped in coloured paper and silk ribbon tied in elegant bows.

'It's a bomb!' Surat exclaimed at once.

'Not necessarily.'

'We must stop him taking it into the box.'

'If we do and it isn't a bomb, we betray the fact that we are keeping a watch on the box.'

'Then what should we do?'

'We must rely on the director-general to use his discretion. You see he has taken the king's place in there.'

Surat looked mystified but he was too caught up in the tension of the moment to ask any questions and Gautier did not offer any explanations. Instead they watched together as the attendant knocked gently on the door of Madame Stahl's box and then, using a key which he drew from his waistcoat pocket let himself in. Minutes passed and when the man came out he was no longer carrying the parcel. Gautier told Surat to follow him and find out what had happened when he had delivered it. As he waited, ill-at-ease on the sharp edge of expectancy, he wondered how many other people in adjoining boxes the explosion, if there was one, would kill or maim. But when at last Surat returned, he was laughing.

'It seems that a beautiful woman gave the attendant the packet and asked him to deliver it to the box where Madame Stahl was entertaining a friend,' he told Gautier. 'It was addressed to a Mr Windsor.'

'Mother of God! I wonder how many people in Paris know the king is here.'

'The director-general opened the packet while the attendant was still there.'

Gautier refrained from swearing with difficulty. One had the right to be courageous with one's own life but not with the lives of others. All he said was, 'Go on.'

'It was a box of marrons glacés. And do you know what?' Surat laughed incredulously. 'On the top layer the lady had placed one of her garters.'

Gautier smiled but he did not laugh. The incident had shown him only too cruelly the loopholes in the precautions he had taken and the weaknesses of his plan. A would-be assassin might well be

169

able to get another person, an innocent third-party, to carry out the assassination by delivering a bomb, suitably disguised, to the box where Madame Stahl and Courtrand were waiting. It did not even have to be a bomb. Why not poisoned chocolates or poisoned marrons glacés? What if Courtrand's well-known love of sweet things had overcome his prudence and the cyanide was now even beginning to take effect? Gautier winced. He ought to have seen the loophole and now all he and Surat could do would be to place a guard on the door of the box preventing anyone else from getting access to it, and that would wreck his whole plan.

As he was brooding over his carelessness Surat, as though to drive home the lesson, nudged him. 'What's this, Patron? Could this one be making for the king's box as well?'

He pointed towards a waiter who, coming up the stairs from the buffet gallery, was carrying a tray with an ice bucket and two glasses on it.

'Champagne!' Gautier exclaimed.

'That will have been ordered for the king without a doubt. There would have been another bottle ready for him in the box before the opera began, you can be sure of that.'

The whole of Paris knew that champagne had been the favourite drink of Edward when he was Prince of Wales. Rumour had it that he would have a bath filled with Mumm champagne at a certain establishment in Rue Richelieu for the girl who was his choice that evening. One might assume that becoming a monarch would not have changed his taste for the aristocrat of sparkling wines.

Immediately Gautier found himself trying to remember whether the manager of the opera house had made any mention of the waiters working in the gallery buffet. He had said that all the attendants were known to him personally and had checked to find out if any of them were missing from duty. But had they discussed the waiters? Gautier thought not. The waiters might not even be on the payroll of the Opéra for the concession of the buffet might well be granted to outside caterers.

He studied the waiter as he reached the top of the stairs and headed towards Madame Stahl's box. He was a large man, with very black hair which he had plastered down on to his skull with brilliantine, close-shaven except for a small moustache. As one would have expected in a waiter working at l'Opéra he was dressed correctly, his apron was spotlessly white and so was the

170

napkin draped over his left arm. He carried the tray with the champagne bucket and glasses balanced on his left hand while holding the neck of the champagne bottle with his right, as though he were afraid it might slip. His shoes creaked, either because they were cheap or new or both, but otherwise he made no noise at all as he walked towards the box in which Madame Stahl was now entertaining, if that was the right word, the Director General of the Sûreté. Gautier wondered whether he too was afraid of making any noise which might disturb the performance.

When the waiter reached the box he knocked on the door and presently it was opened. Gautier could just make out Courtrand's face in the shadows behind the door. He spoke to the man but whatever words they exchanged were said in a whisper. Everyone it seemed had been drawn into this conspiracy of near-silence and it had began to irritate Gautier. Something about the lack of sound was bothering him, about the waiter's unnaturally quiet walk and the way he had held on to the neck of the champagne bottle. Suddenly he saw the explanation as the truth erupted.

Leaping out of the shadow of the column in which they had been sheltering, he began running towards the box. 'This is it!' he shouted at Surat. 'Hurry!'

It took no more than a few seconds to reach the door to the box, which stood slightly open, but even as he did he heard the shot. By some irony its report seemed no louder than the pop of a champagne cork. Dragging the door fully open, Gautier hurled himself inside.

The waiter was standing there, armed with a heavy American revolver. The shot he had fired had struck Courtrand in the left shoulder, hurling him against the wall of the box from where he had slumped to the floor. Blood was gushing down his white shirt-front. As Gautier knew, he had been carrying a pistol concealed beneath his top hat which he held balanced on his knees. He had not been given enough time to fire it, but the unexpected sight of a weapon brandished at him, coupled with the fact that Courtrand had leapt to his feet, had put the assassin off his aim. Now he lifted the revolver, pointing it at Courtrand's head, ready to finish his work.

Leaping at him, Gautier grabbed for his wrist. He was too late to prevent the second shot being fired, but in grabbing knocked the gun aside, deflecting the bullet so that it struck the wall on one side of Courtrand, ricocheted across the box, narrowly missing

171

Madame Stahl and finally buried itself harmlessly in the carpet.

By that time Surat had arrived and he and Gautier seized the man in waiter's uniform and snatched the revolver from him. The man struggled only briefly, accepting with the fatalism of the Slav—for it was Kratov—the inevitability of capture now that his mission had failed. Meanwhile Madame Stahl, recovering from the shock that had kept her silent throughout the melodrama, helped Courtrand to his feet. His courage deflated sharply by fright and shock, Courtrand stumbled over his speech and when at last he could articulate, could only find words of hysterical anger.

'Holy Mother, Gautier! Why did you take so long to get here. Were you trying to have me killed?'

'I'm sorry, Monsieur. I should have realized earlier what the man intended.'

More policemen were called and they took Kratov away. A doctor was found among the audience, and he staunched the flow of blood from Courtrand's shoulder until a horse-drawn ambulance arrived to take him to the nearest hospital. Madame Stahl was given the only sedative to hand, a large glass of cognac and sent home to Neuilly in her carriage. The whole incident was over in a few minutes, unnoticed by almost everyone in the audience as the closing scenes were being played out on the stage, with first Tristan and then Isolde singing their last dying arias.

Gautier did not wait for the end, as the Prefect of Police had taken charge of what had to be done in the opera house. Meanwhile he had to act swiftly.

As the two of them walked out of the building into Place de l'Opéra, Surat said to him, 'I cannot see how you could have been expected to realize that the waiter was an assassin in disguise.' He may well have been surprised that Gautier had accepted Courtrand's rebuke without protest.

'The director-general was right. I should have realized what was happening much sooner.'

'But how did you guess what the man was about to do?'

'He made no noise. There should have been at least a chink of ice from the champagne basket. And he was holding the bottle to stop it rolling about. If the bucket had been full of ice, the bottle would have been firmly bedded in it. There was only one plausible explanation. There was no ice in the bucket because that was where he was hiding his revolver.'

172

20

A CROWD OF several hundred people, almost all of them men, had gathered in Rue Miromesnil outside the home of Madame Pasquier. Some were there by arrangement, instructed to assemble outside the house by agents who for the past two days had been quietly recruiting supporters for Pierre de Jarnac from among the discontented. Others had come, drawn by curiosity, following the crowds as they converged from all directions, wondering what momentous event they were about to witness.

Gautier had difficulty in reaching the door of the house, elbowing his way through the crowd, and when he did reach it, the manservant who opened it did not appear disposed to admit him.

'I wish to see Monsieur Pierre de Jarnac.'

'There is no one of that name here, Monsieur. This is the home of Madame Simone Pasquier.'

'Don't play games with me!' Gautier said harshly. 'The house has been under police surveillance for hours. We know exactly who is here and what is happening.'

'Well I don't,' the manservant replied stubbornly.

'Possibly, but you will be dragged off to St. Lazare prison with the rest, if you impede the police.'

The man gave way. Upstairs in the drawing room Gautier found about a score of people, most of whom he did not recognize, but among whom were de Jarnac, Denise de Richemont and Madame Pasquier. Everyone was talking, their conversation not the polite, reserved and often bored small talk which one heard in drawing rooms, but pitched to a note of expectancy. De Jarnac was moving from group to group, exchanging a word, patting a shoulder, kissing a woman's hand. He was the only one in the room who appeared

173

totally relaxed. In the general excitement no one noticed Gautier entering the room, and the manservant led him across to Madame Pasquier.

When she saw him she was obviously alarmed and took shelter at once in anger. 'Your visits are becoming tedious, Inspector,' she said. 'What right have you to intrude on a social occasion?'

'Come, Madame. This is no social occasion. And I am here to see Monsieur de Jarnac on police business.'

'The Prefect of Police will hear of this.'

'I have just left him at the Opéra. I have come here with his authority.'

As they were speaking de Jarnac came over towards them. Unlike Madame Pasquier he seemed neither surprised nor disconcerted to see Gautier in the room. 'Inspector Gautier,' he said. 'What brings you here?'

'He says he is here on police business.'

'I did not imagine, my dear, that he could have any other reason for coming to your home.'

'I came to suggest, Monsieur, that it would be prudent for you and your friends to abandon your little adventure. It has failed.'

'Adventure?'

'Your plan to take over the government of the country.'

'By what wild piece of deduction, Inspector, have you concluded that this is what I intend?'

'Do you deny that you and your supporters are planning a coup d'état?'

De Jarnac did not reply immediately. It was a calculated pause, as though he were giving himself time to balance the value of a denial against a partial admission which might at least help him to find out how much Gautier really knew. Finally he said, 'It would be idle to pretend that some of my friends do not believe that the Republic should be rescued from the morass into which an incompetent and cowardly government had led it and they have asked me to lead them.'

'But you have not yet decided whether you will?'

'No. That's right.'

'In that case,' Gautier said, 'it may help you to reach a decision if you know that the attempted assassination at the Opéra tonight did not succeed.'

He was watching Madame Pasquier as he spoke. De Jarnac, he

174

felt certain, was too practised a politician to betray his feelings, but a woman might. He was right. Madame Pasquier's eyes widened and then she blinked rapidly several times. It was a symptom of alarm Gautier had noticed in other women.

'What is he talking about, Pierre?' she asked.

'Assassination? Why should anyone try to kill the President?' de Jarnac demanded.

'I never said the attempt was aimed at the President.'

'I assumed it must have been him, since he was going to the gala tonight. Why should anyone wish to make a martyr out of a harmless nonentity whose term of office can be forcibly ended whenever we choose?'

Gautier sensed that by naming the President as the most likely target for an assassination attempt de Jarnac was not trying to put on a show of innocence but to manoeuvre Gautier into revealing how much of the truth he knew. Gautier for his part was playing for time so he made no reply.

'Come with me, Inspector.'

Walking over to a window, de Jarnac opened it so that they could look out on to the crowded street outside the house. As the window opened and light from it fell on the people below some of them looked up, saw de Jarnac and recognized him.

A man shouted, 'Vive de Jarnac! A bas Fallières!'

Others in the crowd took up the cry and began to chant de Jarnac's name. Presently from another part of the crowd a different cry was heard and this too was turned into a chant.

'Down with the government! To the Elysée Palace!'

Within a few minutes it seemed as though everyone in the crowd was chanting, some of them waving at de Jarnac as he stood by the window, beckoning him to come down and lead them, de Jarnac turned away from the window but did not close it.

'As you can see, Inspector, there can be no doubting what the people want.'

'We anticipated that you might be planning to march on the President's palace. Extra police have been placed on guard there.'

'But will they be loyal to the government?'

Gautier could not be sure of the answer to his question. Some policemen were discontented, others might be bribed and if it came to violence most would be reluctant to use force on unarmed civilians, even in self-defence.

175

'There's another factor to consider,' de Jarnac said. 'The army will support us.'

'You would be unwise to count on that.'

Before he had left the opera house, Gautier had received a report from the policemen who had been keeping Colonel Charles Roussel under surveillance that evening The colonel had left his home and gone to the Cercle Militaire, an exclusive club for army officers. Surprisingly for a Monday evening in late autumn, an unusually large number of officers, mostly young officers, had been seen arriving at the club at about the same time as Roussel.

'Colonel Roussel was arrested at the Cercle Militaire together with a number of his friends not long ago, before they could put on whatever show of support for you they were intended to make,' Gautier continued.

He was not certain whether by that time Roussel would have been arrested, but officers from the Sûreté had been sent to the Cercle Militaire to make the arrests before he had left the opera house and would have certainly reached there by that time. De Jarnac must have been disconcerted to hear the news, but he concealed his feelings well. He made no immediate comment and one sensed that he was hesitating, trying to assess what chance of success an attempted coup d'état might have without the support of the army. Gautier felt sure that other operations, of which he knew nothing, had been planned for that evening. Other bands of supporters might even then be ready to seize key centres of government or to disrupt the administration of the country in different ways. In that case a coup d'état might well succeed even though the assassination attempt had failed. The timing of these operations and of the march on the Elysée Palace would be crucial to its success and the conspirators might well be waiting for a prearranged signal before they made their move.

Gautier had his own problems of timing, but he too must wait before he made a move. He had come to Rue Miromesnil on foot while Surat had left for the Faubourg St. Germain in a police waggon and he should be back after carrying out his mission at any moment. Gautier was beginning to wonder whether anything had delayed him when he noticed that the shouting and chanting in the street outside the house had stopped.

He crossed to the window to look out. A police waggon had forced its way through the crowds to a point about 50 metres or so from

176

Madame Pasquier's house but, hemmed in by people, it could get no nearer. As Gautier watched, a figure which he recognized as Surat climbed out of the van followed by his prisoner and two policemen. The crowds in the street watched silently, wondering what this new development might mean.

Returning to the centre of the room, he saw that Madame Pasquier and Denise de Richemont had taken de Jarnac on one side and were speaking to him, earnestly it seemed by their manner and persuasively. Madame Pasquier had laid one hand on the politician's arm and, as he drew near to them, Gautier noticed for the first time that her fingers were bent and thin and the back of her hand wrinkled and covered in unsightly brown spots. They were the hands of an old woman and a remarkable contrast to her almost unlined face, with its soft skin and youthful complexion. He was surprised and amused to find himself recording such a trivial observation at a moment of such tension.

'We must make our move now, Pierre,' Madame Pasquier was saying. 'Do not delay any longer. The crowds outside are ready. Soon they may begin to drift away.'

'But you heard Gautier say that Charles and his friends have been arrested.'

'He was bluffing,' Denise de Richemont interposed. 'And in any case we don't need the army to declare its support. The people are behind us and that will be enough.'

'Perhaps we should wait a little longer,' de Jarnac suggested. 'Then we will know exactly what did happen at the Opéra.'

'No, we must strike now. The moment will not come again.'

Would history repeat itself, Gautier wondered. Would de Jarnac lose his nerve as Boulanger had done and finish up in exile, discredited and broken, taking his own life over the grave of his mistress?

'Before following the ladies' advice, Monsieur,' he told de Jarnac, 'why not wait until you hear what advice your other colleague, the Prince de Chaville has to offer.'

'The Prince? He is not here.'

'He will be immediately.'

Gautier looked towards the door of the drawing room and de Jarnac and the two women did the same. It opened, and Surat came in followed by the Prince de Chaville flanked on each side by a burly uniformed policeman. The policemen were holding his arms, an unnecessary precaution for the Prince was handcuffed, but no doubt they were only obeying the instructions of Surat who had a penchant for theatrical touches on occasions like these.

'My God!' Somebody in the room could not restrain his surprise. 'It's the Prince de Chaville! In handcuffs!'

De Jarnac turned on Gautier angrily. 'What is the meaning of this outrage?' he demanded.

'The prince has been arrested for complicity in an attempted assassination,' Gautier replied.

'An assassination!' Another man exclaimed incredulously.

Not all of de Jarnac's supporters, it seemed, were aware of the carefully staged events that were meant to lead up to the coup d'état. Everyone in the room looked towards the Prince de Chaville who was pale and shaken by the manner of his arrest. All he could find to say was 'This man Gautier is mad!' He spoke in the same tone, with the same arrogance as he always showed, but the words were curiously empty of spirit.

'The Russian, Kratov, whom you paid to shoot the king has confessed,' Gautier told him.

'You mean the Shah,' Madame Pasquier said involuntarily.

'No, the King of England. He too was at the Opéra tonight. Kratov was arrested in the box where the king was being entertained by a lady friend.'

De Jarnac stared at Gautier, uncertain of whether to believe him, and then at the prince. Gautier continued, 'Why you should ever have imagined that the prince was committed to your conspiracy, escapes my understanding. He was only using it and you for his own ends, for a cowardly act of personal revenge.'

'Is this true?' de Jarnac asked the prince quietly.

'What difference would it have made?' The prince asked contemptuously. 'The Shah or the King. The effect on the masses would have been the same. In fact shooting Edward would have served your purpose better.'

'Scoundrel! Traitor! You betrayed us!' In her anger Denise de Richemont's voice rose to a pitch approaching hysteria. Losing control she leapt towards the Prince de Chaville, her fingers stretched out as though to claw his face. When Gautier stepped between them and held her back she attacked him instead, thumping his chest with clenched fists.

'The prince is right,' Madame Pasquier told de Jarnac. 'It makes

178

no difference. When people hear that an attempt was made to assassinate Edward, they will be outraged. We can easily bring the government down, but you must march on the palace now, at once.'

De Jarnac was looking at her but he seemed incapable of speaking. Gautier was astonished in the transformation in his bearing. The man's whole personality appeared to have disintegrated, his poise replaced by confusion, his authority by doubt and hopelessness. The discovery that the Prince de Chaville had treated him with such cynical contempt appeared to have shattered his belief in himself and in his destiny. He may have been wondering how many more of his supporters had been using him for their own ends, how many others might have already betrayed him.

'We must act now, Pierre,' Madame Pasquier implored him 'Lead us to the palace.'

Slowly de Jarnac shook his head. Then he crossed the room and opened the window that overlooked the street. The crowd outside looked up and fell silent.

'Go home, Messieurs,' he said and then, realizing that his voice was no more than a weary croak, he repeated the words, shouting. 'Go home! Go home, my friends!'

'Why?' A voice shouted from the street below. 'What's happened?'

'It's finished,' de Jarnac replied. 'It's all over.'

21

TWO DAYS LATER Gautier called once again at Madame Le Tellier's home. This time it was in the middle of the afternoon, but when the same maid admitted him and when once again he found Michelle Le Tellier in the hallway dressed ready to go out, he had an uneasy feeling that history was repeating itself. Someone, he seemed to recall, had once said that it was only the mistakes in history that were repeated and he began to wonder whether he had been wise in obeying an impulse to make a visit for which he had no plausible reason.

'Monsieur Gautier!' Michelle Le Tellier exclaimed when she saw him. 'I was hoping you might call.'

'Why? Do you wish to see me?'

'Yes. I thought of sending you a message but I supposed you would be too busy. They tell me that Pierre de Jarnac and all his friends have been arrested.'

'Yes and they will be brought to trial in due course.'

'Then France must be indebted to you.'

'You exaggerate, Madame!'

'I'm sure I don't. One does not know exactly what happened at the Opéra the other night but I have no doubt that it was you who saved the country.'

'Perhaps the government. Certainly not France,' Gautier replied drily. Governments in France were frequently being toppled but the country seemed to survive without too much disruption. 'And without your help I would not have succeeded. I came here today to thank you, officially, for your help.'

'Now it is you who exaggerates.'

As she was speaking Michelle Le Tellier lifted the veil she was wearing and looked at Gautier. Since she must have been able to see him clearly through the veil, he supposed that her motive for raising it must be to let him read in the expression on her face a meaning or nuance in what she was about to say which words alone would not convey. But all she said was, 'Once before you called when I was about to go out and you accompanied me. Would you be willing to do so again today?'

'Enchanted, Madame,' Even as he spoke Gautier remembered it was the same answer he had given to her question the last time and he wished that he had at least used a different expression.

'Are you sure you can spare the time?'

'Yes, my afternoon is free.'

It was only by chance that he was free that afternoon. The process of bringing Pierre de Jarnac and the other conspirators to trial had begun and all the previous day, as well as that morning, he had been present while a juge d'instruction had interrogated the prisoners in turn. The questioning would go on for weeks, perhaps even months, but that afternoon the juge d'instruction had been obliged to attend the funeral of one of his cousins and the examination had been suspended.

As they were walking downstairs, Madame Le Tellier remarked,

'Am I right in thinking from what you said that you disapprove of the government?'

Gautier was about to reply that a policeman's responsibility was to uphold governments not to criticize them. Then he decided that the remark would sound both insincere and pompous. Michelle Le Tellier had treated him frankly and as a friend and he should respond in the same way.

'I believe the government is doing what it believes is necessary to protect the country and to ensure the stability of Europe.'

'But you have sympathy for de Jarnac and his colleagues?'

'Why should I have? Three of them are greedy men who were trying to promote their own ambitions; the fourth was obsessed with a spiteful revenge.'

'But as a professional at least you admire the ingenuity of their plan?' she persisted.

'The plot may have been cleverly worked out, but for Madame Pasquier and the three original members to admit the Prince de Chaville to their intrigue was an act of folly.'

'How did he come to join them?'

By questioning the four men and two women who were under arrest, the juge d'instruction had already established how the Prince de Chaville had become involved in the conspiracy. De Jarnac, Valanis and Roussel, who had first conceived the plan had decided, unwisely perhaps, to ask Madame Pasquier to join them, partly because she could contribute generously to the funds needed to finance the operation and partly because, by posing as the old lady's admirers, they would be able to conceal the nature of the meetings they would be holding in her home. Madame Pasquier was indiscreet enough to tell the prince of their schemes and at his suggestion she had then persuaded the others to recruit him as a member of the group.

Gautier explained this to Michelle Le Tellier and then added, 'And they compounded their stupidity by agreeing to the prince's suggestion that he should be made responsible for arranging the assassination at the Opéra. They may have thought it would be a test of his loyalty, but how they could ever have imagined that he was committed to their cause escapes me! How could anyone be so naïve?'

'He must have hated King Edward bitterly to wish to have him killed.'

181

'He did. When he was Prince of Wales, Edward stole the affections of Geneviève Grasset, the prince's mistress.'

'But that must have been years ago!'

'Twelve years. He nursed that grudge for twelve years and then he saw how he could use de Jarnac's plot to get his revenge.'

'Was it not a convenient coincidence that the King should have been in Paris at this time?'

'It was no coincidence. The prince planned it. First he pretended to effect a reconciliation with Madame Stahl and then suggested that she should invite Edward to spend a few days in Paris. He would not have been difficult to persuade. The best time for him to come here incognito is when there is a state visit by other royalty. It is easier then to escape attention.'

When they reached the street they found Michelle Le Tellier's carriage waiting for them. She said something to the coachman which Gautier did not hear and after they had climbed on the carriage moved off, northwards up Rue Miromesnil at first, then turning into Rue La Boétie and straight on into Boulevard Haussmann. When leaving her apartment Michelle Le Tellier had lowered her veil again. Having her face concealed from him seemed in some way to heighten Gautier's awareness of the sensual attraction of her body as she sat close to him in the carriage. She showed no sign of feeling any similar attraction nor of knowing what effect she was having on him.

'De Jarnac faces a long prison sentence. He must be regretting ever becoming involved with the prince,' she remarked.

'No doubt, but ironically his treachery nearly paid off. We were expecting an attack on the Shah or the President. Had the King of England been assassinated the government would certainly have fallen and de Jarnac might be in the Elysée Palace today.'

'It was brilliant of you to guess what he had done.'

'I should have realized it sooner. I should have asked myself why, after having nothing to do with her for twelve bitter years, the prince should suddenly have generously offered his box at the Opéra to Madame Stahl. She said to me that her husband had proposed marriage at a time when she was the mistress of a prince and I assumed she meant the Prince de Chaville. That was thoughtlessness. Her breach with Chaville came at least two years before she even met Monsieur Stahl.'

Gautier did not add that he should also have realized the Prince de Chaville was not likely to have taken offence if his mistress had left him for the security of marriage. That would not have damaged his pride. And marriage need not have prevented them from continuing their liaison, particularly as Madame Stahl had admitted to not loving her husband. Such arrangements were common enough in society.

After continuing along Boulevard Haussmann for some minutes, the coachman turned into Rue La Fayette. Gautier had been wondering why they were heading towards the north-eastern part of Paris, for it was not a district in which ladies usually took their afternoon drives. No one of any consequence would live there and it had no woods or parks or even gardens. When they turned up Rue La Fayette, he suddenly guessed that they were making for Jacques Le Tellier's garçonnière in Rue Lamartine.

Immediately he decided that there could only be one reason why a woman would take a man to an apartment used for secret assignations in the afternoon. Michelle Le Tellier, while she might not be bold enough to seduce him, was placing him in a position where she might expect him to seduce her. The attraction which he felt for her was sharpened into desire. He could imagine her naked body lying next to his, imagine his fingers stroking her throat, moving down to cradle her small breasts, imagine the smoothness of her belly, the inviting curves of her thighs.

Almost at once desire subsided, assailed by inner constraints and by images that he was reluctant to accept. The notion that he would be making love to Michelle Le Tellier in the bed in which her dead husband had lain with his mistresses was distasteful. He could also not stop himself thinking of Janine and the persisting twinge of guilt which he felt would become even more uncomfortable were he so soon to start an affair with the woman whose company he had been enjoying while vitriol was flung in Janine's face. To reinforce these scruples was the feeling, which he recognized as mere masculine vanity, that if he were to seduce Michelle Le Tellier, it should be at a time and place of his own choosing.

As the carriage was turning into Rue Lamartine, she remarked, 'The newspapers say that the Director General of the Sûreté was wounded during the fracas at the Opéra.'

'Yes, he was shot in the shoulder.'

'Then he saved the King's life?'

'In a way I suppose he did.'

The newspaper reports of the incident at the Opéra had said little more except that an anarchist had been arrested and that shots had been fired in the struggle to overpower him. It had been generally assumed that Kratov had gone to the Opéra to assassinate the President, for nobody even knew that King Edward had been at the performance. The Prefect of Police had decided that no statement should be made to correct this impression and it was unlikely that the truth would ever be known by the public. The king had been hastily smuggled back to England and at their trial the conspirators, including the Prince de Chaville and Kratov, might hope for less severe sentences if it were believed that they intended to assassinate the President rather than visiting royalty. So Gautier felt he should not tell Michelle Le Tellier what had really happened.

The carriage drew to a halt outside the building in which Le Tellier had kept his garçonnière. Gautier was aware of a nervous excitement, of anticipation, but the feeling was stifled by a growing depression. As they were leaving the carriage Michelle Le Tellier asked him, 'If the de Richemont girl was not having an affair with my husband, how did he learn about her father and get hold of the compromising letters?'

'That was skilfully managed. Had Denise de Richemont offered the story to your husband he would surely have been suspicious, for he already knew that Roussel was one of the members of the group who were meeting secretly at Madame Pasquier's home and that he had been military attaché to her father in London. So they bribed one of the duc's servants to approach your husband, offering to sell him the letters and pretending that he had been badly treated by the duc.'

'I knew that Jacques would never start an affair with a woman simply for what information he could get out of her. He did have some scruples.'

There was an almost aggressive emphasis in her tone which seemed out of character and for that reason artificial. It was as though she were trying to convince herself that what she was saying was true. Gautier, who suspected that Le Tellier's motive in arranging an introduction to Geneviève Stahl and in making her his mistress had been to extract all the information he could about the circles in which she moved, said nothing. A widow was entitled to her illusions.

On entering the building they passed the concierge in her little cubby-hole and it seemed to Gautier that the woman looked at him as he passed with Michelle Le Tellier, with rather less respect but with more interest than before. But it may have been just his imagination, because when they reached the apartment he saw it was not empty. A team of three men were hard at work under the supervision of a foreman plastering and painting the bathroom and kitchen. The living room and bedroom had already been re-decorated and refurnished.

The bookshelves which had been the main feature of the living room and the huge bed which had dominated the bedroom had both disappeared, the shelves torn out and replaced by a small bookcase, the bed changed for one of more modest proportions and less extravagant appearance. The effect of these changes and of a new colour-scheme was to give the apartment a style and an elegance in startling contrast to the blatant suggestiveness which Jacques Le Tellier had managed to achieve.

'What do you think of the redecoration?' Michelle Le Tellier asked him.

'I like it. And if I may say so without disrespect to your late husband it is a great improvement on the old décor.'

She left him to admire the living room while she went to give instructions to the workmen in the kitchen. The walls of the room had been painted in a delicate shade of pale pink which set off perfectly the pink and blue motif of a beautiful Persian carpet, and they were hung not with erotic pictures but with paintings of more conventional themes: landscapes, still-lifes and a seventeenth-century portrait of a young girl.

When they left the apartment and were once more in her carriage, Michelle Le Tellier said, 'You may be wondering why I went to the trouble of having the apartment redecorated.'

'I was curious, yes.'

'A young cousin of mine is coming to live in Paris. The place will suit him very well.' She paused and then added, 'Perhaps I also wished to erase the memory of what used to happen there.'

'One can understand that.'

She turned her head to look at him and he sensed that behind her veil she was smiling. 'With your policeman's mind you probably suspected that I intended to use it to entertain my lovers.'

'Policemen do not always assume the worst.'

His evasive reply, or it may have been a defensive note in his voice, sparked an idea in her mind. Lifting her veil she stared at him and then exclaimed, 'Good Heavens!'

'What is it?'

'Did you think that was why I was taking you there this afternoon? To make love? You did not know the decorators would be in the apartment.'

'I am ashamed to say that the thought did cross my mind.' Gautier decided to be honest. She could laugh at him if she wished. 'It was a piece of unforgivable conceit.'

'Not at all.' She hesitated for moment and then, like Gautier decided to be frank. 'Since the first time we met I have felt somehow that one day we might be—how shall I put it?—close friends. Do you think me shameless for saying that?'

'Of course not. I only hope your presentiment is right.'

'But not yet. It is too early. After so many years of being married I need time to grow accustomed to being a single woman again. I need time to find myself.'

'I understand.'

Unexpectedly she leant forward and kissed him lightly on the cheek. 'Be patient, Jean-Paul,' she said earnestly, 'please be patient!'

Gautier could have told her how the feelings she had expressed so nearly matched his own. He might have explained the conflicting emotions which he had not yet mastered, the inner constraints that held back the attraction which he felt for her. One day he would tell her, but instinct suggested that it was not the time for wordy explanations and that a banal gesture might be more effective in conveying the feelings he wished to express. So he simply took her hand and lifted it to his lips.